To Xavi, the sexiest cheerleader I could ever wish for.

CONTENT NOTES

Dear Reader,

While *Love, Lines, and Alibis* is an uplifting rom-com mystery, some themes may be triggering for certain people. If you prefer to bypass content warnings and find them spoilery, please feel free to skip this section and dive right into the story.

Although there are no graphic scenes, this book includes off-page death, mentions of sexual assault, profanity, and explicit sexual content.

PROLOGUE

When I finally made it home that February evening, I was freezing. I was tired. I was hungry. And I probably smelled—and by that, I don't mean that I could still sense my lover's fragrance on my skin, but an actual unpleasant odor caused by too many days of unwashed frenzied activity. I sweat when I'm nervous.

I went straight to the shower, turned on the faucet, waited patiently, then remembered what had happened a few days previously—right before all this mess had started —and made a turn for the kitchen. I filled every big pot I could find with water and set them to boil. And, since a watched pot does indeed *not* boil, I rummaged through the refrigerator and the cabinets for something that could appease my stomach rumbles. I settled for a jar of hearts of palm dipped in almond butter. It wasn't slices of avocado on cassava flour crackers—that would be my actual favorite snack but I was out of both valuable ingredients, since I hadn't exactly been able to shop for groceries or anything else—but it did calm my hunger momentarily. I was still craving a lentil burger with sweet potato fries though.

I chugged two big glasses of water and realized I had been parched only after I drank. I couldn't remember the last time I had paid attention to my proper hydration, and it had been one of my mantras since the move to California. That's what you learn when you are a Los Angeles transplant: use sunscreen daily, keep a tatty cardigan in the car all year round, and carry a reusable bottle of filtered water everywhere.

Some of the water on the stove started boiling then and I transferred it to the bathroom, carefully. I've read all the statistics about fatal accidents caused by silly home mishaps. It would have been extremely unfortunate to have endured—and survived—the previous seventy-two hours only to burn myself when it was finally all over.

I poured the hot water into the black-tiled bathtub and added some cold water so as not to scald myself. I slipped out of the satin strappy dress and dipped my whole body in the warm water. That had to have been fated. I had rented a one-bedroom, one-bathroom apartment with a big bathtub I'd always considered ridiculously disproportionate for the space, and it had to have been for the purpose of living that moment. I finally relaxed. I submerged my head fully in the water, having a very cinematic experience. I was the flawed and tired hero having made their Odyssean way home and finally been able to rest. I half smiled, reached out of the bathtub for a nearby notebook—I keep them scattered all around the place as you would expect for someone in my line of work—and started scribbling.

I guess if I'm going to tell you the story of how I found myself inside a hot bathtub after days of unwashed undertaking and with a broken water heater—and after one dead body and two failed murder attempts against me—I should go back to the morning it all started.

1

Two days before, Thursday, February 22nd

I was still in bed and had been snoozing the alarm on my cell phone diligently for what probably was a good hour and a half.

Don't judge me.

I'm not necessarily lazy—if ever the procrastinator. But procrastinating is almost a duty when you call yourself a writer. And I'm that. More specifically, at the time of this tale, an in-between-gigs television screenwriter.

I was repeatedly snoozing my alarm in part because I was technically unoccupied and with nowhere to go until the 1 p.m. lunch meeting I had with my agent that day. She'd assured me she had good news and an offer. I was disinclined to believe that whatever the offer was could be considered good news. I don't know how many times I had to tell her that I was *not* going to take a job as a writer on another broadcast network police procedural with no room for character development or relationship building.

I wasn't that desperate. Not yet. My overall deal

wouldn't expire for three more months, and I was keeping my fingers crossed for a renewal. I still had some money left from the latest residual check from the two seasons I'd been working in an actual broadcast network police procedural with no room for character development or relationship building. The best-paid job of my career. I was working on my spec script—perhaps not while I overslept, but still pretty consistently typing. And even if at thirty-four I wasn't proud to admit that I was a bit of a disappointment to my parents, I knew they'd still help me if things were tight.

The reason I was in no shape to wake up that unseasonably chilly Thursday of February was that I had gone to bed quite late the night before. But that's irrelevant to the story right now. I may have to come back to it. I'll do it only once it's necessary.

I guess I should tell you now that I always aim for the truth. I'm not a so-called unreliable narrator, and none of my stories have ever employed one. If I lie to you, it'll be because I'm also lying to myself. So you don't need to mistrust me.

When I finally stopped my alarm that Thursday morning, I rose from bed, put the moka pot on the stovetop to get the coffee going, and went to the bathroom to take a shower. I was wearing my favorite plaid flannel pajama pants and a two-or-three-sizes-too-big UCLA T-shirt I didn't recall having ever bought—and I had purchased my fair amount of merchandise from the university where I earned two degrees. I took the T-shirt off and couldn't help myself. I smelled it.

See, I told you I wouldn't do it, and I just did. I'm lying.

I didn't just smell it. I *inhaled* its scent. I would have probably buried my face in it had the coffee pot at the stove not started boiling, alerting me that my dose of single-origin caffeine for the morning was almost ready.

I poured the coffee into a mug and allowed it to wake me up. Inside the fridge, I found a slice of the vegan Margherita pizza I'd gotten at Pizzanista a couple of nights before. I was patient enough to microwave it for a total of eleven seconds then devoured the lukewarm pizza with my hot coffee. I made my way back to the bathroom, still having breakfast. I was hoping for the water in the shower to finally be at the right temperature. Only it was still freezing.

I realized the water heater was probably broken, and at some point I'd have to call the company that managed the building so someone would fix it. I would normally shrug it off and get dressed, but I thought about the meeting with my agent where I would need to look mildly presentable. I was even thinking of forgoing my staple combination of sweatpants and flannel shirts and maybe stuffing myself into a pair of high-waisted flare jeans and a cropped T-shirt that Marta had gotten for me. Sure, I needed to shower before that. Even if it was a cold shower.

I cursed the day I had decided to lease an apartment in a 1930 Art Deco building. It had lots of charms but sometimes seemed to lack the amenities of the twenty-first century, running hot water being one of them at the moment. But it was too late to keep wondering if I should have taken a cookie-cutter, synthetic-carpeted unit in one of the many new apartment buildings that had popped up in DTLA over the past few years. I was here now, and I hated moving. Plus, I had other reasons to stay at the Eastern Columbia even if I didn't want those to be acknowledged.

I was saved from the cold shower just then, as the fire alarm started blazing and fully roused me into wakefulness —something the strong espresso hadn't managed.

2

The last thing I needed that cold gray Thursday morning—other than the fucking water heater being broken and having to contemplate the possibility of (maybe) taking a cold shower—was for the fire alarm to go off. I didn't have the energy to deal with it. I hadn't planned on leaving my place until twenty minutes before my lunch meeting.

I opened my front door slightly and peeked outside. My neighbors were making their way downstairs. I found it bizarre because my experience living in earthquake-prone Los Angeles was that people didn't take seriously things like sirens, drills, or even the actual earth shaking if it was below 5.5 points on the magnitude scale. But they were somehow not ignoring this alarm.

Still wearing my pajama pants, I put on my blue Writers Guild of America West hoodie, donned a pair of flip-flops and, before descending to the street, grabbed my keys, cell phone, and laptop and stuffed them inside a LACMA tote bag. I have separation anxiety issues if I am far from either of those two electronic devices for any extended amount of time.

I lived on the tenth floor and knew enough about fire alarms—because of a brief stint on a TV show about sexy firefighters—to be aware that I shouldn't take the elevator. So I made my descent to the street slowly and almost alone. I might have been one of the last residents to exit the building.

The stairway felt eerie. The fire alarm was still blasting but there was not a single person in sight. It didn't feel safe. I wasn't scared of the possibility of getting trapped by fire in the building; I couldn't even smell smoke. It was something else. A creepy feeling made me accelerate until I reached the exit.

I'm not one to recognize many of my neighbors—I'm terrible with faces and use my cell phone as a conversation-avoiding tool when in the elevator or other public areas—but I guessed the throngs of people garbed in different informal styles crowding Broadway Street by the building's main entrance must all live there.

Of course, there was one person I did recognize, even if both of us seemed to be doing everything in our power to avoid one another. I'd even taken the stairs up to my apartment on many occasions to prevent being stuck with him in the elevator. And I'm not exactly your always-take-the-stairs-and-count-your-steps health-nut Californian.

David was there on the street as well. Now, please don't read his name the American way (DAY-vid) but the Spanish way (dah-VEED) as he's a proud third-generation Angeleno of Mexican and Argentinian descent.

David, naturally, was being his most obnoxious, helpful self. He assured everyone there was nothing to fear and that the fire department was already on its way. I'm sure he'd checked to confirm that was true. He might have even had more than one source who corroborated that fact. He was thorough if anything else. He kept asking by name about neighbors from whom I hadn't heard in my life, making sure they were all accounted for. The guy was leading a head count, for fuck's sake! He even went as far as taking his own light-down jacket and giving it to a woman in her seventies who was wearing a T-shirt and shorts. Sure thing, she hugged him. I can't blame her. He's all six feet of manly huggable splendor.

I guess you can draw your own conclusions now. I'm a socially awkward screenwriter who'd just woken up that day and whose idea of a nightmare is having to call a restaurant to make a reservation. David is a city reporter who'd probably been up since five that morning, gone for a run, volunteered in some place or other, and already filed an error-free story and sent it to his adoring editor.

Go ahead, take his side. All our former common friends did it anyway. I'm told he's more fun and engaging to be around.

David gets on my nerves because I'm a heartless spoiled bitch. That and, you may have guessed it, there's an entangled backstory. I'm gonna make this short because I hate when a tale gets stopped for the exposition dump portion, and I interrupted the narration when a possible fire was developing.

David and I were friends in college, and then we were best friends, and then we made out and kept doing it and then, at some point, we sort of started officially dating. We even moved in together and shared a cramped one-bedroom Art Deco bungalow in Central LA with a historically original (if malfunctioning) kitchen. We broke up about two years ago, left the bungalow, and by some mischievous turn of fate ended up renting separate units in the Eastern Columbia during the same week. They were having a sale.

Now you know.

Back to the spillage of humans on Broadway Street.

The firetruck arrived then and, to my dismay, most of the neighbors started clapping and cheering. We still had to wait for almost forty more minutes though. If it wasn't because my agent had agreed to meet a fifteen-minute walk away from there—she was willing to drive from Beverly Hills to Downtown with the excuse of trying a vegan ramen spot in Grand Central Market—I'd be calling her and asking for a postponement. But even if the firefighters took the rest of the morning, I could simply drop by as I was, though I didn't recall having checked myself in a mirror that day. If I told Beatrice (my agent) that I'd been in a fire, I'm sure she wouldn't mind me looking a bit disheveled. And she would not be able to accuse me of not taking my career seriously.

She'd complained about that on a couple of occasions during the last few months, but I'm focusing again on unimportant things.

Returning to the fire. We were informed by one of the firefighters that there was no trace of actual flames anywhere in the building. They believed the alarm had been triggered by accident. I wasn't surprised. The least interesting or exciting possibility tends to be the one that happens. As a screenwriter, I was well aware that real life tends to be far duller than fiction. Also, with the ability humans have to do things they aren't supposed to do, I wondered why fire alarms weren't triggered accidentally more often.

But of course, with my bad luck that morning—cold, unshowered, and improperly attired—everything wasn't over yet. Rumor had it (and rumor at the Eastern Columbia always arrived via the apartment 10B tenant—our resident gossip) that there had been a death in the building.

A violent one.

3

"They found a body!" the apartment 10B tenant kept proclaiming as a small group of residents gathered around him. "That's why they're not letting us back in."

"What do you mean they found a body, George?" asked David in a taking-charge tone. I rolled my eyes, irritated at him. He'd been talking to another elderly neighbor but had obviously kept his ears open and was now coming to inquire about this unexpected development.

Let me tell you, the only reason I know the face of the tenant at apartment 10B, other than the fact that he's a fucking blabbermouth and impossible to ignore, is that he's my next-door neighbor. I live in 10A. David is in 2D, yet he knew the dude is called George. He may have even known his last name and where he'd moved from before coming to the building.

"I was making my way downstairs to get my car since the firefighter captain had told us there was no fire in the building," started George in his perfectly modulated tone. He loved an audience. I recalled him telling me that he was a voice actor who mainly did audiobooks. "I took the stairs because there's still a lot of activity around the elevators, but I couldn't make it past the basement door. I heard something about a body they found at the underground parking area."

"Again, what do you mean a body?" insisted David. I knew his journalistic instincts were piqued. He'd grill George until he got a satisfying and clear answer out of him. A quotable answer.

"I don't know. The firefighters saw me then and forced me to get out. Apparently, we aren't allowed back inside yet." George sighed. "But I think I saw a dropped shoe. And blood," he added dramatically.

One of the neighbors gasped. Another one said he felt faint. David promptly grabbed the potentially fainting person by the elbow and guided him to sit on one of the chairs from the sidewalk coffee shop at the corner of the Eastern Columbia. David then promised to return with water for everyone. I rolled my eyes for the umpteenth time.

Only once David was out of my sight and not distracting me did I realize a man was staring at me from the other side of the street. I can't explain why, but he made my hair stand on end.

Cars from the LA Police Department started arriving then. Some were patrol units with uniformed officers inside but others were unmarked black SUVs with agents garbed in the most odious business wear. It almost looked as if we were in a low-budget episode of *Bosch* or some other Michael Connelly TV adaptation. I even checked for cameras. But they were not there—not yet. And when I checked again, the creepy dude standing on the other side of the sidewalk was nowhere to be seen.

"Brought water," said David, distributing the plastic

bottles among the neighbors. He made sure the person who had actually *not* fainted got one first.

"Toma," he told me in Spanish, handing me a bottle. That was a new precedent: David talking to me in plain daylight for the first time since the breakup.

"Thanks," I replied, stunned, but he'd already moved on to other people in need of hydration and comfort.

The police cordoned off the entrance to the building with yellow tape, and it occurred to me that George may have been telling the truth after all and not just trying to be the center of attention.

"What happened?" I asked one of the uniformed officers. When I didn't get a reply, I added, "Someone said there was a body . . ."

"You a neighbor?" The officer, a woman in her thirties, pen and notebook in hand, asked me.

"Yes, I live in 10A," I answered.

"Name?" Her eyes were on her notes.

"My name, you mean?" I couldn't see how that could be of any relevance.

"No, the name of the guy suspiciously handing water to elderly residents," the officer answered with a chuckle.

Even though I consider myself witty, I don't do well with humor directed at me sometimes. Especially if I'm feeling nervous because I'm dealing with law enforcement or some other authority figure. I blame it on my parents.

Everyone had advised them to do it while I was still a young child, but by the time they decided to move to LA from Spain, I was already seventeen. My year of high school in the States was a nightmare. I tried keeping a long-distance relationship with my boyfriend in Barcelona. Spoiler alert: he started going out with my best friend and didn't even bother breaking up with me. Fortunately, my friend fessed up. College was better, but I was still dealing with culture shock—and heartbreak. Marta, my much younger sister, was five when we moved, and you'd never say she wasn't born here. But I have a thick accent and sometimes I just don't get the humor.

"Elena Freire," I answered the cop's request.

Of course, should I have chosen to brandish my full legal name, the one that included my mother's last name, things could have been more pleasant. But I didn't want to play that particular card. I spelled my name and last name for the officer and waited for her next question.

"Where were you last night?"

"Home," I said.

"Alone?" Her eyes were still buried in her writing.

"Uh-huh."

"When did you leave?"

"This morning when the fire alarm started blasting." I took a sip of water from the bottle David had given me. How could he know that I too would be thirsty?

"Did you see anything or anyone unusual?" the officer continued without making eye contact.

"I mean, there were a lot more people taking the stairs than usual because of the alarm." My dry brand of humor didn't land. "I didn't see anything."

"Okay. You'll have to wait for a bit longer, but we're planning on letting you folks in within the next hour," the officer said, her manner softening, and she moved on to the next neighbor.

David was still in the middle of things, handing out the remaining waters and being asked, I assumed, what were similar questions to mine by another uniformed officer.

I hoped he didn't decide to offer any unnecessary details.

4

My toes were almost completely frozen—flip-flops are *not* advisable all year round in California regardless of what you may have heard or seen—when the city's media team arrived in another black SUV. Something big had to be going on.

Victor hopped out of a city-hall-owned vehicle. "Elena, you look chilled to the bone!" I wasn't surprised to see him there.

He came to me, forgot about his PDA-avoidance rule, and kissed me. On the forehead, mind you. He took off his tailored Tom Ford blazer and covered my shoulders with it. Even if it wasn't a heavy-duty puffer jacket, the woolen garment was still warm from his body, and I welcomed any heat I could get just then.

"You're here on official business?" I asked.

"Yes." Victor looked around, his expression unreadable.

"What happened?" I insisted, but he could be tight-lipped when dealing with matters pertaining to his job as Public Relations Specialist II at the City of Los Angeles. "Someone said there's a body." One of his eyebrows twitched up, briefly unsettling his otherwise composed features.

"We believe there's been a death in the building, yes," he said. Why was he so fucking secretive?

As you may have gathered, the nature of my and Victor's relationship was more than simple acquaintances since we had in fact been dating for almost a year. But the whole thing was still in its early stages—or its late ones—which was why he wasn't sharing with me something another boyfriend would have no qualms explaining. Before you judge me, and since I know most readers have a deep aversion for the cheating trope, no one had cheated on anyone. I'll fill you in on the particulars later.

Fortunately, I wasn't the only Eastern Columbia resident vying for Victor's attention. My neighbors gathered around him, one extremely competent city reporter among them.

"Who died?" asked David, his journalist hat on.

"It's still early to tell," Victor told him, his PR smile fully at play.

"Nonsense," David countered. "The city wouldn't have sent the whole PR squad if it wasn't someone important. But I can't think of anyone you would deem notable enough who lives in the building."

Did he seriously know all the residents at the Eastern Columbia? I barely managed to recognize the faces of the dude in apartment 10B and one-half of the couple who lived in 10C. The wife was a remarkable redhead who reminded me of Amy Adams. The only thing I knew about apartment 10D was that their tenant—or tenants—had impeccable taste in music and favored jazz and blues. As for the rest of the place, I would not be able to recognize them if I ran into them on the street or at the checkout line at Whole Foods.

It's not that I'm face blind or anything like that, I'm just a social calamity.

Back to the daytime drama unfolding on Broadway Street. Victor wasn't answering David's question, and the journalist wasn't finding new ways of challenging the PR expert. Verbally, at least. The two of them were engaged in some sort of staring contest. They knew each other well through work and openly disliked one another. The connection they shared with me had always been ignored and unmentioned by the two of them though. They maintained that their mutual disdain came from the fact that they worked on opposite and irreconcilable sides of the municipal knowledge-gathering-and-divulging business.

Allow me to try and paint the image for you. I'm a screenwriter, after all, and I write in images. Victor and David stood one in front of the other in all their tall, athletic, mid-thirties magnificence. You may think I have a type, and I may, but their similarities ended in their indisputable handsomeness and face symmetry. David was wearing thrifted but nonetheless well-fitting jeans and a T-shirt. His black hair and several-day stubble gave him the air of the perfectly disheveled yet sexy rebel-with-many-causes that he was. Victor was in a $5,000 navy suit—minus the jacket, which he'd so generously but uncharacteristically given to me—flawlessly shaved, and sporting his dark-blond hair styled in a precisely coiffed pompadour.

I was perhaps enjoying gazing back and forth from one gorgeous man to another too much when the guy from apartment 10B decided to talk again.

"It's Dashing Henry!" he proclaimed in his perfectly pitched bass voice. "There's a body in the building, and it's Dashing Henry!"

"What?" I couldn't avoid saying. All the high from

shamelessly staring at the two men I was romantically intertwined with suddenly came to a brutal crash after hearing that name. An uneasy tightness gripped my chest.

I hate doing this because I can't stand nonlinear narration, but I'm going to have to interrupt myself *again* to explain something.

I knew Dashing Henry.

Hell, in the universe my story takes place, the whole country knows the two-time Emmy winner. He'd been the lead actor for fifteen seasons of *LA Misconducts*, where he played a seasoned and corrupt police commissioner charged with covering new political and corporate scandals every week.

I also happened to have worked as a staff writer in *LA Misconducts*—the previously mentioned police procedural whose residuals were still paying for my bills—and had known the deceased personally.

And so had David.

5

"Who's your source?" David asked George, and I sent the most glacial stare my ex's way. He just couldn't help himself.

"My source?" George hesitated.

"Now, now, David Ramos. Are you really going to harass a neighbor for information?" Victor said.

"No, you're definitely more my style," David replied with a wink.

If it wasn't for the shock I was still in after having heard Dashing Henry's name, I'd have been enjoying all the professional foreplay between those two. But I couldn't. I was frozen. I had a headache that was morphing into a migraine, and I needed to get home. So I left.

I didn't care if the police were still inside the building, if there was a body, or if the building was off-limits to residents. For the first time in the year-plus since my mother had become Los Angeles's top honcho, I was willing to name drop and employ the daughter-of tactic.

I was stopped before I could cross the building's threshold. Two uniformed officers stood in front of it with unfriendly frowns. I was about to tell them who I was and why I needed to be let inside when I heard the two men at my heels.

"Elena," David and Victor called in unison. One of them did it with a perfect Spanish accent, and the other did his best after having practiced the pronunciation for weeks in front of a mirror. Don't ask me how I know that detail.

I sighed and turned their way. Most times, it was annoying enough having to deal with one man. I was faced with two at present when I most needed to be alone.

"¿¡Qué!?" I said.

Even if I had technically been living for a little longer in the US than I had in Spain, Spanish still came more naturally to me, especially if I was upset. I wanted to believe it was because Los Angeles is the kind of city where you can mostly communicate in Spanish peppered with a word of English here and there. But I wasn't sure if it was that or if everyone had been right in their warnings to my parents and they should have moved here when I was younger.

I guess both David and Victor knew me well enough to recognize the irritability in my tone. Neither of them uttered a single word after my answer. Fucking annoying cowards, the two of them. I breathed deeply, tried to regain my composure, and did my best at a smile as I turned again, ready to talk to the cops. But I didn't get the chance.

The press made their loud appearance in the form of two vans from competing TV stations and a helicopter.

"The press? Who tipped them?" I said more to myself than anyone else, but I thought I saw it all written over David's face. "You couldn't help yourself, could you? Not even in your own home!"

"Are you implying that I warned the competition?" David replied, his brows drawing together. But I didn't give a fuck if I had offended him. We were both aware that one of the reasons our relationship had floundered was my inability to believe him on work-related topics. It's not that I'm mistrustful or paranoid. He lies.

Victor took himself out of my proximity, heading in the direction of the television reporters with his best and most practiced grin. I expected David to follow him and get whatever statement Victor was about to divulge, but David didn't move. Even if my ex's eyes followed my current boyfriend's every move.

"What are you still doing here? Go chase the story," I told David. I was okay, he didn't need to babysit me. With David, the job always came first. Plus, it wasn't like he had any responsibility to me and my wellbeing.

"I'd rather talk to you first," he told me. His dark-brown eyes locked on me and I felt a whirlwind in my belly. How was it possible that I couldn't still think clearly with him in front of me? We'd broken up two years before. But it was kind of strange seeing and talking with him in broad daylight. Awfully obfuscating too. "Can we go somewhere more private?" he added. George from apartment 10B was lurking closely.

"There's nothing else to be said, and the last thing I want right now is to go anywhere with you." Even if that was exactly the opposite of what my body was telling me. But our breakup hadn't exactly been friendly, and we hadn't learned how to talk to one another afterward. "I just need to get home."

"Let me find out if they've reopened the building," David said.

"¡No necesito que preguntes nada! I can ask myself." I told him I didn't need him in a harsher tone than I'd anticipated.

He looked at me again and his eyes caught me completely off guard. There wasn't offense or anger but real concern. It was as if he was worried about me, so fuckingly worried that I was pretty much sure he was neglecting his work.

I was considering telling David I was sorry when I heard, "Elena."

I was getting tired of hearing my name. I turned and saw Victor coming my way. He was the one who'd called me. "The police want to talk to you."

"I've already talked to them," I snapped. I didn't need a second man trying to organize everything around me. It had been annoying enough seeing David asking questions and handing out bottled water all morning.

"The detectives in charge of the investigation want to talk to everyone again," Victor said. "But especially you—and David. Given your relationship to Dashing Henry."

"I guess they want me to tell them again that I was home alone all night," David said, directing his gaze to me one last time. My breath caught in my throat. Then he made his way inside the Eastern Columbia and approached one of the police detectives.

...

"Name?" the police detective, a tall Black man in his fifties, asked me as we took a seat in two of the low-profile midcentury modern chairs of the Eastern Columbia's main vestibule.

He'd introduced himself as LAPD Detective Alex Rooney. Or it could have been Clooney or Phooney. I think it's been previously established: I'm bad with faces and worse with names.

"Elena Freire Valls," I answered.

"Valls as in Aurora Valls?" I could see the curiosity in his face as he tried to find some physical resemblance between my mother and me.

"The mayor is my mother, yes." It was better not to play coy once people had already figured it out.

"You look nothing like her," the officer went on, and I could only take that as a slight.

My mother is a gorgeous sixty-four-year-old. Think Tilda Swinton or Kristin Scott Thomas kind of arresting and enviably well preserved. She'd taken LA by storm almost two decades before. She was tall where I was shortish, she was skinny where I had hips. Her hair was a perfect white bob that was regularly maintained. I hadn't seen my stylist in months and was at present sporting a messy bun of brown and not necessarily clean hair. She was always impeccably dressed in Balenciaga and Ralph Lauren pantsuits with the occasional Chanel classic tweed skirt suit thrown in. Even if I'd had time to change out of my pajama pants that morning, it wouldn't have been a huge improvement. It's not that I'm a fashion agnostic—I can almost always tell what people are wearing. But most of the time I don't care enough to make an effort.

"I take to my dad," I said, putting the officer out of his doubts.

"I see," he said. "And you live in apartment 10A."

"Yes."

"What time did you get home yesterday?" He opened his top-bound pocket notepad.

"Around nineish?" I answered, trying to remember. "I went to this Q&A session with Shonda Rhimes at the Television Academy—I mean, I didn't go *with her,* I went to see her and listen to her talk. I grabbed a bite with a couple of colleagues at Sugarfish after that." I didn't add that I like their cucumber roll and their seaweed and kikurage salad, but it's still hard to go there if the rest of your party is going hard on the raw fish. Sugarfish is not a destination for vegan sushi like Shojin, after all.

"Which Sugarfish?"

"The one on Ventura Boulevard? Both my colleagues live in the Valley and that one is close to the Academy. Is that relevant?" The detective didn't reply and kept taking notes.

"What did you do when you got home?"

Detective Clooney's question was rather impertinent. I sure wasn't going to tell him that when I arrived home, I had an edible, undressed, and proceeded to power on one of my favorite toys before I got an unexpected—but thoroughly welcome—surprise.

"I brushed my teeth and did a bit of reading before going to bed," I said.

"What are you reading?"

"*Get Shorty*," I answered. I had recently reread a paper-back copy of Elmore Leonard's Hollywood-set dark comedy, although I hadn't done any reading the previous night. But there would be no digital trace of my doing it—or not—like there would have been if I said I had been watching Netflix or writing on my computer. Two years as a screenwriter in a procedural show, and I thought I had become an expert at duping the cops.

"That book any good?" he asked as if testing me.

"I'm doing some research on gangster tales."

"Is that for something you're writing? We know you're a screenwriter," he added.

I hadn't told the other police officer anything about my profession, so I assumed they had checked all the residents of the building. Or at least, they'd done it with *me* and

Detective Clooney had clearly been playing the fool when he pretended he didn't know that my mother was the mayor of Los Angeles.

"I'm working on a spec script," I told him, preferring to leave it as vague as possible. I wasn't going to volunteer any information unless it was demanded. Also, as any other decent writer in town, I got awkward and cagey the moment people asked the dreadful question, *What's your script about?*

"Is it going to be anything like *LA Misconducts*? Never been much of a fan of the show," he continued, and I wasn't surprised. The LAPD wasn't exactly thrilled with the image of endless police corruption represented in the show.

"Nothing to do with that," I said.

"You worked on *LA Misconducts* for two years?"

"Seasons twelve and thirteen."

"Why did you leave?"

That was even more impertinent than when he'd asked about my nightly activities.

"Screenwriting is a transient profession, and my dream while pursuing it wasn't to make a whole career writing about LA cops," I said. I hoped I sounded as sharp as I had intended. I wasn't liking Detective Clooney one bit.

"So you voluntarily left a well-paying job for the possibility of writing a spec script?"

"Correct," I said with my perfected California smile. I wasn't going to give him the victory. "That and I got an overall deal, of course."

Don't call me cocky or obnoxious, but I do love bringing up my overall deal in conversation often. In my defense, it's a rare thing for a minor screenwriter to have a studio willing to pay them just so they get first dibs in whatever they write, even if they don't like any of it.

"What was your relationship with Dashing Henry?" the

cop asked then, and I almost choked at the sound of that name and the word *relationship* in the same sentence.

"So George was right and you found his body then?"

"George?"

"The tenant in apartment 10B. He has a way of finding stuff out. Lucky us, because George has been the only one keeping the residents informed. We've been freezing on the street for more than an hour and still haven't heard an official word from the police or the city about what is going on."

"I guess you can air your complaints about the city with your mother," Clooney said, chuckling. But he soon realized his comment hadn't exactly landed. "I can't divulge anything except that when the firefighters came to the building this morning, they found the body of actor Dashing Henry."

"Was he killed?"

"What makes you say so?"

"I can't imagine all this secrecy and need to investigate if he died of a heart attack," I said, and I started to wonder if my lawyer should have been present. He would *not* be happy when I told him I had been having that conversation without him in the room.

"So what was your relationship with the deceased?" the detective asked. Somehow, the lack of the deceased's name made it possible for me to answer this time.

"None, as such. Of course, I'd known him during my tenure at *LA Misconducts*, but I haven't talked to him or seen him since I left the show."

"Why so?"

"I've kept in touch with several of the screenwriters at the show and the showrunner, but I don't necessarily connect with actors that much unless we have something in common."

"Like Amelia Sanchez?" he said, referring to one of the

former stars of the show. Amelia had left *LA Misconducts* around the same time as I had and had found enough success both in indie films and prestige TV after that for her to be repeatedly photographed on the red carpet. Her good looks may have played a part besides her undeniable talent as a performer. I'd been her plus one on more than one occasion, and it was no secret that we'd become fast friends after meeting on *LA Misconducts.* She'd even talked about it in interviews sometimes.

"Amelia is a woman, an immigrant, a fellow Spanish speaker, and roughly a year older than me. So yes, we found ourselves connecting over a few subjects and have kept in touch since I left."

"Of course," he said. "You've told one of our officers that you were home alone all night."

"Uh-huh."

"And you don't recall anything out of the ordinary?"

"Not until this morning when the fire alarm threw us onto the streets."

Detective Clooney took a few final notes without meeting my gaze or giving any hint that I could leave.

6

I had managed to wrap the chat with Detective Clooney without deviating much from my first statement to the police. I returned Victor's blazer—it always makes me nervous to wear borrowed expensive garments when I'm a well-known stain magnet. I didn't drop by my own apartment to put on socks, sneakers, and a second, warmer sweatshirt though. Instead, I was now knocking on David's door. And even if it was a well-practiced gesture, it still felt bizarre.

"Querías hablar," I told him when he opened the door, letting him know I was there to talk.

"Pasa." He let me in.

And just like that, I was inside David's apartment for the first time.

Not really.

Technically, I'd been in his studio apartment many times. Only it had always been late at night, and I have a sort of doctrine: What happens around midnight is all the fabric of dreams.

Since I'd only been there in dreams, and for very

different purposes than a chat, I didn't know how to act or what to say when I crossed David's front door. There was a smirk on his face as if he saw I was being bashful and thought it hilariously hypocritical of me.

"Can't find my favorite T-shirt. Did I leave it at your place?" he said, the smirk still on his lips. I was dumbfounded.

"You wanted to talk," I repeated, this time in English in case he hadn't heard me the first time. I had no intention of breaking our unspoken rule of never acknowledging what went on between the two of us at night. And I had no plans of returning his T-shirt anytime soon. I was there because he'd seemed quite adamant about his need to talk and even if I pretended I didn't care, I couldn't resist him. The thought of him being distressed pained me. And he had looked sort of uneasy when he'd told me he needed a chat.

"Should we perhaps synchronize our police approach going forward?" he finally said.

"Probably," I conceded. "You've talked to Clooney as well, right?"

"Clooney?"

"The detective in charge of this investigation," I said, impatiently. This visit to David's place in the middle of the day was taking way longer than I had previously anticipated, and I needed to be out of there.

"Elena, en serio. He's called Rooney. Could you please not color everything with a Hollywood veneer?"

And there it was. Another one of the many irreconcilable differences that had broken us apart. He wasn't exactly a showbiz fan.

"Okay, Mr. Serious Reporter. But tell me, why aren't we using the perfect alibi that we have for last night?"

"Do you think we need an alibi?" he asked.

"You tell me! Detective *Rooney* was all nosey and asking all kinds of questions about Dashing Henry," I said, feeling sullied just by speaking that name. "I'm a bit confused about something though."

"¿Qué te tiene confundida?" he asked me in his LA-accented Spanish with notes of Mexican and Porteño.

Tú, I almost blurted out. *You are the one who's confusing me.* But I didn't.

"What was Dashing Henry's body doing here? Did he live in the building?" I hadn't asked the cops that because I didn't want to sound more clueless—or more guilty-looking—than I already was.

"You literally have no idea who lives here, right?" He laughed.

"Nope, and I intend for it to remain that way. But seriously . . ."

"To the best of my knowledge," David said, and I knew that was code for *I have three sources who've confirmed it,* "he didn't live here, no."

"So what was he doing here?"

"I'm afraid that's what the cops want to know. Also, apparently he was found right next to where my car is parked, and that's made them suspicious." I remembered George mentioning the body was found in the parking area of the building.

"David, we should have told the cops the truth," I said then. I didn't like the idea of him being a suspect in all of this.

"Aren't you worried about your boyfriend finding out that you spent the night with someone else?"

I gaped at him. This was the first time he'd referred to Victor as my boyfriend or anything else, really. But the word *boyfriend* coming from his mouth when it wasn't to describe his relationship to me felt bizarre. Then again, David and I didn't exactly do much talking lately.

"We'd be telling the police, not him," I said.

"Police talk," David continued.

"Right," I said, realizing I wouldn't mind that much if Victor found out. Is it bad to say that, by then, I was quite frankly bored with Victor? In any case, David didn't have to know that. "What are you up to right now?"

He was searching all the surfaces of his apartment, looking for his notebook. His favorite black rollerball pen was already in his hand, and I had an inkling about his intentions.

"Nothing," he said sheepishly, but I knew he was lying. Add that to the long list of irreconcilable differences: When it came to his job, David lied. Or, at least, he wasn't always completely honest. But I've told you about David's lying tendencies already, right? They rub me the wrong way.

"I know I was wrong before, when I accused you of calling the press," I told him, trying to affect as much of a serious tone as I could. "I know you didn't call them because you're the one who wants to write about what happened."

He blinked at me and opened his mouth, likely to say something defensive, but I cut him off.

"Don't. I'm not telling you not to do it. I'm only asking you to let me help you. For all we know, right now you're at the top of the cops' list. Let's figure this out together, investigating as a team so we can prove you had nothing to do with it. I'm sure telling them that you were home alone all night is not helping your situation." I didn't want to question the reasons behind it too deeply, but I *needed* to help him investigate and make sure he'd be all right. And we both knew that wasn't the first time we'd cracked a case together.

"I appreciate the offer," he said, and for an instant I

thought he was going to accept it. I felt thrilled about the idea of helping him. It was a sensation I hadn't felt in a long time. I was genuinely concerned about him. I knew that in the cops' eyes he was probably the most plausible perpetrator, and I needed to dissuade them from that notion.

But David didn't take me up on my proposition.

"Listen, there's still something I need to tell you. The reason I told you we needed to talk. It's important." You can add his flair for melodrama to that running list of irreconcilable differences. I hate drama. I write drama, but I don't want it in my life.

I didn't even try to conceal my exasperation at his words.

"I know you *still* don't want to talk to me," he said. "Pero no podemos seguir así."

I didn't see why things couldn't stay the way they were, but I relented.

"Okay, but we have to have this conversation at my place because I need to change. I'm meeting my agent in less than an hour and can't be late for that—again."

...

"Are you worried at all about this?" I asked David.

We'd both come up to my apartment using the stairs—the elevators were thankfully still off-limits. I don't think I could have been inside such an enclosed space with him even for half a minute.

I was in my bedroom, smelling the clothes piled in different states of cleanliness around the space and trying to unearth the one top my sister had gifted me not even two weeks before.

"What should I be worried about?" David answered from my living room. He was fishing for his misplaced

UCLA T-shirt among the wreckage that was my apartment. I hadn't exactly had time to tidy up that morning. And he'd still not let out a single word about whatever he thought we needed to talk about.

"About Dashing fucking Henry appearing dead where you live a week before the trial was about to start." I kept my volume loud from the bedroom.

I finally found the top I needed buried under the pillows of my unmade bed. Had I worn the garment the night before perhaps? In any case, it didn't smell too bad to me.

"The trial was going to be a total sham. My lawyer is confident we were going to get a win or even a dismissal of the libel charge," David said, as if both of us didn't have a close relationship with said lawyer and knew well that the attorney in question wasn't exactly an expert in defamation law.

I was going to call David out on that but I caught him.

He was eyeing me through the open space between the kitchen/living area and my bedroom. One thing about the Eastern Columbia: the whole building had been designed with a wall-less concept in mind.

"Are you checking me out?"

I'd taken off the WGA West hoodie and was wearing just my pajama pants and a bralette from the now defunct les girls les boys. I may be awful when it comes to outerwear and have committed such crimes as wearing Birkenstock sandals with socks, but I have impeccable taste in underwear. And David's eyes were fixed on my body in my bedroom mirror.

"Should I not be staring at you?" He locked eyes with my reflection in the mirror.

I turned around and walked in his direction, still in nothing but my sheer mesh bralette and my low-hanging pajama pants. I stopped in front of him, a mere few centimeters between the two of us. My eyes were playfully fixed on his the whole time.

Something electric crackled in the air. It was always like that between the two of us lately, but seeing each other's faces during the daytime heightened it. So did the fact that we were somehow talking and not just communicating in grunts and monosyllables. The temperature in the room heated even more than it had on previous recent occasions.

I thought he was about to kiss me. I know *I* was going to kiss him.

But the doorbell buzzed.

"Elena, it's me!" I heard Victor's voice on the other side of my front door. He knew I *never* answered the doorbell or opened that door unless I was zealously waiting for a package to be delivered.

Fuuuuck! I thought but managed not to say out loud. I wanted Victor to leave and for me and David to be about to kiss in plain daylight. But the moment had been fleeting.

"Right," I said and, against my own desire, left David standing in the middle of my living room. I went to my bedroom to grab the top I was supposed to be wearing. I hurriedly put it on and went to open the door.

"Been looking for you all over the building. You weren't home before," Victor said when he saw me. His eyes fell on David. "Ah, you're also here."

"I was actually leaving," David said. He exited without attempting to make an excuse. "I'll text you later. We still need to talk," he told me.

David left and I realized he was going to start investigating the case without me. I had asked him to join in, and he wasn't interested. He only seemed to want to talk to me about something even if he wasn't telling me what it was.

I assumed that Victor wasn't going to ask about David's presence at my apartment or what we supposedly needed to talk about. The nature of my relationship with Victor had always been uncomplicated, incurious, and open. (See, I told you there had been no cheating.) He made his way to the kitchen and opened the fridge.

"What was that about?" he asked, checking the sparse contents of my refrigerator.

"What was *what* about?" You can decide whether to believe me, but I truly had no idea what he meant.

"Why do you need to talk?"

It didn't escape my limited deducing skills that he was not looking at me but pretending to be thoroughly hypnotized by the non-contents of my fridge because he was avoiding conflict.

"Why don't you go and ask him?" I told Victor, annoyed. "He's the one who says he wants to talk. For all I know, he may be having second thoughts about letting me keep the fifth season of *The Wire* on DVD when we split up. It's the one about a newsroom."

Victor opted for a change of subject with judgment still directed to my fridge. "Where do you keep the sparkling water?"

"I don't."

"What?" he exclaimed as if not having sparkling water could be equated to not having Wi-Fi—or running hot water. "You have a SodaStream or something, right?" He sounded distressed. On second thought, maybe the source of the distress wasn't my lack of posh water but the fact that I had been caught with my ex and wasn't going to talk about it with him. But at the time, I remained unaware of that possibility.

"Nope. I hate bubbles." My tone lacked even a hint of apology.

And that said so many things about our relationship of convenience. He didn't know that I abhorred fizzy liquids. I'm sure he was still convinced that because I was technically European, I *had* to like sparkling hydration.

I was aware of his water preference but made no effort to keep any in the house. My sister would be able to find her favorite kind of chocolate—Hu Hazelnut Butter Crunch Milk Chocolate bar at the moment; Amelia knew the diverse array of kombucha cans inside the fridge was there solely for her enjoyment; and I kept Guayakí loose leaf yerba mate for those rare nights in which David felt like having it. But there was no sparkling water.

I was certain Victor wasn't at my place to pick a fight or to talk about our relationship—he just wanted to tell me something about the case. But I'm going to make you wait for it since I guess this is as good a moment as any to tell you a bit more about him. About *us*. Because I know you must be wondering, What is she doing with him exactly? And perhaps more specifically, What is he doing with her?

To be completely honest, I'm not sure.

Victor arrived in my life the moment I most needed him. He was like no one I had dated before. I didn't even know I liked blonds until I met him and his eternally freckled if perennially tanned skin.

Of course, it was my mother who introduced us. She approved of him, which was much more than I could say about any of my previous partners. And I didn't hold that against Victor. He's sexy, he can be funny (in private and when he's completely sure that nothing he says will end up online and ruin his future political prospects) but, above all, he's easy.

I'm perfectly aware that he was probably with me because of how well connected I am. He'd never leave me so he didn't lose access, and that made the relationship quite effortless. I never had to worry about saying the right thing, buying the right birthday gift, or wearing the right clothes. He didn't mind that I don't even try. Our relationship felt almost like work, and I know how to work.

Which was why I expected Victor not to say a single thing about my ex being there when he arrived. And then he did. And I can genuinely say that I didn't see that plot twist coming.

"I know David and you are friends or whatever," Victor blurted, and I would have been a bit taken aback by the euphemism if I didn't know how much of a true politician he was. He was a master in the art of not saying what he implied. "But you should probably be careful."

"What do you mean?" Was that his way of telling me he was jealous or something? Did he want to have the exclusivity chat? Because I sure wasn't interested.

"Too many things against him. First, he bylines an article that gets Dashing Henry canceled but somehow David ends up being fired by the newspaper where he published that article. Then Dashing sues him for libel. And now the actor turns up dead at his door a week before the libel trial was set to start."

"If you put it like that . . ." I don't think Victor realized how much the mention of Dashing Henry unsettled me. I was hit with a wave of discomfort at his name and not because I thought Victor could be jealous of David. "I mean, it wasn't technically his door but the parking area."

"Same thing. The cops like him for this. Don't be seen or photographed with him," Victor continued. "I don't think your mom would appreciate the fact that her oldest daughter was linked to a suspected killer."

You have to give it to politicians. Victor wasn't really worried about my safety if David was indeed Dashing Henry's killer. He wasn't even jealous or, if he was, he was making an effort not to show it. What concerned my pretend boyfriend was the possibility of my image—but especially my mother's image—getting potentially damaged if I was seen in the company of the wrong person.

I'm embarrassed to admit that even though I'm a writer and I think myself clever, I couldn't come up with anything sharp enough to counter Victor's comment. So he probably thought I was acquiescing to his advice. In reality, I was simply stunned—and fuming.

After that, I asked him to leave.

7

As if conscious of the fact that I had needed him that day but hadn't reached out, my lawyer called the moment Victor left my apartment.

"Papá," I answered, as my father is also my legal counsel, and tried to make him understand I couldn't talk then. "No tengo tiempo de hablar ahora mismo. I have a meeting with my agent."

"Estoy bien gracias, hija," he answered and proceeded talking in Spanish, ignoring my curt answer. "And your mother and sister are also doing great. How are you?"

"Busy," I answered, rolling my eyes.

"Because you're meeting your agent, yes," he continued. "But *how are you?* I saw Dashing Henry's body was found at your building."

"The police were here. It's been a bit hectic," I conceded. I needed people around me to stop saying that name.

"I can't say I'm sad Henry is dead. He was everything but dashing and a real creep. So much so that his lawyer had finally left him. But you still haven't answered my question," my dad continued. The only people who could beat him at persistence would be my mother and sister. *"How are you?"* he repeated.

"I'm not sure," I finally admitted.

"Why don't we do something. Call Beatrice and tell her you need to reschedule your meeting."

"I can't. The meeting has already been rescheduled twice—by me," I added before he asked. "She's even driving all the way Downtown to make sure I won't have any traffic hiccups."

"Do I want to know why you've already rescheduled it twice?" he asked, the tiniest bit of frustration in his voice even if I knew he was doing everything in his power not to sound judgmental. While both my parents could be described as overachievers, Dad has always been the most understanding and flexible of the two when it comes to my many shortfalls.

"You don't." And he didn't.

The first time I'd postponed the meeting with my agent, I had feigned menstrual cramps, when in reality I'd been too hungover. I didn't even remember what had happened the second time. I think, for a change, I may have been experiencing a rare good day of writing and didn't feel like interrupting the flow.

"Okay, go meet Beatrice. Make it short and then come home. There's a pot of kale soup waiting for you." I almost said yes on the spot. Caldo de berzas was my favorite comfort food, and my dad had started substituting the chicken broth for veggie stock to accommodate my latest dietary activism.

"I'll try to drop by tonight or tomorrow night, but can't promise anything," I said. I didn't feel like having the conversation I knew he thought I needed.

"That soup may not be waiting for you tomorrow. Your

sister is going to find it before that. By the way, how's David doing with all this?"

"How should I know? We're no longer together, remember?" I told my father. It was no secret that David was his favorite boyfriend. I knew Dad was helping him on the libel case free of charge.

"If you say so . . ."

That was more than I was going to endure.

"I say so and I really need to go now."

But my dad kept me on the phone for a good minute more while he sent me hugs and kisses and all manner of affectionate reassurances.

As I hung up, finished changing, and made my way to my meeting, I recalled something I'd managed to put aside until then. It was a day I didn't necessarily want to remember, but present events were bringing it all back.

I hope you are ready for the first flashback portion of this account. Please don't tell me you think flashbacks are lazy storytelling and bad writing. I don't know how to tell you this part of the story any other way—or at any other time.

David and I were still together then. It must have been a bit more than two years before the day of the triggered fire alarm at the Eastern Columbia. We were both home, at our cozy bungalow, watching TV, hugging on the sofa under a blanket or affecting some other quintessential expression of basic millennial domesticity.

As we were lying on the couch, he got a message. I was on top of him and made room so he could take his cell phone out of his jeans pocket. He read the message as I teasingly kissed his collarbone and neck. But the moment I saw his face, I knew we wouldn't be watching another episode of *Mindhunter*, we wouldn't be having a conversation about

David Fincher's many talents as a thriller director both in film and TV, and we certainly wouldn't be making love on top of the imitation midcentury sofa or any other faux midcentury surface in the house that night.

David had the expression I'd learned to associate with a thirst for the truth: He'd been tipped off about something and wanted to chase the story. I was sure he was about to make some kind of excuse and tell me he needed to go work when he didn't.

"Have you heard anything about Dashing Henry misbehaving on set?" he asked, pausing the laptop where *Mindhunter* was playing on top of our recently purchased coffee table.

"Misbehaving?" I asked. My heartbeat rapidly accelerated and I feared David could feel it too.

"We got a tip a few weeks ago from Henry's former personal assistant. She'd only been at the job a few weeks because she said Henry tried something with her and she left," he continued.

I had sat up on the sofa and was now at the farthest edge from David. My heart was a nervous mess.

"David, you keep talking in euphemisms. *Henry tried something with her.*" I was frustrated about his choice of words and echoed them to him so he heard his own lack of clarity. "And why are you telling me all this? You never tell me anything about your job until a story is about to get published and you need me to read the final draft to reassure you . . ."

"I work with lots of confidential and vulnerable sources, and I like respecting their privacy and safety," he said.

"Thanks for the vote of confidence." I was probably being harsher than necessary. Or perhaps I wasn't.

"It's not that. You know it's not that!"

"Do I?" I asked. "What's different this time?"

"My source is getting tired of waiting for me to find another source. You know I need several accounts from different people before thinking about writing or publishing an article, let alone something that could potentially ruin someone's reputation. And I thought since you worked with Henry, you may have heard something."

I felt almost relieved about his ignorance but also strangely betrayed by it.

I had left *LA Misconducts* a mere few weeks before, and he hadn't bothered inquiring about it much. I felt he assumed I had gotten tired of the long hours and hard work. And now that my former job would suit his reporting pursuits, he was all nosy about it.

"I've heard nothing," I said. And that was true. There had been no gossip, no warning regarding Dashing Henry and his taste for younger women, who he saw as easy prey—especially those still trying to establish themselves in showbusiness.

As I arrived at the restaurant where I was meeting my agent, I shook off the memory of that day like I'd been shaking off so many others. But I had a notion I'd be having to recall more stuff from my past and my link to Dashing Henry. And I didn't know if I was ready for it.

8

I'd been seated at the bar of Ramen Hood for ten minutes, waiting for my agent to find a parking spot big enough to fit her supersized Rivian SUV. I used the wait to write and rewrite a message for David. It may sound ridiculous to you but bear in mind that we hadn't just stopped talking since the breakup. We had halted all forms of digital communication as well, so this was my first text to him in more than two years. Our last text exchange had been about the division of stuff post-breakup. We had both claimed possession of the 1991 paperback edition of *The Catcher in the Rye* in our common bookshelf. In the end, I had lost and had to buy another used copy of the Salinger novel at The Last Bookstore.

After some drafting and redrafting, I was about to send a very uncompromising and boring text to David that read:

> Should be done with my agent in 1 hour.
> Want to talk after that?

But I surprised myself by deleting it and writing something closer to what I really wanted to tell him.

Need you to make me scream like yesterday

Between the non-fire, the dead actor, and all the unpleasant memories, I was starting to feel the stress from the day. All I wanted was a hot shower, a phenomenal fuck, and a siesta.

"Can't believe you actually want to meet with me today, honey," Beatrice said, making one of her grand entrances and kissing me on both cheeks.

Well, I don't, I caught myself thinking but not saying out loud. I wondered, once more, why everyone in Hollywood assumed I was touchy-feely and liked physical contact based solely on my country of origin. I wanted to tell them, I've been living in the US since I was a teenager. I have a blue passport too. I have the same qualms about germs you do. Can we please stop with the kissing and the hugging?

I didn't say a single word though.

"How are you doing?" Beatrice continued. She hadn't even realized I hadn't answered her previous comment. "OMG! What a day you must have had! You need to tell me everything."

I was going to tell her some redacted version of the story and try to see if I could make any sense of what had happened that morning while doing it. I've always believed in the power of vent therapy.

But in the end, it would be *her* telling *me*. How did she have more details than I did? I was there when the body was found. Well, in the proximity of it at least.

"You know they think he was killed, right?" Beatrice continued with her nonstop talking. "They've expedited the results of the autopsy, but it wasn't a shooting or a stabbing. He was run over by a car and they're treating it as a murder."

I was about to ask something but there was no need. Beatrice had already anticipated it.

"They don't think it was simply a hit-and-run—he still had his cell phone and wallet with all the credit cards. But his watch was missing. It was a Patek Philippe worth north of eighty grand. I guess that was difficult to leave behind . . ."

Although Beatrice was talking about the gruesome death of a person—and not recapping all the clients she had been able to place in the latest season of *The Gilded Age*—I'd have sworn my agent was enjoying herself.

"I know, I know. How did they know it wasn't an accidental robbery gone terribly wrong? If there's something we know in Southern California, it's that parking lots are a total hazard!" She never missed a beat. "Apparently, there was some sort of message from Henry."

Again, no need for me to react with a follow-up comment. Beatrice knew I was enthralled even if her gifts as a storyteller left a bit to be desired. Storytelling 101: You can't keep ignoring your audience and their needs for the whole length of your tale. Yes, that's my not-so-veiled manner of telling directors to stop making three-hour-plus movies. People need to pee whether you acknowledge it or not. But I digress.

"When the police notified Henry's attorney about the death," Beatrice continued, "he told them about a voicemail the actor had left him presumably before being run over. The message advised the lawyer to contact the cops as he suspected his life was in danger."

"The fucking prick!" I finally managed to say. "Annoying even when he's dead. Telling everyone what to do."

"I gather you weren't much of a fan?" Beatrice asked, suddenly interested in what I had to say.

"I wasn't," I admitted.

"I hear you're not alone. It doesn't look like he had many friends left. Pretty much everyone in Hollywood detested him." That was news to me. I'd been convinced he was a well-regarded actor. His career vouched for that. "The only ones who hadn't deserted him yet—his agent and manager —were going to ditch him now that he's been fired from *LA Misconducts*. He'd long been without a publicist . . ."

"And I hear he was also without a lawyer," I managed to contribute. I wondered if that was why Henry's attorney hadn't alerted the authorities immediately after getting his call. Henry was no longer his client, and he wasn't picking up his calls. But there was something else Beatrice had said that called my attention. "He was fired?" I'd heard something around town but thought it was some unfounded rumor.

"Very much so."

"What happened?"

"I'm dying to find out about it but haven't been able to— yet," Beatrice said. It made me wonder at her methods—or reasons—to possess so much information about Henry's death. "But perhaps your boyfriend was right after all with that exposé article of his about Henry."

The mention of David had blindsided me, but I was still able to react. "Not my boyfriend anymore," I said.

"That's right! You told me or someone else did . . ."

She wasn't even remotely ashamed that she'd probably been openly gossiping about me and my relationship status behind my back.

"So, honey, we need to talk about the offer," she said, getting in agent mode while we were served two plates of the OG Ramen with vegan eggs. And, in case you were wondering, I don't know what the vegan egg is either.

"Tell me about the offer," I said unenthusiastically.

"With Dashing gone from *LA Misconducts*, they're gonna be wrapping the show but want to bank on its popularity. So they're developing *NYC Misconducts*, and the showrunner wants you back on the team."

"Is Fred also running this sequel then?" I said, referring to my former boss at *LA Misconducts*, showrunner Fred Appleton.

"He is and he loved working with you," Beatrice said. "There's one caveat though. Fred feels that, in order to write about the NYPD, he needs to *inhabit* New York. So the writers room is going to be based there."

"Yeah, I'm not moving to New York," I said. Even if *NYC Misconducts* sounded remotely attractive to me, which it didn't, my whole family was in Los Angeles and my life had already been uprooted once. I was not going to do that again.

"I'm gonna give you a bit of time to think about it," Beatrice replied.

"I'm *not* moving to New York," I repeated, trying to sound even more assertive.

"I know you're an LA girl, honey." That was not even true. I was a Barcelona girl turned Angelena by her parents. I didn't feel the need to turn into something else and become a New Yorker. "But the weather there is not *that* bad," my agent continued. "I'm sure Fred will let you work from home if there's a big snowstorm. And New Yorkers really grow on you once you get to know them. I'm a New Yorker, aren't I nice?"

She was all fake niceness and actually from New Jersey —not that there's anything wrong about that, it's just not even in the same state as New York City—but I shrugged in acceptance. I avoided conflict like the plague.

"Now Elena, honey, I hate to be the bearer of bad news, especially today," Beatrice said.

Then don't, I thought but, again, I didn't say it out loud.

"How are you doing on that high-concept spec of yours? What was it . . . *Godfather* meets *90210*? Is it anywhere to be read?"

"Almost there," I lied.

I said I didn't lie as a narrator—I didn't say anything about not lying as a regular person. The script about a teenage girl and daughter of a mafia leader, who moves with her family from Miami to Beverly Hills and is forced to make new friends, was nowhere near ready to be read. I was stuck with writing a story I thought the market may find amusing—and some streaming service an absolute must to produce—but I wasn't feeling it anymore even if I tried to continue typing.

"I need something from you *pronto*, honey," Beatrice said, and I'm not even going to try and describe her pronunciation of the word *pronto*. I can only imagine that, because she was meeting with a Spaniard, she thought its use appropriate. Never mind that I have dual citizenship, speak four languages, and my English—if accented—is more than proficient. "Either you write something extremely sellable and commercial, or you accept the *NYC Misconducts* offer you're being all snobby about. But I can't have you doing nothing for much longer. Per the conditions of your overall deal, you owe the studio something. Something they like," she added before I could protest and bring up the four projects I'd pitched and written and they had rejected. Perhaps this was why I wasn't feeling my latest spec script attempt. I'm perfectly aware that having thick skin is the number one quality to being a successful screenwriter, but who can take so much rejection?

"And I assume I don't have to remind you that the overall deal runs out in three months. The chances of the studio renewing it are getting slimmer as the market for overall deals is getting colder. So take the job they're offering you or get me something juicy."

There it was. The not-so-veiled threat behind a mask of fake smiles and concerned *honeys*. Either I delivered something soon or I could start thinking about shopping for a new agent, because Beatrice was going to put me in client Siberia.

9

I would be lying if I didn't admit I was worried about Beatrice's words. It wouldn't be the first time she chastised a client whose output wasn't to her satisfaction. She was known for her ruthlessness in contract negotiations and getting the best terms for her clients—but also for asking said clients to produce their best work and be their best selves.

I knew she'd been extremely generous and patient with me. Quite lenient too, for her standards. I also suspected she'd only done that because of who I was. And by that, I don't mean my natural talents as a screenwriter or the fact that I had all the markings to become the next Michelle King or Jenji Kohan, but who my parents were and their position in the city and the Hollywood industry.

I was walking home, still worried about my prospects if I became a screenwriter whose agent was actively ignoring her—or even an unrepped one—when I realized the perfect story was waiting for me. It had everything: a glamorous setting, the tragic death of a famous actor, and all the ingredients of a riveting whodunnit. I just needed to figure out who actually did it and write a script about it. And who better to help me figure all of that out than a hunky investigative reporter with whom I shared a lot of history?

He'd already told me no when I'd asked to join the investigation of the case that morning. But he couldn't say no to me again, right? I wasn't going to give him the option this time. I couldn't afford it. I needed to work on this with him and get the perfect tale on which to base my next project.

I called David from the street, ready to leave him a voice-mail, but he answered right away.

"Where are you?"

"Why?" he answered.

"Because I'm obviously coming. You need help, Scribe."

I hadn't used the affectionate term with him since we'd broken up. Hell, I probably hadn't used it for weeks or even months before the separation, and I knew he couldn't resist it. He'd always loved it when I used tender words with him, perhaps because I'd rarely done it.

"I'm at the swimming pool," he said, and I rolled my eyes.

Why couldn't he work from his desk at the newsroom or at home or even from his sofa, like a normal writer? He always needed to be out and about, writing from the weirdest places. I did most of my writing directly from bed and had never been able to understand the coffee-shop and public-space dwellers.

I accelerated my walking cadence and made it to my destination in ten minutes. The swimming pool is on the rooftop of the Eastern Columbia, overlooking the building's turquoise and gold-embellished clock tower. Sadly, the elevators were still not functioning and by the time I made it to the rooftop, I was sweating and breathing heavily.

It wasn't even that hot, but David was lounging on a lawn chair, his computer propped on his lap, his T-shirt missing.

If this was some sort of strategy on his part to look sexy and make me ogle, he was succeeding.

Extremely.

"Have news about the pecs—about the death!" I stumbled. My subconscious has always been treasonous.

"Please sit down and tell me," he said, smiling and signaling the lawn chair next to him.

Let me restate that he was shirtless.

"I have conditions," I managed to say firmly, standing at a distance and trying to look only at his face. I don't think I managed. I also don't think anyone was buying my pretend apathy toward him.

"Of course you do," he said, putting his laptop aside and sitting upright.

"I'll share everything I know, and I'll make use of all my access at city hall and with the production team of *LA Misconducts*, but you can't shut me off. I need full access to your investigation. We're working on this together."

"What's in it for you?" he asked, and that was a good start. He wasn't saying no outright.

"I think there's a script in this story," I explained. "And I want to be the one to write it. But there needs to be an article worth adapting first. And I'm counting on you for that. Let's work together to make all that happen."

"And you're willing to share all your contacts?"

"I am."

"Dale," he agreed. He put his T-shirt back on, and I wasn't ready for the ease of the situation—or the sudden disappearance of a shirtless David.

"¿Sí?" I was unsure I'd heard him correctly. I sat on the chair next to the one he occupied.

"Elena, don't make me regret this. Why are you doubting?"

"I'm not doubting. I just didn't think you'd say yes so easily," I said. "You've never let me help you before."

"You never offered your connections before." And there it was. It appeared I was nothing but my connections.

"So we've got a plan then? I help you investigate. We clear your name. You write an article. And I adapt it into a script." I needed to make sure we were both on the same page.

"We have a plan," David said.

I reapplied sunscreen—I may have an olive Mediterranean complexion and tan well but I was still aware of the dangers of the Southern California sun even in winter—and proceeded to tell David everything Beatrice had shared with me pertaining to the case.

"You don't look mildly surprised," I said once I finished my account. It was as if nothing I'd said was news to him.

"I have a source at the LAPD."

"Ah," I grumbled. Of course he did. What exactly was I doing there? So far, helping didn't seem to be my thing.

"Are you going to keep pretending you didn't send me a very explicit text?" he asked me then. I was astounded by his words—and the turn of events.

"What are you talki—" The text I had been drafting earlier popped into my brain, and I wanted to die. "No! No, no, no, no . . ." I took my cell phone from my back pocket, unlocked it, and went to the message history to reaffirm that I hadn't sent that last draft.

But I had. There it was: a green bubble. David, of course,

was an Android user to my iPhone. A green bubble of shame that read, *Need you to make me scream like yesterday*.

"I sent this by mistake when my stupid agent arrived. It was like a butt call but a butt message, only it was sent with my fingers—I think. Never mind. Can we pretend this didn't happen?" I pleaded.

"As we've been pretending we haven't been fucking each other for the last half a year?" he said. "I liked the message. Is it that terrible to tell your lover what you want?"

"Is it what we are now? Lovers?" I could feel my cheeks burning and my heart beating furiously.

"I prefer *lovers* to *former-partners-turned-booty-call*," he said.

I had been avoiding that conversation with him since the night six months before when I took the elevator to the second floor, knocked on his door, crossed my fingers, pulled him by his T-shirt the moment he opened the door, made sure he was okay with the situation, kissed him, helped him out of that T-shirt and the rest of his clothes, undressed myself, pushed him to the sofa, put a condom on him, got him inside me, fucked him with an urgency I hadn't known before, had a stupendous orgasm, made sure he also did, and left without saying a single word.

"Is that what you've been trying to talk to me about all day?" I asked.

"Not really, but since we already started. Tell me, what does Victor have to say about this arrangement of ours?"

"Nothing, we're non-exclusive. Not that it's any of your fucking business!"

That was a red line for me. If he really needed it, I could —reluctantly—talk with David about how, after that first night, I had kept going to his apartment, looking for sex but never for a conversation; how at some point he'd also started coming to my place; and how we'd managed to exchange keys to each other's places while uttering no words but both understanding that would make our nightly visits easier— and perhaps more frequent.

If David needed it, we could talk about how not having any strings attached had meant a more audacious sex life than when we'd officially been a couple.

We could talk about how we were never this hot, horny, and needy for one another when we were in a formal relationship except perhaps in those first weeks when we were still friends messing around.

We could even go over the fact that I trusted him completely when it came to the two of us together in a dark room with only the goal of pleasure in mind, but I still couldn't find it in me to trust him for anything else.

But we were *not* going to talk about Victor.

10

We stared at one another for what felt like an eternity, daring the other to be the first to say whatever needed to be said between us. I was about to call a truce and ask him to leave the pool—let's not forget we were in February and that's technically also winter in perennially sunny SoCal—and go to my place. I was still craving a shower, a fuck, and a siesta, not necessarily in that order.

But, of course, as it was always the case with my and David's story—and the reason why I had wanted to keep things as non-verbal as possible those last few months—he got a call. A work call.

In the past, he would have walked away from me under the pretense of not wanting to disturb me, even if I knew what he wanted was for me not to overhear his conversation. But he didn't do it this time. He remained exactly where he'd been and answered his phone, a pained look of apology on his face.

"Hi. I'm sending it in the next hour, but it's short and mostly speculative," he said to who I assumed was his editor. "If we had more time, I'd prefer to wait. But I know we don't."

It had to be bad if David was thinking of bylining something he had qualified as *speculative*.

But every local, state, and national big outlet and minor blog had been reporting nonstop about Henry's death since that morning. So even I understood that David would want to write something about it too. He'd been the reporter who had uncovered Dashing Henry and had gotten him canceled. David had probably had something, or a lot, to do with getting Henry finally fired. And he was there when the body was found.

"Perhaps I shouldn't have used that adjective . . ." he continued as if trying to make a point with his editor.

Did he look tense or frustrated? He was so annoyingly calm and balanced all the time that I hadn't learned to recognize the signs of stress in him. He didn't appreciate that and had probably added it to our extensive list of grievances and differences.

In my defense, it's just so difficult to tell. He doesn't sweat, he doesn't fidget, he doesn't pace restlessly. He doesn't stutter, avoid eye contact, or become irritable. You can only tell he's not happy by the clench of his jaw. And since I happen to be partial to his sharp jawline, sometimes I find myself not recognizing that he's not trying to be sexy but mad.

I realized something must be wrong with David that afternoon when his jawline started looking sharper than Matt Bomer's and Henry Cavill's combined.

"I *know* I'm not impartial. Nobody expects me to be in this case. They want me to write about it precisely because I'm not impartial—and the body was found at my building."

The blade from the fancy Japanese mandoline that my

dad had gotten for me the previous Christmas looked duller than David's mandibles at the moment, yet his voice was perfectly measured. I'd probably be screaming if I was in his situation—or simply not saying a word.

He hung up after that and I thought I perceived the slightest trace of frustration in his eyes.

"Everything okay?" I asked. For some reason, I wanted him to know I had perceived his unhappiness this time.

"My editor doesn't think I should be writing about Dashing Henry's death. He's passing me for another reporter."

"What? That's bullshit!"

"I know. That's why I'm going to ignore him and keep doing my job. There's no way I'm not reporting this story." I knew that, as a not-so-young-anymore reporter, he kept an inner checklist of grievances against past and present editors.

"What editor is that? John Diaz at the *LA Gazette*?"

"Michael Townsend from the *Los Angeles Voice*," he said, referring to the *Gazette*'s main competitor. "The *Gazette* fired me after the big Dashing Henry article, when the actor sued me and pretended he'd never coerced sexual favors from his staffers."

"Right, I knew about the *LA Gazette* being done with you. I always thought they were a bunch of self-centered idiots," I said.

"John Diaz is actually a nice guy. His hands were tied when they got rid of me." I couldn't avoid rolling my eyes. I'd never been a fan of Diaz, even though David adored him. Too many late-night deadlines, weekend assignments, and endless rounds of editions.

"So you're working with the *Voice* now?" I asked.

If we'd been talking for the last few months, I wouldn't

have to ask such basic questions. Those were the kinds of things you were supposed to know about someone you . . . cared about. But we hadn't been on speaking terms, and I'd been actively avoiding him online as well. Not only his social media but all of his writing. It reminded me too much of him.

"I'm only freelancing for the *Voice*," he said, and I thought he was about to tell me something else, but he didn't because my cell phone rang.

Chances are that, if you phone me, your call will go straight to voicemail. Same happens with any other unknown number. Same with most of my friends and acquaintances, same with Victor, same with my agent even. I do pick up the phone at least half the times my dad calls because he's threatened to write me out of the will if I don't. My mother never calls—I'm told she's a very busy woman—so that doesn't count.

But there's one person for whom I'm always telephonically available—unless I'm flying or seriously undisposed. She even gets her own personalized ringtone (Chvrches' "The Mother We Share"): my little sister Marta.

And that was exactly the identity of the caller that wretched Thursday of February when me and David were still inexplicably by the swimming pool of the Eastern Columbia.

"It's Marta," I told him before picking up the call.

"I recognize the ringtone," he said, and it dawned on me that we had so much history together, even if I wanted to keep pretending we didn't.

"Hola," I answered the call. Most of the conversations between me and my sister happen in the best kind of Spanglish. We always understand one another and never find strange the need to keep mixing languages.

"Oh, dios mío. ¡Hola!" she said. "Are you okay? I saw there was a murder in your building!"

"News travels fast, but yes," I said. "Estoy entera."

"Oye, I don't actually have time to talk right now," she said. "I'm driving and my copyright law class starts in less than twenty minutes. ¡Llego muy tarde!"

She'd come home from Berkeley the previous summer —to the relief of the whole family; we never understood the Northern California allure—to follow in my dad's steps and study the same branch of law as him after a stint as a theater fellow at Berkeley Rep. She'd been *temporarily* living at my parents' property since her return, and no one seemed to be pretending any longer that she wanted to find her own place and move out of their guest house.

I can't blame her. My parents' cabañita de la piscina is a 1,500 square feet bungalow outfitted with its own kitchen and full bathroom. It has a separate entrance, full access to the swimming pool and the main house's cooking services— a.k.a. breakfast, lunch, and dinner are included and deli- cious—and is regularly cleaned and maintained.

If it wasn't because I have this thing going with one of the residents at the Eastern Columbia—and I'm a mess to live with anyway, and my sister has expressed her desire never to share a house with me again—I'd probably move in with Marta.

"I'm calling because I overheard Mamá having a sneaky conversation when I went to the house to grab my merien- da," Marta continued, referring to her afternoon snack. She was twenty-four, had a Bachelor of Arts in Theater and Performing Studies, had been an exchange intern for a year at Teatre Lliure in Barcelona, and was currently enrolled in the law program at UCLA. But she could still sound like a little girl sometimes. "Mamá was meeting

Victor and the whole PR crew over Zoom. Ha sido todo muy raro."

"What do you mean raro?" I asked her.

"They're having issues with the rogue councilmen again," she said, referring to the two council members, with the same party affiliation as my mother, who'd been recently accused of having made sexist comments about one of their female colleagues from the opposite party. "There's a new insensitive text message from one of them or something like that."

"Okay, are you calling me to gossip about the latest city council telenovela occurrence?" I said, confused.

"Of course not, tonta." I could hear her honking viciously. Marta was one hundred percent Californian mellow vibes in all but one thing: her driving instincts. She was all Mediterranean intensity when it came to her skills behind the wheel. "The PR peeps and Mamá don't want any more headlines about dysfunctionality at city hall. They're gonna leak to the *LA Gazette* the fact that the police are working under the assumption that David is Dashing Henry's killer. They're building a case against him."

"What?" I yelled.

"David doesn't have many friends at city hall. Everyone is still mad at him because of the article he wrote six months ago uncovering Henry just when they'd hired the actor to promote the city's image," Marta said. Just as David's article was published, the whole of Los Angeles had been covered in billboards with Henry's creepy face on them paired with the Los Angeles city logo. No wonder no one at city hall had a soft spot for my ex.

"They can't throw David under the bus!" I protested. David looked at me and raised a questioning eyebrow. Did he really *need* to look so sexy while doing it?

"You know they don't have many qualms when it comes to distracting the press. They hope that by giving them David's story, they won't give that much space or attention to the one about the council's sexist members," she said.

Even if I didn't want to admit it, being the daughter of a politician, I understood the bizarre logic behind that way of acting.

"I need to go now," my sister said.

"Okay. Talk later?"

"Yes. Will you do me a favor?" she asked. "Will you let David know about all this? He still has friends at the *Gazette* and maybe he can talk to them and get this stalled."

"Why not let him know yourself?" I asked, even if David was currently in front of me and watching me with interrogating eyes. I was very aware that my sister still had David's number memorized among her favorite contacts, and they kept in touch regularly. But I knew she'd called me and not him because she was looking for not-so-subtle ways of forcing me to get in touch with him.

"You do it," she said.

As I hung up and looked at David, I was reminded of another moment in our past. A very different one. Probably the opposite circumstance to the one we presently found ourselves in.

It had been four years before. I had just gotten my job as a staff writer at *LA Misconducts*. He'd been offered a contractor position at the *LA Gazette* with the option of becoming a permanent staffer. It looked as if things had started working our way and we'd finally managed to figure out our careers. But, of course, that moment was actually the beginning of the end of our story together.

11

After the chat with my sister, we went downstairs for a coffee to talk things over—not things about *us*, but everything each of us knew about the case —and I informed David about my mother's intentions toward him. Marta was right about David still having friends at the *Gazette*, something that would have never crossed my mind. David made a call to John Diaz, his former editor there, and seemed unfazed at the prospect of his name being in tomorrow's newspaper not as a byline but as a headline. Perhaps Diaz was a nice guy after all, even if I'd never liked him.

Debrief coffee at ilcaffè morphed into the need for something stronger, and I managed to drag David all the way up Bunker Hill to the Conrad Hotel with the excuse of getting drinks at their rooftop restaurant, Agua Viva.

He grumbled and protested about the bougieness of the place but in the end was content when we were seated at an outdoor table with views of city hall and he tasted his Fernet-Branca cocktail. As for me, I move with ease through luxury hotels (even unshowered), had been a regular at the place since it opened a couple of years before, and had a suspicion that David would love the spot too if he ever gave it a chance.

We were now on our second—or perhaps third, we had shared at least one glass of Albariño—drink, and I was euphorically tipsy. Not even the order of patatas bravas and eggplant toast I had devoured were making me sound any less drunk—or uninhibited. And, to my partial astonishment, David didn't seem at all preoccupied about the murder case.

"You left my place annoyingly early last night," I finally told David, downing the last of my aptly called Tornup Tiki Punch and wondering why we didn't go out more often.

Right, we were no longer a thing.

"I'm sorry about that," he said with a smile that had me blushing, but I could see he was nonetheless surprised. "Frustration is the least thing I want to elicit in you when we're together. But I'm happy we're finally talking about this."

"This?" I said with a chill.

"You know? Those visits that you've been cataloging as oneiric because they always happen at night and where there are two mandatory terms: no words and loud orgasms."

I ignored his incisiveness. I hate it when he gets me so well. "Why did you leave so early yesterday?"

"Sleepovers have never been on offer," he said.

"I wasn't offering you to sleep when you left," I pressed.

We both knew that, since we'd started hooking up again a few months before, the previous night had been the first time I had indicated I wanted to have sex again. I had sensed he was also eager, but he'd left anyway.

"There was something at work," he said.

"Ah," I said, suddenly not wanting to know more.

There was a brief and slightly uncomfortable silence during which I was tempted to order another drink even if more alcohol was far from what my system required. We both avoided each other by looking once again at the beautiful city as sunset had given way to night.

"I saw your neighbor after I left your apartment yesterday," David finally said.

"Not fucking chatterbox George, please!" If the tenant in 10B had seen David leaving my place at 1 a.m., by now the whole building would know that we were "sleeping" together—and I hate being the object of gossip.

"No, the guy in 10D."

"I don't think I've ever seen him."

"He politely greeted me with a nod. We took the stairs together in silence. I exited the stairs at my floor, and he continued making his way downstairs. He was dressed in medical scrubs, so I assumed he must have been going to work."

I suddenly realized something that perhaps I should have detected before. You may have been wondering about it for a while. I've never been the fastest at this deducing game, so pardon my tardiness.

"Do we know what time the police think Henry was killed?"

"My source at the LAPD said anytime between 10 p.m. and midnight," David said. He'd been in my apartment since 9:30 p.m.

"And you're sure you don't want to tell the cops you were with me?"

"I don't know what looks worse: not having an alibi or

coming up with one after admitting we've lied," he reasoned.

I was going to protest when, even if I was still incredibly inebriated, more stuff started clicking.

"What was Dashing Henry doing at the Eastern Columbia?" I asked.

"I don't know," he said. "My LAPD source is a bit spooked and has been very tight-lipped. I'm trying to get them to tell me more because I feel the police know more than they are letting on."

"Of course they do! David, remember that there's a chance they think you're the killer. Don't you think perhaps that's why your source is a bit shy all of a sudden?"

"We've known each other for a long time. I doubt they would believe me capable of murder."

"I'm so drunk, I don't think I'd be able to walk home. But even I can realize how naïve what you just said sounds," I told him, worried.

"Let's go. I'll take you home." Once again, he was shutting me down. I was so used to it by then that I didn't even try bringing up the subject again. Plus, it had technically been me who had given him the perfect excuse to change subjects when I mentioned how wasted I was, so I could not complain.

We walked silently for the few blocks between the hotel and our building. My steps were so unbalanced—especially going down the hill—that David got closer and put his arm around my waist to make sure I would not fall. Since I promised you transparency, I'll go ahead and admit that I may have overplayed the drunk role. I may have even been able to walk in a straight line for at least half a short block. But I was too thrilled at his body being so close to mine.

"Are you wearing my deodorant?" he asked, as the closeness between our bodies allowed him to sense not only my heat but also my fragrance.

"No, but my heater broke and I was trying to get a shower this morning when the alarm went off—and you know the rest," I explained, not explicit enough to add, *So, it's you that you're smelling on me because I still haven't showered since last night.*

When we got inside the Eastern Columbia, we saw that the elevators were finally working again. I may not have been as inebriated as I was pretending to be, but I still don't think I could have climbed ten floors. We both got inside one of the elevators and David pressed the ten but not the two. Lusty, wanton anticipation grew in my body.

"So, we're working on this together," I said, trying to keep my mind cool and my thoughts steady. There was a chance I would start undressing him inside the elevator otherwise.

"It looks like we are, yes."

I wondered if he could see my desire.

"Let's not do a podcast though," I said, feeling an urgency to pretend I wasn't craving him with all my body. "I don't want to be *Only Murders in the Building, LA Edition.*"

"I don't even know what you're talking about."

Of course he didn't.

The elevator finally made it to the tenth floor and the doors opened. I could feel the impatience between my legs. David walked me to my door.

"Are you coming inside?" I asked, tired of pretending I wasn't starved for him.

"You're still very drunk," he told me, and I suddenly hoped I hadn't stopped feigning disinterest because I knew that was going to be a no. "I've walked you to your door because you literally can't stand straight, and I wanted to make sure you made it home safely. We both need some quality sleep tonight."

"I hate it when you sound reasonable."

And I did.

So I kissed him playfully on the cheek while tugging the waist of his jeans, told him good night, and closed the door of my apartment behind me.

I was still tipsily elated, so I undressed and proceeded to power on one of my favorite sex toys. There would sadly be no unexpected surprises that night.

I couldn't avoid reminiscing about the previous evening though.

Don't get ahead of yourself. This is *not* the chapter where I tell you what happened between David and me on Wednesday night. We're still barely at the beginning of the second act and we've almost already kissed on the page once and have had a handful of mentions about how unbridled our orgasms are. We cannot have a sex scene so early in the story.

Please don't hold that against me. Writing smut is hard and awkward but I enjoy the process anyway. It's just that it goes against all the rules of slow-burn narration to have explicit content among the two main cast members so early in the story, and I'm a stickler for procedure and abiding by the genre's formula.

But don't be too disappointed. I promise I'll be persuaded to tell you all about our night together before this manuscript ends. It's relevant for the story, as a murder was taking place while we were shamelessly frolicking.

What I can tell you now is how incredibly disappointed I felt by that Wednesday night's end.

David and I had fallen asleep after sex. And so that I'm clear, there was zero frustration to report up until this point. It was the first time that we'd slept together—literal meaning here, not the euphemistic one—since breaking up. He'd been incorrect in his assessment while we were having drinks at Agua Viva: Yes, sleepovers had never been on offer before. But they somehow had been the night of the murder.

We woke up in a jolt to what sounded like fireworks but could have equally been some shots. The noise startled me and then I realized that David was still in my bed. It was reassuring, having him by my side. He'd also woken up. We sought each other's eyes in the darkness of the room—as if realizing what had happened and searching for certainty that everything was still okay. I took my hand to his jaw, closing in on his lips with mine.

I can't shake the feeling that had I managed to kiss him then, our situation would be different at present. Perhaps we'd be sharing the same bed now.

Not only did I want to sleep with him on Wednesday, actually sleep, but I was even tempted to break the silence vows I seemed to have made with him and talk about whatever our relationship status was. I knew he'd been wanting to do it for a while now.

But I didn't get the chance to kiss him. Right when my lips were brushing his and I could sense the notes of spices and honey on his breath, he moved away from me, from my mouth, my body. I keenly felt the absence of his warmth. I didn't understand what was happening at first and grabbed his forearm, pleading with him to stay. He removed my hand from his arm, looked me in the eyes again, and we said the first words we'd exchanged since the breakup.

"Don't go yet," I begged.

"I need to," he replied.

I guess now you'll understand a bit better why I was so cross with David the following morning when a fire alarm threw us onto the streets and he started playing the exemplary neighbor.

12

Friday, February 23rd

On Friday morning I woke up to a splitting headache, dry mouth, and the notes of "The Imperial March" drumming incessantly by my ear. I groaned as I lifted my cell phone from where it had been lying on my pillow. I saw my mother's name on the screen even though I had recognized her ringtone. Something had to be *very* wrong for her to be making the call, and I needed to double-check it was actually her.

Don't get me wrong, Mayor Valls does call me—sometimes—when she needs to confirm my attendance to an event or instruct me about my wardrobe for another event. It's just never her calling from her own phone anymore but her press secretary, or her first assistant, or her second assistant, or her intern, or someone else in her seemingly limitless entourage.

But she was *personally* calling me that day at the unseasonable time of 6:47 a.m.

"Hi," I answered as assuredly as I could mutter.

"Hungover?" she asked. Unlike with the rest of the family, and to better integrate in American society, my mother and I had ditched our pre-US-move communication language, in this case Catalan, and now solely spoke to each other in English. And let me add, how the fuck did she know I was hungover?

"No, but you woke me up. It's a bit early." I tried playing it cool even if I was still lying in bed.

"Early? I've been up since 5 a.m." I rolled my eyes. She would have never woken so early when we lived in Barcelona, but then we moved here and she transformed into this political animal who woke up early, never drank, never said the wrong thing, had a fake smile perpetually plastered on her face, and was always working.

"I gather you haven't checked the news," she said.

She had repeatedly talked to me about how disappointing it was to have a daughter who was only interested in reading the Arts & Entertainment section of any newspaper or media outlet. So I had added Travel & Fashion after that to my news regimen and she was still not happy. I suspected she wanted me to read about local, national, and international politics, but I didn't want to undermine my undeniable talent for constantly disappointing her.

"As I've said, you woke me up, mother," I told her. "I haven't even peed yet—let alone read anything."

"Check the *Los Angeles Voice*." It sounded like an order.

"Anything in particular?" I asked as I fired up my laptop. Other people sleep with their significant others or their fur babies, but I have to do with my devices. I typed the name of one of the city's main newspapers into the browser.

"You'll know when you see it," my mother said. "Go to the restroom, have a coffee, and read the article I'm calling you about. I expect you'll report to me in five minutes and tell me what you'll do to fix this."

She hung up.

Don't think I'm a terrible daughter or anything if I tell you that I didn't follow those terms and I didn't call her back. For one thing, I didn't want to be yelled at—yet again. Apparently, I can be quite the dissatisfying daughter.

On the other hand, this time she may have been right in scolding me. After reading the article I *knew* she was referring to, I realized this wasn't exactly like the time I'd turned up high to a campaign event and had eaten *all* the chocolate chip cookies of the press buffet or the occasion in which I'd worn platform sneakers, low rise jeans, and a daring Vivienne Westwood corset to a black-tie political function. In any case, I wasn't looking forward to whatever nagging was coming my way.

But, of course, evading Aurora Valls is no easy task.

"Still haven't had time to pee," I answered the phone when my mother called again a mere twenty minutes later.

"I don't care," she said. She hated it when I made what she considered *vulgar* comments—and talking about physiological needs always fell in that category for Aurora Valls.

I waited patiently on the phone. If she wanted to confront me about the story on the cover of the *Los Angeles Voice*, she'd have to phrase what had inconvenienced her so much. But that would also fall in the category of *vulgar* chatter.

"Did you read the article?" she said, tentatively.

"I did," I replied. "I saw that your strategy has been successful. Not only is the *Voice* not saying anything about the problems you're facing with two of the council people at city hall, you've managed to distract everyone with this juicy tale of the murder of Dashing Henry."

"If only that juicy tale stopped at mentioning David's involvement!" my mother fumed. She didn't even try to conceal the fact that she'd leaked my ex's name to the newspaper.

"*Alleged* involvement. But don't tell me you were expecting they'd just publish whatever story your people fed them without reporting it themselves?" I filled my voice with as much scorn as I could affect at such an early hour and given the somewhat serious circumstances.

"I wasn't expecting said reporting would lead to them writing about my firstborn and dragging her into a salacious story about murder! Especially considering said daughter is *supposed* to be broken up from a relationship with David Ramos for two years now," she said, still eluding the sticky subject. "PR is going to reach out to you to come up with a strategy to counter this."

"Not interested, especially when there's nothing to counter. The article is completely fabricated when it comes to the association of David's name with the murder of Henry. But absolutely accurate when it comes to his *connection* to me," I said. Finding the right code word could be so thrilling sometimes.

"I was hoping for a different version of the events," my mother said, not even trying to conceal the frustration in her voice.

"You got the actual facts," I said.

I'm not exactly timid or amenable. I do whatever I want. But I try to avoid confrontation at all costs, especially with my mother. That's why I didn't add what really had me fuming that morning: the fact that she couldn't care less if she'd leaked the name of an innocent man to the press. She was only concerned because I'd also been linked to that man and—by extension—her.

"Will you tell my lawyer I'll be calling him in a bit?" I asked my mother, trying to sound conciliatory.

"I'm sure he'll be thrilled." I'm still not sure whether she meant it. Sarcasm has never been her preferred or strongest suit.

When she hung up, I refreshed the website of the *Voice* again. The article that had caused my mother to irately wake me up was still placed atop their frontpage. I gave it a second read, holding my almost finished cup of espresso.

Investigative Reporter David Ramos Linked to the Death of LA Misconducts Actor Dashing Henry

The LAPD is working under the assumption that the former *LA Gazette* contributor David Ramos could be behind the death of Dashing Henry. Ramos is said to be having a relationship with Mayor Aurora Valls's oldest daughter, the unemployed screenwriter Elena Freire Valls.

By Gloria Kingsley

It reads like the script of a bad formulaic genre show. It could be an episode of *LA Misconducts* but it's actually a true crime tale.

LA Misconducts troubled actor Dashing Henry was found dead at the parking area of a Downtown Los Angeles apartment building this Thursday, February 22nd, in a suspected hit-and-run. The case is being investigated as a murder.

Henry, 62, had recently been fired from the network procedural show after 15 seasons leading the cop drama. The actor had come under scrutiny six months before when a series of articles by then *LA Gazette* reporter David Ramos were published. In the articles, Henry was said to have made unwanted sexual advances toward at least three members of the *LA Misconducts* cast and crew.

Among the people who came forward making accusations against the actor was *LA Misconducts* associate producer Brenda Lee, then girlfriend of *LA Misconducts* former series regular Amelia Sanchez. Sanchez and Lee both left *LA Misconducts* at the end of season thirteen and are now married.

Ramos's articles were published more than a year after that, and once Lee no longer worked on the show. Henry maintained the accusations were false and had sued Ramos for libel. The trial was set to start next Monday. It's not clear why the *LA Misconducts* team had decided to rescind Henry's employment in the show now, but a source close to the show's production team is citing showrunner Fred Appleton's appetite for change with the development of a sequel set in a different city.

Scandalous Hit-and-Run

According to sources not authorized to discuss the murder investigation, law enforcement is working under the assumption that Ramos could be the one who ran over and killed Henry with his car. The body of the actor was found at Ramos's residence building at the Eastern Columbia Lofts on Broadway Street.

Ramos was fired from the *LA Gazette* shortly after his contested articles against Henry were published and after the repeated denials from the actor and the *LA Misconducts* network. He was an occasional contributor of this newspaper. The journalist was romantically linked to Mayor Aurora Valls's oldest daughter, Elena Freire Valls, a few years ago but they were no longer a couple, at least not openly. According to a resident of the Eastern Columbia Lofts, Ramos and Freire Valls could be involved yet again as the two of them spent Wednesday night together at Freire Valls's apartment. She's also a resident at the Eastern Columbia.

"They pretend like they don't know each other but they've been *seeing* each other for a while," said the Eastern Columbia Lofts resident with knowledge of the case who wishes to remain anonymous. He says he shares a wall with Freire Valls's apartment unit. "I could hear them humping like rabbits on Wednesday night. They're so loud, it was impossible to sleep."

Freire Valls, who coincidentally was a writer for two seasons of *LA Misconducts*, has been mostly unemployed after leaving the show also at the end of season thirteen.

It's still unclear whether Ramos would have acted alone or could have been aided by his jobless girl-friend while allegedly running over Henry.

"Fucking chatterbox George!" I grumbled when I finished reading. "And fucking Gloria Fucking Kingsley," I added, referring to the reporter who'd written the article. "I never fucking liked you. Was it really necessary to include that I'm unemployed *three times* in the fucking article? I have an overall deal!"

I realized that something had to be intrinsically wrong with me when I was more upset about being called out for my lack of an occupation than the insinuation that I could be complicit in a murder.

Call it extreme careerism.

I was about to call David and tell him what I really thought about his former coworker Gloria Fucking Kingsley, when I saw the incoming call from Beatrice on my phone's screen. Could my day get any worse?

I finished my coffee, breathed deeply three times, and did what all good in-between-projects writers do when their annoying agents call: answer the phone and pretend they actually like them. Fortunately, I didn't have to say much.

"Honey," Beatrice said when I picked up the call and even before I could mumble a simple *hello* or even a *hi*. "You're on the news!" she said enthusiastically. As a seasoned Hollywood acrobat, she was a firm believer of the whole *All news is good news* mantra. "Fred is thrilled!"

"Is he?" I asked incredulously. It was one thing for my agent to pretend any headline was good publicity for me. It was another for my prospective boss to agree.

"Of course! He loved the idea of your name being linked

to a murder investigation. He feels that will give your name even more *cachet*," she reasoned. You don't want to know how she pronounced the word *cachet*. I just hoped I would never have to hear her say it out loud again.

But the whole thing with Beatrice and Fred loving my PR problems sounded so convolutedly Hollywood that even I thought I saw the logic in it.

"Fred has finally told me what happened with Henry and why they decided to fire him now as opposed to six months ago," Beatrice said. The woman loved to gossip even more than talking shop.

"They finally realized he really *is* a sexual predator," I said.

"They did! How did you know?" But Beatrice didn't need or want my input. "Apparently, Dashing tried taking advantage of Archie Eisenberg's niece. Archie's been Fred's producing partner in the show for a few seasons and his niece was interning on *LA Misconducts* this year."

"Did something happen to her?" I asked, an anxious tone in my voice.

"To the niece?" she asked, as if my question wasn't the most relevant, and compassionate, to make at the moment.

"Yes, of course, to the niece," I answered, trying not to sound exasperated.

"Oh, she's fine," Beatrice assured, minimizing whatever had happened. "But Dashing messed with the wrong twenty-something-year-old. Archie was beside himself and he even threatened Henry. Apparently, Charlize Theron taught him hand-to-hand combat."

"Who? Henry?" I asked. I was getting lost in Beatrice's Hollywood tale.

"Archie, of course! Why would Charlize want to teach anything to Henry? But Archie feels awful about the whole thing. I've been told he regrets his past maneuvering on Henry's behalf." Beatrice was whispering now, implying conspiracy.

"What past maneuvering?" And how did this woman always know everything?

"I was hoping you could tell me more about it, actually," Beatrice went on. Apparently, she didn't know everything after all. "As it pertains to something that happened to your not-boyfriend."

"Who? David?" I was intrigued. What could my ex and my former boss's producing partner have in common? Archie Eisenberg wasn't even one of the producers working on *LA Misconducts* when I was there. He'd joined after I left.

"Yes, the one you're *seeing*," she said, not even trying to conceal the insinuation. "When Archie started working on *LA Misconducts*, he did a lot to put the show on the map again, to make it look refreshed and cool. He was the one who got Dashing Henry the gig as the face of the city of Los Angeles that backfired a little on city hall."

"Because they unveiled the campaign the same week David published the first article uncovering Henry," I filled in. "I still can't see what you're hinting at."

"Archie knew David was working on a damaging article against Henry, and he tried shushing it," Beatrice explained. "He didn't want the bad publicity after all the work he'd done revitalizing the popularity of *LA Misconducts*."

"Shushing it?"

"I'm told he went quite out of his way so that David's piece wouldn't get published. Archie wasn't successful in the end, but I would love to have more details. If you ever find out..."

"Oh, you want me to ask David about it."

"And indulge my gossip, yes. Information is a valuable

tool in this town. Anyway, I didn't call to gossip but to tell you that Fred wants to meet you to talk about the job."

I felt a bit blindsided by the sudden change of conversation. "I still need to think about it."

"Honey, you need to make a decision." Beatrice sounded less pleased than before. "I can stall the meeting with Fred, but you need to give me an answer by tomorrow."

I could give her an answer right then and there. But, if I said no, she'd drop me on the spot. What I could do was keep helping David report on this fucking bullshit murder and come up with a fresh-from-the-headlines treatment for her by tomorrow . . . or something similar.

"Why the rush?" I asked, trying to sound as professional and unbothered as possible.

"I'm going to the SAG Awards," she said, referring to one of the many awards-season functions happening in the city from the beginning of the year and concluding with the Oscars. "Fred and Archie Eisenberg are also going to be there. They started working together only a couple of years ago, but they've been busy! They also produced that indie movie with Amelia Sanchez, and she's nominated for it. I thought it was awful, but . . ."

I'd had it with the woman. Was she really trashing my friend's work in front of me?

"Oops! You two are friends, right?" she asked.

"We are," I said, trying to sound as stern as possible.

"But don't you agree with me? I mean, she's normally superb but this last movie of hers . . ." I was about to tell her how much I didn't agree with her but, of course, she didn't give me the opening. "Anyway, Fred is going to be there and then he'll see me, and he'll want to know whether you are taking the job in New York or not. It's one thing to avoid people by phone, but in person . . . I can't play hide and seek all night. I'm wearing Vera Wang!"

"Of course you can't," I said, and it came off a bit flippant, but can you blame me?

"Honey, I need an answer from you," she repeated. "Either you come up with a script no one can say no to, or you take this offer."

"And I promise you'll have an answer," I said.

"By tomorrow at 5 p.m.," she replied. "I'm not taking any calls when the ceremony has started."

It was going to be a tight deadline. But I thrived on them.

13

After telephonically braving first my mother and then my agent, I just wanted to go back to sleep. Maybe even take a long hot relaxing bath and doze off in the bathtub. But that Friday morning would not be the day to do it. It wasn't even seven thirty yet. I'd barely had any coffee. I needed a proper breakfast, a long shower, and some naproxen to help alleviate the hangover.

I drank two full glasses of water and made my way to the shower when I heard my phone buzzing. I went back to my bed, looking for it, and saw Victor's name on the screen. I let the call go straight to voicemail. I guessed he'd also read the news. But I couldn't have another conversation about that damned article that morning. Especially not with him.

I was again heading for the shower when the doorbell rang. I didn't have time to swear under my breath or even think about pretending I wasn't home.

"I brought vegan donuts from Donut Friend and almond milk macchiatos from Verve," David yelled from the other side of my locked front door. I stopped in my tracks and went straight to open it.

I don't know how he'd done it, but David had somehow learned that I'd gone vegan since we quit living together and had chosen the surprise breakfast accordingly. Also, for the record, that's exactly how you should aim to wake someone up: with fried sugary dough and hot comforting beverages.

I opened the door, only partly aware that I was wearing a two-or-three-sizes-too-big UCLA T-shirt and not much else. I didn't even think about how it looked that I was dressed in his favorite college garment, or whether I was showing too much leg. When you're five foot three, you can hardly be described as leggy.

He gave me a stare that at the time I interpreted as knowing—he was conscious that I had his T-shirt and was glad to have found it even if it wasn't clear that I would give it back—but I now think his look was more on the side of appreciative. I may not be leggy per se, but I sure am sexy. Did I mention I wasn't wearing a bra?

"I have a plain glazed, one covered in passion fruit, one covered in matcha, their version of Boston cream, and some donut holes for good measure," he said, not acknowledging my state of dress—or rather undress—while I was still standing at the door. He held a black donut box and a to-go tray of coffees in one hand, clutching his laptop with the other.

How could someone look so ~~good~~ scorchingly hot at 7:33 in the morning and after having way too many drinks the night before?

He wore faded jeans and a dark knit sweater. His hair was still wet from a shower. He smelled of soap, recently applied deodorant, donuts—and him. I felt hungry and realized it had nothing to do with my need for food but my need for him.

Céntrate, compórtate, I ordered myself to focus and

behave. *He's not here for a morning fuck and breakfast. He's here to work on the case, and he's brought food because he knows you're the worst and the only thing you keep in your refrigerator is wine and expired mustard.*

I let him in. He went straight to my round dining room table and started making room for the food and his computer, setting some of my stacks of badly organized scripts, notebooks, and books on neat piles on the floor.

"Relax, I've seen the articles," he told me then, sitting at the table and keeping his perpetually collected and cool façade.

I breathed a bit more easily. I didn't want to be the one to break it to him that his name was splattered across the front page of the newspaper he was supposed to be working for.

I allowed my tense shoulders to go back to a resting position and sat at the table, as far away from him and his intoxicating and pheromone-laden smell as I could while still having full access to the donuts. I bit into one of the holes, had a long sip of coffee, and allowed myself to savor the bliss. Only then did it hit me.

"Articles?" I asked. "*Plural.*"

"Articles," he said, the hint of a smile still on his lips. Was he clenching his jaw at all or had it always been so sexily sharp?

"Okay, my mother woke me up this morning and forced me to read the one on the *Voice* with your name all over it."

"Your name is also there," he said.

"Fucking George. I never liked him."

"He wasn't lying." He sent my way one of the most mischievous, lust-filled stares in our history together.

"He wasn't," I admitted, doing my best at an equally nonchalant but sexually charged stare.

Not only had we been loud on Wednesday night, I'd

texted David after that and asked him to make me scream like that night again. But he still hadn't obliged. And it didn't look like that was going to happen any time soon—if ever again—considering we had bigger preoccupations and he seemed to be the main suspect in a murder investigation.

So, very much against my primal needs, I asked him about those preoccupations.

"What's the other article? Or is it also *articles*?"

"Singular this time," he said.

"Menos mal," I said, relieved.

"No te creas, the article in question is quite damning in itself."

"Fucking press!" David looked offended, but I didn't care.

"Dashing Henry's email account was hacked, its contents leaked online, and someone has already had time to go over more than twenty years of correspondence," David explained.

"Is there any link to a possible reckless driver in those emails?" I asked.

"Yes, if you count me as that."

"What?" David could be described as many things—exasperatingly detailed-oriented, organized to the extreme, quippy, and a bit egocentric—but he was a responsible, careful driver. And he was incapable of murder.

"Apparently there are some emails from an account with my name on it sent to Henry. The fake David Ramos arranged to see Dashing Henry at the Eastern Columbia the night of the murder."

"What?" I repeated.

"Henry's emails were hacked and leaked online. Someone using my name asked him to come to the Eastern Columbia on Wednesday night. That same someone told him I wanted to discuss the upcoming libel trial. Someone else found all the emails and has written about it."

"Fuck!" I managed to say. I took a sip of coffee to appease my nerves after that bombshell, but I could see my hand trembling as it approached my lips.

"Elena, the messages in my name are fake. I never reached out to Henry." For a moment, I thought I saw him gritting his teeth.

"I know, Scribe," I said, feeling the need to comfort him but preventing myself from reaching out. The man had rejected me two nights in a row. I was wearing his T-shirt and I had called him the one word he knew I only used with him. I wanted him to know I knew he was innocent and I'd be there for him, but I also needed to protect myself from the situation and stop showing how much I still cared about him.

"Who wrote this second article?" I finally managed to ask.

"I don't know them," David said, and that sounded weird to me. He'd been a city reporter even at his high school newspaper in Inglewood and then during college. He knew pretty much every other LA-based metro journalist either by name, reputation, or even friendship.

"Who published it?"

"YouReallyDontKnowWhatsOutThere.com," he said.

"What? Some random website? How did you even find this?" I asked.

"I have a Google alert with my name," he said sheepishly.

"Of course you do." I tried to suppress my smirk.

"Elena, please be considerate. I've been fucking accused of murder," he said. "And you know you also have a Google alert set up with your name in case something flattering gets published about you."

"Of course I do!" I relented. "Listen, I get it. We're writers, we're a bit self-absorbed. But should you really be worrying about what some random person says about you? Should you be calling whatever they published an *article*? I thought you had a limited definition of journalism and blogs weren't part of it."

"I've never been such a snob!" he protested.

"You have whenever you've defended the essence and purity of news writing, Mr. Two-Time Finalist of the New America Award in public service journalism."

"Okay, but it won't take long for an actual journalist to find this garbage piece of writing and publish it in a bigger outlet."

"Your reasoning is extremely flawed. If they're an actual journalist, they shouldn't echo anything without reporting it first and reaching out to you for a comment," I said.

He looked at me, defeated. But I understood why he was worried. I'd be too.

...

We'd been working at my place for a good two hours. David kept making calls to colleagues and former editors. He wanted to see if there were more stories about him about to hit the virtual presses and I realized that, even when he was talking to some of his friends, he didn't mention anything about the so-called article at YouReallyDontKnow-WhatsOutThere.com. He obviously didn't want to be the one pointing anyone in that direction.

He was also trying to find an outlet for the piece he was working on with me. The article where he'd explain that it wasn't him who ran over Dashing Henry and that plenty of people would have reason to want to do that. A piece that would read even better if we managed to find out who the terrible—or very intentional—driver was.

He was making all his calls from my living room table. You may think I would be annoyed by so much babbling. But he'd been so secretive and cagey in the past when it came to his work that I was almost thrilled with the present and constant chatter and the fact that he no longer felt the need to hide any aspects of his professional life from me.

Even if I was using my noise-canceling headphones on and off to block his voice at times and be able to focus on my own task, I was almost certain of something: David hadn't called and wasn't calling Michael Townsend, his editor at the *Los Angeles Voice* and the one person ultimately responsible for having approved and published the damning article that got me thrown out of bed that morning. It didn't look like David was going to try to publish at the *Voice* anytime soon, and it didn't surprise me after the frontpage article where me and my job status were also mentioned. Well, and where he was blatantly accused of murder.

Despite the fact that David no longer worked there, John Diaz of the *Gazette* had avoided the story planted by my mother. But Townsend hadn't been able to resist the sensationalism of the tantalizing possibility that his reporter ran over Henry and was in bed with the mayor's daughter, even if it wasn't true. Not all of it, anyway.

I was particularly jubilant that David wasn't reaching out to someone else in particular. Someone I'd upgraded to the top of my most-actively-loathed-people list. I just hoped it remained that way. Not my hating of that person, I'm a constant and dependable grudge-holder if anything else, but David's lack of attempts in trying to contact said person.

But don't assume I was eavesdropping on all of David's conversations or non-conversations. I was working too. And by that, I mean that I'd found Dashing Henry's dumped emails online and I was going through them to see if I could find something else in there.

I wasn't confident that any of that could be relevant or trusted. First, I had to make sure the emails were actually Henry's—especially considering the exchange with a fake David. But I found several emails from years before that I had written to the actor when I was still working at *LA Misconducts*. They were mostly impersonal messages where I would send a new version of the script or explain why we'd changed a specific line of dialogue. I recognized those communications and assumed that at least part of what was online were Henry's real messages. But rereading those messages wasn't exactly a pleasant trip into the past. It made me feel itchy.

At least I was relieved to see that, so far, YouReallyDont-KnowWhatsOutThere.com seemed to be the only place to have discovered the email dump and to have written about it. I just hoped no one else did.

"I think I found something," I told David after he finished furiously typing. He had moved on from calls to angry emails.

"Someone else published something about me emailing Dashing Henry?" he asked, his jaw *definitely* on the side of ridiculously chiseled.

"No, don't worry about that. No one else has picked it up."

"Yet," he said.

"Haven't you just been on the phone for the last two hours making friends with everyone so that they call you before something like this happens?" My tone was just shy of exasperated.

"You can't really trust a reporter once they've got a scoop," he said.

"Scribe, not sure if it was when people started accusing you of not knowing how to drive or of making way too much noise at night," I told him, playfully, "but you're starting to sound like me when it comes to the mistrust in your profession."

"As I recall, it was *you* making most of the noise," he said, also playfully. At least I had succeeded in getting his mind off things a bit.

"We'll agree to disagree on that," I said. "Now, can we temporarily table all this naughty banter and go back to the issue at hand? I think I found something."

"So you keep saying," he said, and that really aggravated me. I wasn't sure if we'd be able to work on this together, to be honest. "Yet you keep burying the lede and not telling me about it."

As I've committed to being transparent with you, I'm going to admit that it had long been established that David and I were the opposite kind of writers. I did commercial fiction on film and TV, and he was a print reporter of facts. But even if we dabbled in different kinds of prose and mediums, we could still both be insecure, self-centered, overly sensitive, and obsessive when it came to our writing.

All qualities that didn't exactly promise a smooth collaboration. Add that to our convoluted history together—both as an official and nonofficial couple—and we were a surefire disaster waiting to happen.

"You're the most conceited, arrogant, insufferable person I've ever met!" I finally told him. My face wasn't showing a hint of rage or any other sentiment though. I'd been trained in the art of the poker face by Aurora Valls herself, and the woman was masterful. "I'm willing to put all that behind us and work together. And we both know collaborating is going to be a big challenge, but can we at least try and be civil?"

"We can try," he conceded, which was as close to an apology as I would get from him since the whole being-written-about affair was making him uncomfortable—and irritable. "Now tell me what you found?"

"When was the last time you wrote about Dashing Henry?" I asked.

"I think when he sued me for libel, we ran something. I didn't write that personally, but I was involved in some of the reporting."

"And over the last months, reporting about Henry, have you ever found something about a superfan of his—veering on stalker—called LA Troubelmakr?" I asked him, looking at my screen. "And I need to show you how this dude spells Troubelmakr because I'm not sure whether they're trying to be funny or if they're simply an orthography tragedy."

If David and I could agree on something—other than the correct way of brewing coffee, the superiority of coastal cities with Mediterranean climate, and how *not to* parallel park like an asshole—it was on the utmost importance of proper orthography.

"Not sure, the name kind of sounds familiar somehow," David said, referring to the shameless misspeller.

"They'd been writing to Henry nonstop for at least two or three years it seems. I think they're some sort of big fan of *LA Misconducts* and have mystified Henry's character in the show. Even if the character, same as the person, was an absolute bastard. Anyway, Henry answered their emails first. You can see that he felt flattered by the attention."

"The guy was a total narcissist," David said.

"But then something must have happened, and Henry must have gotten tired of the LA Troubelmakr, who sounds like a high-maintenance, whiny idiot. Henry stopped replying to their emails. That hasn't stopped the Troubelmakr, who's been writing to Henry at least twice a day and demanding to meet in person."

"So Henry had a stalker. How is this relevant?"

"Some of the latest emails, from like only a week ago, sound quite aggressive and confrontational. You can see that the Troubelmakr was quite frustrated about Henry's silence. And they make it clear that they've followed the actor several times and know where he lives. Could it be that they followed him to the Eastern Columbia and confronted him in the parking area?"

"Now you're speculating a bit too much, no? Ms. Fiction Writer."

"Perhaps, but you have to admit it's worth checking it out!"

"I do."

"You do?" I said, almost surprised. Had I actually been good at this investigating stuff?

"But let me check something first, because that ridiculous name does sound familiar," he said as he searched his email. "Here. He wrote to me when my first Dashing Henry story was published. He was upset and called me all sorts of colorful things."

"*Spinless nincumpoop, snowfleek server of the cancellled culture, hater of all things matcho . . .*" I read on David's computer screen from one of Troubelmakr's emails. "He has a flair for the dramatic. If only he could spell. And I guess we can assume it's a man."

"We can assume, yes. I can show you even more colorful stuff. He kept emailing me for a couple of weeks. In the end,

I talked with the security team at the newspaper, and I don't know exactly what happened. I guess they reported him to the police and sent him some lawyery letter, but he stopped emailing me."

"And that was before they fired you?"

"Yes. But whatever legalese they threatened him with must have been scary enough because he didn't make contact again even after I was fired."

"What if it was him who pretended to be you and lured Henry here with those emails in your name?"

"Why would he do that?" David tried protesting.

"I don't know! To make sure Henry finally showed up. He must have known he'd sued you."

"You haven't convinced me, but we need to keep looking into this Troubelmakr."

"So, what do we do now? Try to find him and make him confess?"

If that were a screenplay I was writing, this would be the perfect time to insert a chat between the sexy, pining-for-each-other investigators and their first suspect. But I assumed in real life things tended to be a bit different and most certainly slower—and happened in a more boring fashion.

"We can see what's out there," David said, and what he did next astounded me a little. I hadn't anticipated a seasoned, award-winning—perhaps only award-finalist, but still—investigative journalist like him doing something so basic and mundane, but he did. He went to Google, typed "LA Troubelmakr," and browsed through the results.

"You need to start somewhere," he told me when he saw my disbelieving expression. "Or do you have any better ideas?"

I didn't, but he didn't need to know that. Up until that

moment, I'd been convinced he'd have some secret investigative method known only to his profession. Like some ultra restricted browser with which to find the geographical location of every possible source or person of interest, or some other made-for-TV nonsense like that.

"Why does this guy look familiar?" he asked me then. David was reviewing the Google search results and had found a couple of images of someone responding to the name LA Troubelmakr. He looked like a man in his thirties, of medium build, and wearing an *LA Misconducts* white hoodie. He had short bleached-blond hair and the kind of creepy smile you hope never to see up close in person.

I shuddered uneasily because the fact was, I *had* seen him in person.

14

My phone rang then and made us both wince. The phone identified the caller as *Lawyer*. I answered immediately.

"Elena, your mother said you'd be calling me," my dad said in a concerned tone. It wasn't his signature style to skip over the good-mornings, how-are-yous, what-did-you-have-for-breakfasts, and all of his usual dad repartee.

"I was going to ring you and then things got complicated," I tried to explain. For a moment, I felt I was seventeen again, and he'd caught me smoking a cigarette while picking me up after some party.

"More complicated than the police wanting to talk to you?" He scoffed.

"What?" I said, confused. For someone who prided herself on being articulate, I kept catching myself saying the same interrogative word over and over that morning.

"Fortunately, we have friends at the LAPD and they did me the courtesy of calling me first," my dad explained. "But they want to talk to you again."

"What?" I sounded like an idiot. "Why?"

"Something about a certain article at the *Voice* and you possibly lying to them about being alone the night of Henry's death." A dash of frustration colored his tone.

"Oh, that," I said, still sounding completely dumb.

"Yes, *that*," he replied, unamused. "And Elena, will you do me a favor and tell that irresponsible, idiot *ex* of yours that he's also wanted at the Downtown police station for further questioning?"

"What makes you think I know where he is?" David was standing no more than a few inches in front of me, looking at me with scrutinizing eyes.

"I'll meet both of you there in thirty minutes. Don't be late," my father said with the kind of tone he reserved for the courtroom.

The line went dead on the other side.

"My dad is pissed," I told David. My father had decided to also forget about the take-cares and the hugs and kisses that always accompanied his farewells, and I suddenly realized I missed them.

"He saw the article and wants to have a chat about my intentions toward you?" David asked. I'm still unsure whether he was messing with me or not there.

"What? No!" I rolled my eyes. "But the police may not be as tolerant in their views."

...

I'd caught David up on the contents of my dad's call, and we were out the door five minutes after I had changed into a pair of baggy high-rise jeans and yet another cozy flannel shirt.

"Drive or walk?" he asked me at the landing, in front of

my recently closed front door. I could hear the notes of Miles Davis coming from apartment 10D.

"Drive?" I offered.

"Walk?" he countered.

"Seriously? Sometimes I feel like I'm the Angelena native and not the transplant. He'll kill us if we're late. I think he'll try to represent us both during the chat with the police."

David gave me a confused look.

"He's a lawyer!"

"An *entertainment* lawyer," David said.

"So what? He was good enough for you when you were accused of libel but not now?" David still didn't appear swayed. "You know he's not charging us, right?"

"Okay, but I drive," he allowed.

"Can't I drive?" I asked, sparring for a fight. "You know my car is more eco-friendly than yours."

He growled in assent, and I knew I had won.

...

I was driving us to the Downtown LAPD headquarters and realizing that right there, in front of us, was another one of the irreconcilable differences that could explain our separation. Money. My parents gave me an upscale electric SUV two Christmases before. I love the fact that I won't have to go to a gas station ever again. David thinks it's a blatant expression of my swanky and posh upbringing. He has a 2015 plug-in Toyota Prius.

No matter how many times I told him my family came from an incredibly humble background in Barcelona and both my parents are what you would call self-made, he still tends to see only the somewhat pricey cars; the five-bedroom, six-bathroom home plus guest house in Beverly Hills; and the office at city hall.

He's never bought that I'm as much of a regular kid from a middle-class neighborhood as he is. What's more, he's always considered me a bit hypocritical because I identify as a non-rich child. I'm aware that I have no student-loan debt, that I have a good—and extremely costly—healthcare plan that includes dental and vision, and that the only reason I'm not more worried about my employment prospects is because my parents would have my back if I needed help, and having my back wouldn't put a dent in their finances.

Please don't think I'm posh. I spent my childhood wearing plain, inexpensive clothes, never receiving that toy everyone else wanted and got for Christmas, and not playing video games because we couldn't afford a console.

My parents only started making real money once we moved here. And yes, sometimes they spoil me and give me excessive gifts—like a $60,000 car—but I think it's only because the three of us remember those years in Barcelona when things were tight.

"You've been awfully quiet since we got in the car," David said.

"I was thinking about the creepy Troubelmakr guy." We hadn't yet had the chance to talk about that.

"Does it sound completely delusional or paranoid if I say I think I've seen him around?"

"It doesn't because I *know* I've seen him around," I said, taking my eyes from the road briefly to look at him.

"When? Where?" His tone was worried.

"Yesterday. When we were on the street waiting for the firefighters to let us back into the building. Quite a few passersby stopped and lingered for a bit. They were curious about the people on the street and the alarm and everything else. I was watching them go about their lives and wondering what their occupations and family situations and things like that were—I like playing that exercise. And suddenly I saw this dude standing on the other side of the street looking at me with a creepy smile. It gave me chills."

"What happened?"

"Not sure. Some neighbor or other complained about something and you jumped in to assist them, and that must have annoyed me and caught my eye," I said. "And when I looked again, the weird guy was no longer there and I couldn't see him anywhere. I'm sure he's the same guy we saw today on those internet pictures."

David was doing all his thinking silently, and I didn't want to look in his direction again. In the past, he may have accused me of sometimes being distracted on the wheel. I wouldn't count his mild dislike for my driving style as another one of the things that precipitated our uncoupling, though.

"So, you also saw him yesterday?" I asked.

"Don't think so," David said. "I think I've seen him around our building one or two times these past few days though. I just assumed he was a neighbor. You know how familiar faces keep popping up at the grocery store or the barber shop?"

"Not really," I admitted. David was into community and making a difference in the neighborhood. I can't say I was. Call me selfish, but lending my mother to the whole city of Los Angeles seemed like involvement enough.

Even if we were five minutes early, when I parked at the LAPD visitor's parking area, my dad was already waiting there. He was immaculately dressed in a white shirt, a silk tie, and one of his woolen Hugo Boss suits. He likes nice things but never goes for anything extravagant.

He was carrying an Urth Caffé to-go cup of what I assumed was his usual order of double espresso macchiato. He went to drink from it only to drop an exaggerated amount of coffee over himself, staining his blazer.

Remember when I told the Clooney guy that I take to my dad? I wasn't lying.

"¿Te has quemado?" I asked my dad as I was getting out of the car, worried he may have burned himself. He was trying to drain the coffee stain with a tissue and making it even worse. There was now not only coffee but cellulose residue all over his jacket.

"What? No," he replied, also in Spanish. "But I just picked up this suit from the dry cleaners!"

"Hola, Mateo," David greeted my dad. Did he sound a bit flustered?

"Ah, so you found David! And in record time," my dad said, a knowing look in his expression. "Was the neighbor telling the truth? Were you two together the night of the murder?" Dad was famous for his directness.

There was an uncomfortable silence for a few seconds in the underground garage of the LAPD. The fluorescent lights flickered overhead. Both David and I fixated on our shoes, not answering or looking at my dad.

"Anyone?" our lawyer insisted. "Were you together on Wednesday night?"

David and I may be a couple of Californian millennials used to being evasive and walking on eggshells, but my father is one hundred percent pure Spaniard bluntness and doesn't appreciate lack of clarity.

"Yes," we finally both mumbled, our eyes still fixed on the floor.

"You two better start telling the cops the truth. What exactly made you think that telling them you were alone when you weren't was a good idea? In fact, why the hell did you tell them anything? I should have been both your first calls!" He scowled. "Here's what's going to happen. We're going to get inside. You each are going to amend your statement and talk again to that Clooney guy—"

"Rooney," corrected David, and my dad gave him one of his   don't-mess-with-me-when-I'm-in-my-lawyer-mode looks. "Never mind," David said, and I almost chuckled.

"Do we need to talk to the cops separately?" I asked.

"After having lied to them once, it's not like they trust us a lot, so we'll do it together. Plus, this is only a friendly chat to show them we *now* have nothing to hide," my dad explained. "If they had anything against either of you, this would be a different kind of conversation."

"But we still need a lawyer?"

"Sí, cariño, haven't I taught you anything? You *always* need a lawyer. Especially one that won't charge you by the hour."

15

We sat in one of the police station's windowless, charmless interview rooms. I was appalled by the yellowish paint peeling off from the walls, and I started regretting coming there. I sweated nervously and remembered I hadn't exactly had time to shower that morning. I'd been absent-minded about my personal hygiene before—so many years of drought in California, and you start developing a method for showering every other day if you're feeling lazy. But we'd had two extremely wet winters in a row, and I had no excuse for my lack of washing other than I really hadn't had the chance to get to it. That and no hot water. Plus, the inconvenient appearance of a corpse in the building, I guess.

We sat at the rectangular table in the interrogation room. I sat with David and my dad on one side. Seated opposite us were Detective Clooney and a black-haired woman detective in her thirties who introduced herself as Detective Moreno. I had to do a double take because Detective Moreno was stunning with her fresh face and pixie cut. I checked once again for the cameras because she looked straight out of any network police procedural show, including her choice of an impeccably fitting navy wide-legged, double-breasted suit.

"This is highly unusual," started Clooney, taking me out of my TV reverie. "I understand you want to amend your statements."

The detective was looking only at me and David, but we knew better than to utter a single word without having express authorization from our lawyer.

"My clients Elena Freire Valls and David Ramos wish to amend their statement regarding the night of Wednesday, February 21," said our lawyer. He sounded assertive and confident, even in a stained suit and smelling like coffee.

"Highly unusual," repeated Clooney.

"Come on Detective Cloo—Rooney, don't be a pushover. You know this happens all the time," our lawyer replied, and I was surprised by that piece of information. Did people really change their police statements frequently? My dad never lied, but he had a way of transfiguring facts when it suited his needs as an attorney, so you never knew. "When they were first questioned by the police—without the presence of their lawyer, I may add—both my clients stated they were alone that night because they didn't want to share a personal relationship they didn't think was relevant to the case. They've since come to realize they made a mistake."

Detective Moreno made some notes and chuckled. She looked highly entertained by the whole situation. Clooney continued staring at me and David. I shifted uncomfortably but would have gladly given away my highly prized collection of signed Sofia Coppola–directed movies on DVD to know what exactly David was feeling.

"So you weren't alone all night on Wednesday after all?" Clooney asked David.

Our lawyer nodded for him to answer. "I wasn't," my on-again (or was it off-again?) lover said. "At around 9:30, I went to Elena's apartment."

"He was with me until 1 a.m.," I contributed.

"And we should believe you now because . . . ?"

"You can ask my neighbor George if you don't believe us," I said. "The walls at the Eastern Columbia are apparently quite thin."

"This alibi of yours is extremely convenient," said Clooney. "Were you really together during all that time?"

Both David and I assented.

"There was no chance for one of you to sneak outside Miss Freire Valls's apartment and go meet Mr. Henry in the parking area of the building?" continued Clooney.

"I think they've both already said that they were together at *Ms.* Freire Valls's place," our lawyer established. He knew I found the whole concept of using different titles of courtesy for women depending on their marital status preposterous and sexist.

"Since they haven't been exactly forward in the past, I'd like to hear directly from them about this," Clooney said.

"We were both at Elena's place until I left and returned to my apartment," David said.

"Any reason why you left?" Clooney asked.

Ouch.

"I had no reason to stay."

Double fucking ouch.

"I saw the tenant in apartment 10D leaving his place when I left Elena's," David continued. "Maybe you can check with him. He'll corroborate it."

"How convenient," Clooney said, and it made me think we should have probably knocked on apartment 10D that morning and brought the jazz-listening neighbor with us to this meeting. "But what about before that? Do we have to assume that you were"—he grabbed a copy of that day's *Los Angeles Voice* that had been hiding underneath some folders and read from it—"'humping like rabbits' from 9:30 p.m. to 1 a.m.?"

I cringed. But there's nothing like directness to thwart certain indiscretions. "There was humping followed by sleeping."

"And how do you know that when you were placidly sleeping, your partner didn't take the chance to leave the apartment?"

Our lawyer was going to intervene, but I signaled that I could take care of it.

"First of all, even my neighbor knows who gets in and out of my apartment. Don't you think I would have noticed David if he decided to go exploring in the middle of the night and then came back?" I said. "Not sure if you've seen any of the units at the Eastern Columbia, but there are literally no walls. And second of all, you're implying that David came to my place to have an alibi but then forgot to use it when he talked to you the first time. Does that make any sense?"

"Does any of this make any sense, *Ms.* Freire Valls?" said Clooney. "Let me play something for you."

He opened a laptop, searched for something on it, then started playing an audio file.

"*Matt, I know you said we were done, but I'm sure you'll come to realize you made a mistake and take me back. I'm at David Ramos's building,*" the recording said. I recognized the voice immediately as it made my blood run cold and my skin crawl. It was Dashing Henry's. "*It makes no sense being here, but I have to confront him. Even if he scares me. Do you think he's capable of something against me? Maybe you should call the cops and tell them about the emails. I know, I know! You told me not to come, but I don't always listen."* Henry stopped talking then and there was background noise. I recognized the sound made by the elevators at the Eastern Columbia and the muffled sounds of someone thumping on something. *"The damn hack journalist isn't even here. Been knocking on his door for over ten minutes! I know what you'll say, but I needed to at least try and talk to him ... And I'm already leaving anyway, looking for the car now. Wait, someone's yelling at me from a fucking Toyota Prius!"*

Detective Clooney stopped the audio file.

"This voicemail was sent to Matt Steele, Dashing Henry's former lawyer. Mr. Steele was already sleeping when Dashing Henry called him on Wednesday night and didn't listen to this until Thursday afternoon. He notified us immediately after realizing its content," said Clooney. "What you haven't heard, because I stopped the recording before that, is Henry being run over at around 10:17 p.m. on Wednesday night."

I breathed heavily. I had hated Dashing Henry, but I sure didn't need the picture of his demise in my mind, even if only in audio format.

"Mr. Ramos, do you have a car?" Clooney asked.

"Yes," David answered tentatively.

"And what car is that?"

"Please, let's stop this farce. You know perfectly well, because you've checked his DMV registration records, that my client has had a Toyota Prius for over five years."

"More like ten," corrected David. My dad and I rolled our eyes. We've always found amusing how much David needed to be precise.

"Could that be the same Prius Henry was talking about?" asked Clooney.

"Come on! Half of LA drives a Prius," my dad intervened again.

"Not anymore, now everyone is driving electric," the detective corrected, looking my way. "We could have both of your cars checked, and that could work in your favor if we don't find signs of collision or anything else in them."

"Sorry, but no." Our lawyer was quick. "You'll need a warrant to get near any of my clients' vehicles."

"It looks good to collaborate," Clooney said.

"I don't care how it looks. We both know that if you want to find something, you'll find something."

And that's why you always need a lawyer in the room, I guess. I was ready to tell the cops to go ahead and check my fucking car and leave me alone. And then I realized I'm a terrible parker and both my passenger side wheels have continuously suffered from my inability to parallel park without bumping into the sidewalk. Sure, someone could read so many dents as suspicious.

"Are you aware that there's someone online who's been impersonating Mr. Ramos?" our lawyer told the cops then.

When we'd arrived at the station, we'd explained to my dad that there was a fake email account in David's name and everything about the article on YouReallyDontKnowWhats-OutThere.com. He'd advised to tell everything to the cops since there could be more articles soon.

"What, someone has been writing trashy articles and bylining them David Ramos, and you're upset?" Detective Moreno said. She seemed to have a twisted sense of humor. I didn't like it one bit.

"No, someone made an email account in his name and emailed Dashing Henry. That someone asked the actor to meet at Mr. Ramos's place the night Henry died."

"I didn't write that email," David said.

"Not even considering your career was hanging by a thread with a libel trial on the near horizon? A libel trial that can hardly go forward now that the offended party is dead?" said Clooney.

I needed to get out of there. Writing interrogation scenes was much more fun than living through them, even if I wasn't the main suspect—or perhaps because David was.

"My career is not hanging by a thread," said David. I knew he'd been deeply wounded by those words. "At least, it wasn't before this morning's article in the *Voice*. And I didn't write that email. I have never used the email account from where it was sent. I'm meticulously careful in my digital communications, and you won't find any trace between that account and any of my personal devices."

"What about your work devices?" asked Clooney.

"I'm a freelance contributor. My personal computer and phone are my work computer and phone."

"So, can we take a look at them then and make sure you never sent those emails?" Clooney asked.

"No, you can't," our lawyer intervened. "Unless you have a warrant, of course."

"Your client just said we wouldn't find any trace between the email account that messaged Henry and his devices. But for that, we need to look."

"Which you'd be able to do if you had probable cause and a warrant," Dad said.

"How does your client know Mr. Henry was supposed to meet him at his place if he wasn't the one who sent him the email citing him there?" asked Clooney.

"As part of his duties as an investigative reporter, my client found a series of leaked emails from the deceased," our lawyer explained. "Among them were those sent from an account impersonating him. My client won't reveal any sources but will point to the leaked emails in collaboration with this investigation."

"That won't be necessary." I realized the police already knew about the emails and Dad had been right in telling them about it.

"Great. If that's all, I think we should get going." Dad moved to stand.

"Just one thing." This time it was Detective Moreno chatting us up. "We know Mr. Ramos has a reputation as an investigative journalist, and he may feel inclined to further report on this story himself."

"I'm too involved to even fathom the possibility of writing about this messy story," David said, his melodramatic tone fully on. I had to pinch myself not to roll my eyes. Not only was he terribly overacting, he was lying.

"Good," Detective Moreno said, and I couldn't believe she'd bought David's words. I guess not everyone knew him as well as I did. "You're in enough trouble as is. Let us investigate. It may not look like it when the *Voice* decides to write salacious half-fabricated stories"—she pointed toward the newspaper still on the table—"but we have reason to believe that whoever is behind Henry's death wasn't simply a reckless driver but someone dangerous. You wouldn't want to get tangled with them."

"We certainly wouldn't," our lawyer said, but I couldn't help feeling the detective's words had been some sort of cautionary advice. Also, did I imagine it, or had she been looking at me when she said those words?

etective Moreno escorted us out of the interrogation room and into the busy corridors of the police station. My dad excused himself to go to the restroom, but before that he gave me and David a stern look. *Don't you dare say anything you shouldn't while I'm not here.*

"In case you remember anything else," said Detective Moreno, handing me and David cards, "both my office and cell phone numbers are there."

I checked the card distractedly, learned that Detective Moreno's first name was Laura, then put the card inside one of the pockets of my jeans, never to see or think about it again. My pockets could have that effect on things; they were like doors to a parallel universe inaccessible to this Elena variant.

"And congrats, by the way," Detective Moreno added.

"I'm sorry, for what? The honor of being interrogated by the police for a third time in two days, or having finally figured out that we needed a lawyer when we talk to you folks?" I asked.

"I meant how unapologetic you are about this whole thing of yours. You used to date," she said, gesturing to David and me. "You have a boyfriend," she directed at me. "Yet you two seem to have such an *interesting* relationship."

"I guess," David said, being polite. I don't think he was particularly fond of the singularities of our situation. And he'd always thought *interesting* was the biggest offender in the art of the empty word.

"The thing is, I'm notoriously bad when it comes to this stuff," Detective Moreno continued, seemingly unaware of my and David's lack of interest. Was she being so chatty and nice because she was genuinely like that? Was she working on her inner growth and doing a therapy session with us? Or was she trying to get our guards down so we'd confide in her? The daughter of a lawyer in me decided it had to be the third option: She wanted to pretend she was telling us something private so we'd tell *her* something we still hadn't disclosed to the cops.

"What stuff?" I asked her tentatively. I'd let her talk all she wanted—or needed—but I would listen, not share my own stuff.

"Relationships," Detective Moreno said in her dry, straightforward tone. "What I'm trying to say is, I'm sorry if we came off as a bit judgmental or reproaching before. We were just doing our jobs."

"Getting people to talk is not easy," David said, and I could have stabbed him with my eyes. Did he really need to be so understanding and sympathetic with *everyone*?

"I could never judge your arrangement when my love life is a complete mess." I knew for a fact she was fishing for a candid reaction from us then.

"It's not like our arrangement isn't a bit messy," David started saying, but I interrupted him.

"We didn't feel judged," I lied, and before David could add anything else or tried making friends with the officer currently investigating our possible involvement in a murder, I steered him away. We made a rushed exit toward the parking area. I was sure my dad would be able to find us there.

...

We said goodbye to my dad, who had to run home to get changed and then head back to his office. He was in the middle of some contentious negotiations as two of his musician clients were expecting new contracts—and the royalties resulting from that—once the TV sitcom they'd worked on in the nineties hit a streaming service.

David and I got inside my car and saw my dad's SUV leaving the parking area, but I didn't start driving. We needed to talk first.

I was trying to phrase an elusive thought that'd been plaguing my mind when my cell phone buzzed inside the rear pocket of my jeans. I grabbed the device out of habit and read the message distractedly.

FRED APPLETON

Elena. I just wanted to let you know I'd be honored to work alongside you once again.

Well, I won't be.

I put the phone back in my pocket. Where was I?

"That conversation with the police was . . ." David interrupted my thoughts about Fred Appleton and whatever I needed to tell him.

"Weird?" I ventured. We were both looking at the semi-empty parking structure in front of us.

"That doesn't cover it."

"Awkward," I tried again.

"Closer, but still not precise."

"Uncomfortable."

"You're getting warmer. Torturous, perhaps?" he asked.

I scoffed. "At this rate, not as torturous as this conversation!"

"Sorry. You know I like words," he said, flashing his most irresistible puppy-dog stare.

"And you get especially obsessed with them when you're nervous," I told him. "Now that we've had to go over some of the specifics of our sex life in front of the police—and, let's not forget, my father—can I tell you something?" I'd been holding on to this for way too many years. "I always hated Gloria Fucking Kingsley."

David shifted to face me better. "What? What brought this on?"

"I guess the fact that she was supposed to be your former colleague and friend but decided to throw you under the bus the moment city hall called and spun a fabricated tale about you . . ." My gaze was still lost in the gray semi-empty space in front of me.

"She got a scoop," David said.

"Are you serious right now?" I was too enraged to keep avoiding his gaze and turned to face him. "That wasn't a scoop, that was a bunch of lies. And she had no issue writing them. Also, she said I'm unemployed three times in the article!"

"Well, you're not actively working on any production right now," David reasoned.

"I'm writing my spec script! I have an overall deal! I have plenty of employment. Perhaps nothing is being made at the moment, but that's not the point!" I yelled. My frustration ran deep, and I realized I had been yearning to have that argument for a while. Fred Appleton barging in at the worst moment instead of waiting for my agent to give him an answer hadn't exactly appeased my mood.

"You always get upset because I'm a stickler for precision when it gets to finding the right way of wording things. And then someone describes your situation inaccurately, and look what happens," David said, and that was the last straw.

"That's not what I'm saying!" I said, my voice rising in volume.

"Then tell me what it is!" he said, yelling too. We were both screaming at each other by then, having our first full-blown argument since we'd broken up. And we—I guess, technically me—had chosen the vicinity of a police station for it.

I finally let it out. "Were you having an affair with her?" If only I'd found the courage to do it two years before.

"What? With whom?" he asked, and for a moment there I thought he looked genuinely clueless. I didn't reply though. I just stared at him pointedly. "With Gloria?" he finally said. "Of course not!"

They'd been working together at the *Gazette* when David and I were still a couple, and even though I pride myself on not being jealous, I was green with envy about her. She was witty and hot, she always knew what to say, what to read, and what new places to go. And, above all, she was so self-assured and confident in her own skin. I feared the day David realized she was perfect for him in a way I had never been.

"Are you sure?" I asked, but I was sounding a bit more deflated and insecure than when I'd first posed the question.

"I couldn't be more certain," he said. He wasn't being

theatrical about it, and his jawline looked his usual sexy, so I assumed he was telling the truth. "Why would I have an affair with her when I was with *you*?" He managed to make the word *you* sound like the most special thing.

"I don't know! You tell me!" Believe me, I know. Not my best line. "You could also have started seeing her after we broke up." I was starting to sound deranged and foolish.

"Elena, why would I want to start *seeing* her? All I wanted to do when *you* broke up with me was find a way to be together again," he said. "Also, for the sake of at least trying to appear feminist, what makes you think she'd want anything to do with me?"

"Oh please! Forget about your feminist argument." We didn't have time for that then, not when he'd said what he'd said. "You wanted to be together again?"

"Elena, isn't it obvious?" He needed to stop using my first name in that melodious, tender way only he knew how to do. "We live in the same building!"

"They were having a sale!" I realized how ridiculous it sounded only after I'd said it out loud.

"You have keys to my apartment," David continued, and the calmness in his tone agitated me even more.

"It's just more convenient this way." I was trying to justify the whole situation and hearing the absurdity in every one of my words.

"Whenever you've decided to surprise me with a visit in the middle of the night, have you ever caught me with anyone?"

I looked at him for a few seconds, not knowing what to say next. I was processing everything that had been said between the two of us, and not quite grasping the actual implications.

"What have we been doing all this time?" I asked him finally.

But there was no answer as a uniformed officer knocked on my window then and almost gave me a heart attack.

"Miss, are you here for police business?"

"Yes, we were just inside editing our statements or whatever you call it," I told the officer as I rolled my window down.

"Editing your statements?"

"Adding some revisions, giving notes, punching up our statements?"

"We were *amending* our statements, officer," David intervened.

"I see," the officer finally understood, her gaze shrewd. "If you're done, you should leave. We don't like people lingering in this area. Someone else may need to park."

I checked in front of me at the many parking spaces available. "We were having a conversation."

"The parking area of the LAPD is no place for conversations. It's the place to *park* if you need to conduct police business."

"It was a possibly life-altering conversation."

"The parking area of the LAPD is no place for life-altering conversations."

I drove off then, because I had to admit that she had a point.

17

I drove down Broadway in silence, still going over the last words David and I had said and not knowing what to do next. The questions, *Could we go back to the conversation we were having?* and, *You said you wanted to get back together?* kept writing and rewriting themselves in my mind.

I was just going to let me say them out loud in front of David while he was still in my car, with me, before we got to our destination. Because I felt, otherwise, I'd probably never get to see or talk to him ever again—even if we lived in the same building. I was feeling *that tragic.*

He'd just told the cops he had no reason to stay at my place on Wednesday night. He may have been interested in rekindling our relationship in the past. But I doubted he'd be interested now. Perhaps I'd even misunderstood the whole thing about him having been interested before. And, also, why would I care? Wasn't I supposed to be invested in my relationship with Victor? And even if I wasn't, since when had I wanted to be back with David?

I hadn't said a word of what I wanted to voice to David when my phone rang.

Victor's name displayed on my car's infotainment screen and—for the first time since my parents had given me the new car—I missed my old, dumb 2008 Toyota Corolla. Good luck trying to sync your smartphone to that.

"Aren't you going to pick it up?" David asked as my phone continued vibrating and the car's screen persisted in showing Victor's name.

"Not while I'm driving."

"You know he deserves an explanation, right?" David said.

An explanation about what? I'm not proud to admit that it took me a good minute to realize David was referring to that morning's article and the fact that I was now publicly fucking my *ex*.

"I feel bad for him," David continued. "Don't you feel bad for him?"

"Oh my god! Seriously! You really want to talk about Victor right now?" I was, perhaps, yelling a bit.

"Only because for the first time in months, we're actually talking and you're not shutting me completely off!"

"Okay, I can't!" I really couldn't have that argument with David and drive safely at the same time even if I was only going at 20 mph. So as a car miraculously left a spot on Broadway, I pulled over to park there.

"What do you want to talk about?" I turned to face David and left my car to finish parking itself. My phone had thankfully stopped ringing by then. "I'm very aware that we must be the most LA couple ever as this is the second argument we've had *inside* the car today."

"Let's get out of the car then." He opened the passenger door and got out. I followed suit. "Also, did you just refer to us as a couple?" he added while we stood side by side on a misty Broadway sidewalk.

"Can I actually park here?" I deflected, only partially. I really didn't want another parking ticket.

"You can, but feed the meter," David said, diligently reading the parking signal posted on the street. You could always rely on him for bureaucratic matters. "Two-hour limit."

"Should I pay for the full two hours?" I asked. It's not that I'm stingy or anything, but I hate overpaying for parking.

"Do you feel this is a half-an-hour-, hour-, or two-hour-long conversation?"

"Let me pay for the full two hours."

Once I dealt with the Los Angeles Bureau of Parking Management, we walked aimlessly on Broadway in the direction opposite our respective homes at the Eastern Columbia. It was as if he also didn't want to get home and continue with that life where we pretended not to know each other—a pretense I had forced us to follow.

"Okay, I can't believe I'm doing this," I started. "But you really don't have to worry about Victor."

"How do you know he's not hurt or jealous?"

"He could be, but I seriously doubt it."

"Is that what you think about all your boyfriends? That we don't care?"

"Oh my god. Enough with the melodrama and the accusations! This is why I have been avoiding this conversation for months! Can we please stop mixing things." I may have been yelling. *Again.* "Let's talk about Victor if you *really* need to. I don't think I'm quite done with the Gloria Kingsley thing. And then we can move to *us.*"

"Is there an us?"

"You tell me." We both stopped walking.

We looked at each other in a way we hadn't really in months, perhaps even years. We let our eyes do the talking for a moment, the same way we've been doing those past few months of limited words and unlimited lust. But I hadn't recalled David staring at me with that raw, sexy smirk since we were both barely out of college and had just started fooling around.

For the second time in two days, I thought he was about to kiss me. And for the second time in as many days, I was certain *I* was going to do it.

This could have really happened here, and no story editor would have batted an eyelash or complained about it taking place too early in the heroine's journey. It was the perfect time for a little release and some making out that would leave the reader and me wanting more.

Only, and I'm sorry to let you down here but think about how disappointed *I was*, there was no kiss.

"Why is there a guy who looks awfully like the Troubelmakr coming this way and looking at us?" David said. It would seem that at some point, he'd stopped directing his attention solely to me to gaze over my head.

I turned toward where David's eyes were fixed on the horizon and recognized the same man I'd seen the day before in front of our building. Only this time, I wasn't feeling a chill but actual fear.

"Is he holding a hammer?" David squinted to get a better view of the Troubelmakr. This may not be the best place to tell you about it, but David is a bit nearsighted. He'd never appreciated my belief that with his black hair and squared jawline, he'd look like a sexier Clark Kent if he ever chose to wear glasses. He never does—hence the squinting.

"A cell phone perhaps," I contributed, also trying to see

more clearly, as I suffered from my own myopia and lack of appropriate eyewear.

"I think you're right. I don't like him. Is he stalking us or what? I'm gonna go talk to him," David said with a decisiveness I hardly knew he possessed. "Wait here."

"Are you insane?" I protested, grabbing his arm and stopping his movement. "Since when have you started talking like the overprotective hero in a romance novel? Please sound like the reasonable writer that you are. He could be carrying a gun!"

"No, he isn't," David said, still set on confronting the man headed in our direction.

"It does look as if he's coming for us, and he looks *not* happy," I protested.

This is what happens when you put two people used to typing all day in the middle of an action segment. Not only have we purposely forgotten our rimmed frames at home because we're a bit vain, we take our time to analyze everything and argue. And we don't necessarily react in the most smart or agile way.

"Definitely not a phone," I said as I got a clearer view of what the Troubelmakr was wielding in his right hand. It didn't look like a gun but was weapon-adjacent, and he picked up his speed. "Run!" I shouted.

In all honesty, I had only reached that urgent conclusion once I asked myself the one pressing question: *What would Tom Cruise do?*

David seemed about to protest, but I grabbed his hand and steered us in the direction opposite to the unhinged guy holding an unidentified object. David was forced to follow me. I was *not* going to let the man I may have been harnessing strong feelings for confront a possibly armed person, no matter how brave and full of bravado he felt.

In case you were garnering any doubts—which, if you have been paying any attention, you shouldn't—no, of course I am not a runner. When it comes to exercise, I limit myself to a strict diet of yoga of the stretching-but-not-really-the-push-up-heavy kind on Saturday mornings followed by mimosas and avocado toast topped with mushroom bacon.

So scarcely half a block of running and I was already panting and sweating profusely. Did I mention Broadway was even more full than usual of people pretending LA is a walkable city?

I was straining my neck from all the checking behind to see how much closer the Troubelmakr was getting and, at the same time, trying to swerve all the pedestrians on the sidewalk.

"Market!" David said, pulling us in the direction of Central Market.

"Are you crazy?" I protested.

"We can exit through the Hill Street entrance, and we can easily lose anyone inside!"

"It's hard to lose anyone when we won't make it past the first line of vendors. Too many people!" I jerked his arm, forcing us to continue running.

We crossed at the intersection of Broadway and Fourth Street, and I had to close my eyes because the traffic light had already turned red for pedestrians. That gained us a renewed distance as our pursuer wasn't able to cross until the bulk of the car traffic stopped again.

While we were being chased, I remembered Detective Moreno's admonishing words: Whoever had killed Henry was quite dangerous and we wouldn't want to get tangled with them. A shiver ran down my spine.

I was still holding David's hand, or he was still holding

mine, even though running with our hands joined made swerving incoming pedestrians harder. But feeling him attached to me gave me some silly sense of reassurance and calmness. Nothing bad could happen if we were together.

And then I lost him.

I panicked. I even stopped in the middle of the street. It was something that, as a native urban dweller, I never do because it goes against all the rules of pedestrian flow etiquette.

People kept bumping into me as I was literally in the middle of the sidewalk, and I was checking to see where David was, aware that our pursuer was closing in on me.

18

"Elena!"

David's voice had to be coming from far away since I was lost and alone. Only that, when I checked to see where he was, following the direction of his words, I realized he was literally a few feet in front of me. He extended his arm toward me and I grabbed his hand as if my life depended on it. And it probably did, but I needed to get my shit together nonetheless. *Pronto.*

We started running again after the confusion but, when the traffic light on Fifth looked like it would force us to stop, we both decided to make a right.

A high-pitched voice called from behind, "I demand to talk to you!"

It was the Troubelmakr.

"Don't you dare go and talk to him," I warned David, urging him to keep running. "He's armed and dangerous. And I need you."

"Promise me something," David told me, and he sounded quite breathless himself.

"I'll promise you anything," I replied. Why I had decided to talk when I was already so out of breath is something I still don't understand. It only made my exhaustion worse.

"What did you do to Dashing?" the Troubelmakr yelled, adding to my distress.

"If we ever get out of this: no more fights, no more misunderstandings. Please," David said as we cut across Pershing Square.

"*If?*" I managed to let out.

"*When* we get out of this." David's voice and request were the only things keeping me sane in that moment.

"Hotel, hotel!" I screamed and pointed to the Biltmore in front of us on Olive Street. A group of at least a dozen uniformed police officers stood by the hotel's ornate columned portico and its arched Renaissance Revival entrance.

This time David didn't argue about my *thing* for ritzy hotels. We both accelerated toward the one-century-old LA institution.

"Help!" I shouted as we crossed Olive Street with a total disregard for incoming vehicles. "He wants to kill us!" I gestured at the Troubelmakr behind us. You could probably gauge that I had completely lost it by then and was uncharacteristically being an absolute drama queen.

Only after seeking assistance at the top of my lungs and in a state of complete breathlessness and near exhaustion did I notice the reflectors, collapsible diffusers, rigs, and cameras sprinkled over the sidewalk. We were crashing a movie shoot, and those police officers I had addressed weren't actual cops but actors or extras of some sort. Had I been paying attention and not worried for my life, I would have realized their uniforms and all the police cars parked in front of the hotel looked straight out of the 1950s.

But there's such a thing as movie magic after all. The uniform-wearing people were, in fact, highly trained stunt actors who'd just endured the whole *300* or *Fight Club* or Marvel or some other unrealistic workout program. In a matter of a few seconds, David and I stopped running as our helpers chased down the Troubelmakr, overpowered him, forced him to relinquish what he'd been brandishing at us —it ended up being a pair of extremely outmoded sunglasses—and brought the stalker to us in made-for-Hollywood handcuffs.

We soon learned—thanks to the nervous divulging of an overworked production assistant—that we'd interrupted the shot of a noir film, set in an alternate 1952 Los Angeles in which all the West Coast was actually part of Canada and its colonies as our neighbors to the north were ruled by a creed of vicious alien invaders.

That's when I saw him. I recognized him right away. He was tall, silver haired, and absolutely suave dressed in a three-piece tailored period suit. He was even wearing a fedora. And he was the star of the film we'd just crashed.

Gary Firth was a fifty-something-year-old Hollywood small-time legend who looked at least ten years younger than he actually was—as movie stars tend to do. He'd made a career mainly in TV in the nineties and late aughts, when I had not so platonically fallen in love with him as I watched reruns of his small-town dramedy *Fish Out of Water*.

He'd been steadily working in indie film and prestige TV since then but had never found another enduring and successful show again. I knew he'd been in conversations for the part that had eventually gone to Dashing Henry in *LA Misconducts*, but Firth had turned it down as he lived in New York and didn't want to spend so much time of the year away from his family.

In the end, the actor, who—unlike Henry—was all graciousness and class, had had a five-episode arc in one of the seasons of *LA Misconducts* when I was also working there, which is how I'd met him.

That morning, when David and I so inelegantly bumped into him at the shooting of his latest movie, he also recognized me. And that's when I had the idea of asking him a somewhat strange favor.

...

"What did you do to Dashing?" The Troubelmakr had been repeating the same question for the last twenty minutes.

After the initial confusion, the team of the movie relocated David, me, and a highly shackled Troubelmakr to the hotel's famous Gallery Bar and Cognac Room.

Even if it was barely 11 a.m. and the bar was still very much closed, the crew lent us a stand-in bartender who mixed me and David cucumber mango Cosmopolitans because we were both in desperate need of day drinking.

We were supposed to be trying to make the Troubelmakr confess about his involvement in the demise of Dashing Henry, but the stalker proved immune to all our lines of questioning and kept asking over and over what *we* had done to Henry.

I was starting to believe he was *only* an overzealous stalker and nothing else when the key element of my latest brilliant plan finally made an arrival. Gary Firth granted my favor and stepped in, not seeking attention but catching it anyway.

"Elena, you're swooning," David whispered in my ear as Gary Firth entered the bar.

For clarity's sake, let me tell you that I may have been swooning about my teenage TV crush, but it was David's breath on my neck that caused all kinds of interferences in my confused brain.

"Don't be ridiculous!" I snapped at David. "Gary, thanks so much for taking the time." I donned my best, most affable smile. And somehow, I managed to remember yet again that I hadn't showered or washed my hair that morning—or the previous one.

"Anything for a colleague," Firth said. And I believed him. Or perhaps his facial features were way too masculine and symmetrical for me to ever assume him capable of anything ungenerous.

The actor took one of the tall chairs from the bar and seated himself close to the Troubelmakr.

"Hi, I'm Gary Firth. Pleasure to meet you," the actor told the stalker.

"I'm Marky Fitzsimmons," the Troubelmakr said, visibly starstruck. It looked like I wasn't the only one who had a thing for Gary Firth.

"How do you spell Fitzsimmons? Zee, ess, and two ems?" interrupted David. At some point, he'd managed to produce a pen and a reporter notebook, and he was already taking notes.

"Er, yes," Fitzsimmons said.

"Marky, you were chasing down my friends Elena and David," said Firth. He nailed the pronunciation for both mine and David's names like not many people manage to do.

Okay, perhaps I was mildly swooning, but can you blame me? I was still in shock, and a nice person was taking care of me and David. It was probably that last element that made me realize the reason I was so smitten with Firth wasn't (only) because he was beautiful but because he was helping me help David. I suddenly understood that I'd been quite distraught about my *ex* and his alleged involvement in the murder of a deplorable human being. But I preferred to ignore that realization and bury it under all the other things taking place.

"I want to know what they did to Dashing Henry!" Marky/Troubelmakr answered. I kept being stunned at his insistence that we had done something to Henry. Also, he seemed to genuinely like the late actor, and that was a sentiment I would *never* be able to share or understand.

"Why do you think they've done anything to him? Did you read this morning's article on the *Voice*?" Firth asked, and Marky nodded.

I did feel a bit self-conscious then when I realized that absolutely *everyone* had read about mine and David's dalliance and our propensity to express ourselves loudly while making love.

"The article said Ramos ran over Henry and the jobless girlfriend helped him!" Marky/Troubelmakr said.

"It didn't say that! It was preposterous and poorly written, and I'm not even jobless. I have an overall deal!" I protested. I refused to be reduced to the role of the jobless girlfriend. I was neither one nor the other.

"Don't worry Elena, I got this," said Gary, and I was starting to get a little annoyed. Why was he being so nice when the Marky/Troubelmakr dude was a total ass and a possible murderer?

"Why do you think they had something to do with Henry's death? The police also have a subscription to the *Voice* and could have apprehended them," the actor continued.

"She's the mayor's daughter!" Marky/Troubelmakr pointed at me.

And there it was. The one thing even more inescapable than my ten seconds of micro-fame as an idle screenwriter with a great sex life: my identity as a nepo baby.

19

I stepped out of the Gallery Bar and Cognac Room after the accusation of being a mama's girl. Everyone who really knew me was well aware that nothing could be further from the truth. I was very much a daddy's girl.

"Thanks for always having my back," I told my friend Amelia as I answered her phone call. Her incoming communication had given me the perfect excuse to leave the room where Gary Firth was treating the Troubelmakr way too nicely.

"Not sure if you'll say the same after I tell you why I'm calling," Amelia said. "Also, are you okay? You sound flustered."

"It's been—a day," I said, not quite sure how to phrase what had happened to me. "I'll tell you all about it, but I think I need to get drunker for that."

"Drunk*er*? Elena, you know I don't like to judge, but it's not even noon. Well, I guess it's Friday and the internet is buzzing about you and your sex habits . . ."

"Is it really? Buzzing?" I walked through the Beaux Arts,

paneled-ceilinged galleria outside of the bar and made a right at a random corner.

"A bit yes, haven't you checked it out? Do you want me to lend you my publicist?"

"No need," I said. I preferred not to know what the internet had been regurgitating. "I'm sure it'll die down by tomorrow."

"Keeping my fingers crossed." I knew she was physically crossing her fingers when she said that. Even her toes. She was that nice and that much of a good, superstitious friend. "Listen, that's not why I called. I have bad news."

"Did something happen? Are you okay? Is Brenda okay? Are Bimbo and Troglodita okay?"

"We're okay and the dogs are as dumb and cute as usual. Everyone is healthy and happy—ish," Amelia said. "My dad decided to surprise us with a visit though."

"Lucky you!" Sarcasm rang through my tone.

One thing I had managed to leave out of my conversation with Detective Clooney when I told him about the many things that I had in common with *LA Misconducts* alumna Amelia Sanchez: we both have difficult relationships with one of our parents. For me, it's my mother-turned-political-animal. For her, it's a father who keeps pushing her toward a more ambitious career and still doesn't understand why she'd decided to slow down a bit for the past two years and be more choosy about her projects.

"My dad is adamant, and he wants to be my plus one tomorrow for the SAG Awards," Amelia continued. "And I really don't know how to tell him no."

"Is it that bad? Going with him, I mean? At least the SAG are one of the short-ish ceremonies. Of course, you still have to do the damn red carpet . . ."

"So is it okay if I go with him?"

"Yes, of course. I mean, if you feel comfortable."

"Please don't think that I don't want to be seen with you because of that stupid article! In fact, since my dad has a strict eight-thirty bedtime, you could come to the afterparty with me instead," Amelia said. She sounded a bit anxious, and I was starting to understand why. "Brenda, of course, doesn't want to hear about changing out of her pajama pants or separating herself from the dogs to come either to the ceremony or the party and being repeatedly photographed, but I'd like to have some support there. You know those things are all work and no fun, and that way they can take lots of pictures of us together. The press loves it when the lesbian actress leaves her wife at home and takes her friend instead."

"Don't forget the part where the friend is the mayor's daughter," I said, joining in on the joke and stopping my random walking through narrow halls, brimming with old memorabilia, before I got completely lost.

"It's difficult to forget it. So do you mind terribly that I won't be able to take you to the awards, and would you like to come with me to the party instead?"

I jolted. "To be completely honest, I had forgotten I was supposed to be your plus one for this. I'm not even sure I have a dress," I told her because it was true, but mainly because I wanted her to stop feeling bad about it. I *knew* she wasn't telling me she had to go to the ceremony with her dad because I was publicly toxic. She couldn't care less about that. She just couldn't say no to her demanding father.

"Elena, cariño, eres lo peor," she said, and I knew that, at least, I had managed to appease her.

"That's why you like me," I joked. "I have a question for you, actually. A professional one."

"Dale."

"Fred Appleton has been pestering me to take this job that I know I don't want."

"Is it the *LA Misconducts* sequel? He's also tried signing me. I told him no," Amelia said. "Even if I enjoyed working with him in the movie we did together, I think it's only because of Archie."

"Archie Eisenberg?"

"Yes. He's Fred's producing partner and knows how to keep Fred on his toes. Nice guy."

I narrowed my eyes in thought. "Really? I've been told he tried shutting down David's story about Dashing Henry."

"Did David tell you that?"

"Beatrice did actually," I admitted, and there was no need for me to add a last name as both Amelia and I shared the same agent. "I haven't had the chance to ask David about it yet."

"I'm sure you've been very *busy* with David and all." I could hear the laughter in her voice. "But don't believe everything Beatrice tells you. The woman is a well-known rumor spreader. So ask him about it."

"Okay. Any advice on how to politely tell Fred that I don't want to work with him but I may want him to introduce me to other people in the industry?"

"Oh, just be open and straightforward and adamant in your love and adoration for his extremely exceptional writing," Amelia said.

"So lie."

"It's not lying, just a bit of creative deception and career self-preservation."

I thanked Amelia for her precise Hollywood insight analysis and hung up. And almost as if he'd known I'd been talking about him, I got another one of those annoying text messages from Fred Appleton that I was going to keep ignoring.

FRED APPLETON

I wanted to ask you how everything is at home. I'd hate for you to be uncomfortable.

What the hell did that mean? A regular person would read that and think he was inquiring about my mental well-being after being talked about so publicly in the press. But my former showrunner was big on playing mind games—and pranks. He'd once broken into an actor's house to leave a prosthetic horse head in his bed because he was playing a gangster in the show. And the last season I was there, he'd tampered with the food at craft services, making it so inedible no one touched it. He wanted to see if having a hungry team would make the production run faster. It didn't.

My paranoid side wanted to believe there was something hidden in his text message. Could he be behind my lack of hot water at home? Because I sure as hell wasn't *comfortable*.

I was still musing about Appleton's implausible but on-character involvement in the failure of my water heater when I refocused on the big black-and-white picture hanging in one of the hidden halls of the hotel. It captured the tuxedo- and gown-clad attendees to the Academy Awards ceremony of 1939 that had taken place inside those walls. It was because of moments like that, when you suddenly found yourself confronted by so many decades of moviemaking history, that I loved Los Angeles.

The image made me realize I'd been living in Hollywood for so long, I was starting to have problems telling fact from far-fetched fiction. Of course, Fred Appleton wasn't implying anything about my lack of hot water while he sent me that last text!

...

"What did I miss?" I asked five minutes later when I rejoined the bar.

"Apparently, Fitzsimmons wasn't stalking Dashing Henry but working for him," David stated. I rolled my eyes because from that moment on, Marky/Troubelmakr would be known to David simply as *Fitzsimmons*, given that's the proper way to refer to a source on second reference and beyond. "Remember you found a bunch of emails from Fitzsimmons repeatedly reaching out to Henry? The actor called Fitzsimmons and asked to meet."

"They met? And what do you mean Marky worked for Henry?"

"They met in person. I think Henry didn't want a digital trace of the encounter. He had me followed for days by Fitzsimmons," David explained. "That's why I thought I had seen him around the neighborhood. It turns out he's not good at following people and not being seen."

"Why did Henry have you followed?" I asked David, but then I thought better and turned to the Troubelmakr. "Why did you follow David?!" I was worried and tired—but mostly pissed.

"Is she gonna hit me?" Marky/Troubelmakr asked Gary Firth. He covered his face with his hands. "She's angry!"

"What? Of course I'm not gonna hit you! But tell me why the hell you were following my partner!" Even if he looked quite harmless now, I'd been terrified when Marky had been chasing me and David. The idea of him following David when he was alone sent a chill down my spine.

"I thought your partner was the blondie who always wears expensive suits," Marky/Troubelmakr said. I registered only then that he was younger than I'd assumed, barely in his midtwenties. Yet he'd sent menacing emails to David. Had that quasi post-pubescent creep been following me around as well? He had to, if he knew about Victor.

"Can we please leave my personal life out of this! Tell me why you've been following David," I said in frustration.

"Don't bother," Gary Firth said, waving a hand. "David and I have tried *everything*. I even offered to host Marky at my place if he ever travels to New York. He's agreed not to bother you guys again, but he doesn't want to tell us anything else. We should call his lawyer."

"Has everyone lost their minds?" I said. "Why should we call his lawyer? He's not even been arrested! Those were fake cops! He's wearing fake handcuffs! And you're a fake private investigator who's offered to help me but has gone too far and invited a possible stalker to your home."

I leave for five minutes.

"Marky, the offer is off the table. Gary has been nice enough already. He may give you an autograph, but he won't be taking any fucking selfies with you and he won't be inviting you to his home!" The Troubelmakr pouted. "And now you're gonna tell us what exactly you were doing for Dashing Henry, or I'll get my mother to ban you for life from all the studio lots, premiere red carpets, shooting locations—and Disneyland."

"Can she do that?" the Troubelmakr asked the two men in the room, horror written on his face.

Of course not.

"Do you doubt it?" I raised an eyebrow.

"You are a bad woman!" He looked like he was going to start crying.

"One hundred percent pure evil feminist of the worst kind. If you spend half an hour more with me, you may even become infected and stop being scared of confident women. Now tell me why the hell you were following David!"

"Is feminism really infectious?" Marky/Troubelmakr asked the men again.

"You bet, Marky. But it's not a bad thing," Gary Firth said, and I may have beamed at him in awe. And swooned.

It's just reassuring when some of your early crushes become adorable and sexy fifty-something-year-olds like him, Keanu Reeves, or Winona Ryder.

"Henry wanted to know about the journo's movements before the trial," Marky/Troubelmakr finally said. He looked unconvinced by Gary's words, but he was talking nonetheless. "See if he could use some garbage against him."

"Garbage?" David protested. He would only play the objective observer who was merely taking notes to a point. "What garbage?"

"He was hoping for something big like corruption or links to a gang, since you are, you know, Latino and all that. I kept telling him you were way too boring for any of that." Marky/Troubelmakr's smile was creepy, and I was breathing deeply to prevent myself from killing the bigoted prowler. "You're a total snoozefest and the most predictable and dull person I've ever watched. I didn't even see you litter or go over the speed limit."

"Thanks, I guess," David said.

"Man, I totally missed that you were boning the mayor's daughter. Dashing would have liked to know that." Marky/Troubelmakr was apparently feeling more loquacious now that he'd started telling us what we wanted to know. "He'd have used that as ammo against you."

While I was happy that Dashing Henry had been unsuccessful in his attempt to find something damaging against David, and I was relieved that he was no longer able to hurt him, that last statement from the Troubelmakr made me shiver. David and I had been careful and discreet, but I still didn't like the idea that whatever we had could be used against him.

"What happened the night of Henry's death? Were you also following me?" David asked.

"Yes. I had been learning your schedule and routine the past few days. I followed you until you got home a bit after nine that night."

"What did you do next?"

"I called Henry and told him you were there."

"Had he asked you to do that?" David had shamelessly hijacked my interrogation. But, in his defense, the man-child seemed to respond better to men than women. And Gary looked happy not to play a starring role in the questioning anymore.

"Yes." The Troubelmakr looked at me with fear.

"What happened then?"

"I was hanging out on the street, right across from the building's entrance. Five minutes later, I saw Dashing's Mercedes-Benz pulling onto the parking ramp."

"How do you know it was his car? Did you see him driving it?" asked David.

"He has an AMG G63 in bronze," Marky/Troubelmakr said.

David frowned. "A what?"

"A very big, very expensive, somewhat distinct car," I translated, and I spelled the name of the model so David could jot that down.

"He couldn't have been happy with the Prius tailgating him," Marky/Troubelmakr added.

"What Prius?" David and I asked in unison, possibly too eagerly.

"A Prius tailing Dashing's car, way too close for my liking —and I'm sure Dashing wasn't feeling it either. That bronze paint scratches easily, you know. The Prius followed Dashing right into your building," Marky explained.

David looked at me then back to Marky. "Did you see who was driving it?"

"Dunno. A dude?"

"Age? Race? Ethnicity? Hair color? Any other remarkable characteristics?"

"A regular dude? It was dark, I didn't see much," Marky said, and I could see David's exasperation.

"What happened next?" I asked.

"I kept hanging around because I was curious to see if the mayor would show up to visit you," he said, pointing to me. He had a clear case of Celebrity Worship Syndrome if I've ever seen one.

"My mother doesn't do call visits," I told him. If Aurora Valls wanted to see me, she summoned me.

"So anyway, Dashing hits me up all upset because he's been knocking on the reporter's door and the guy isn't there. I told him I saw him go into the building and I didn't see him come out."

David and I looked at each other. We both knew why Dashing Henry hadn't found David at his place that night. He was already with me.

"Why did he want to see me?" David asked.

"Dunno, to beat your ass probably." Marky/Troubelmakr laughed, and I was getting tired of him. And the idea of what could have happened to David if he hadn't been at my place that night made me uneasy. What did Henry want with him?

"Did you see anything else? Did Henry's car leave or the Prius that went behind it?" David asked.

"Nah, I left. Chris Evans was going to be on Kimmel that night, and I needed to take the Metro to Hollywood and Highland to see if I could catch him and ask for a selfie when he left. They shoot at El Capitan," Marky/Troubelmakr said, as if the whereabouts of Jimmy Kimmel's production company were a big secret.

Before our minor stalker could grab his cell phone and produce the pictures he'd taken with Captain America himself, I gestured at David that we should leave. Fortunately, we'd been perfecting the art of communicating without words for the last half a year.

20

"We agree, right?" I asked David once we were out of the Biltmore and had bid our good-byes to the film crew. Marky had decided to stay at the hotel and harass Gary and the rest of the cast of the movie for a while, but I managed to scare him enough that he'd promised me he'd leave within an hour.

David raised an eyebrow. "Probably. Care to specify what we agree on, though?"

"Better to leave the police out of this. They can find Marky themselves," I said.

"Definitely. Let's stay as far from them as possible."

"Even if a chat with Marky could help them realize you really didn't lure Henry to the Eastern Columbia the night he died but the other way around?" We had to cover all the angles.

"I don't know about that. I still feel there's a way of using Fitzsimmons's testimony against me," David reasoned, which sounded plausible to me. "Plus, they specifically warned us to stay away from this. I don't want them more pissed off at us than they already are."

"And we're always on time to let them know if we change our mind," I said.

David made a humming noise. "You never replied to my ask, by the way."

"What ask?" I was tired, still shaken, and hungry. It was noon and I was *drunk*. I couldn't remember what he was talking about.

"No more fights, no more misunderstandings," he said, recalling the words he'd said to me when we were both running from Marky—zee, ess, and two ems—Fitzsimmons.

"When has there been a misunderstanding?" I asked.

"Apparently when you left me because you thought I was *seeing* someone else."

"I didn't leave you because of that!" I protested. "I didn't leave you. *We* came to an agreement."

"Really? And what would that agreement be?"

"That it was better to part ways considering I was going through some stuff, and being the girlfriend of LA's hottest investigative journalist wasn't exactly helping me overcome my insecurity issues."

"Since when have you been insecure?" David asked me, baffled. And he was right. I'd always been blindly self-assured, until I wasn't. And he still hadn't realized why that had changed.

As I didn't want to have that conversation—our two-hour relationship conversation that had been interrupted by a celebrity-adoring man-child—I picked up the pace, making my way to my car on Broadway. I had a slight premonition.

"The reprobate, revenue-hungry beasts!" I yelled when we finally made it to my car. The meter had run out exactly two minutes before, and I'd already been ticketed.

"Elena, we were finally having a conversation." David

looked at me with disillusionment painted all over his features.

"I know, I'm sorry," I said. "But I just got a parking ticket when I wasn't even a minute late!"

I wanted him to understand my frustration. But he didn't.

"Can't you just tell your mom about it?"

"And what, make it go away?"

"Yes?"

"I don't do that, and the fact that you believe I'd do such a thing is part of the problem." I see now that it wasn't exactly me talking, but the fact that I was equal parts tired and hungry. But, on the other hand, I was right.

"Is it too late?" he asked. "Are we too different now?"

Are we incapable of being together again, of loving each other again, of mending things? I added my own questions to David's words in my mind. But I didn't say them out loud.

"Can we perhaps leave this conversation until after we've been fed?" I seriously thought that was the best way of proceeding and not getting ourselves hurt permanently. "Will you have lunch with me?"

"Of course," he said, graciously. But I could see the disappointment in his eyes.

...

Only after I had devoured half a falafel plate did I finally feel human enough to say something. We were seated at one of the picnic-like outdoor tables from Z falafel, and David was giving me the silent treatment.

"Okay, I'm able to talk now," I said and again, I know, sometimes my lines are lacking. But I'm more of a polisher than a solid first draft writer. So I was giving him a poor first version of what I really wanted to say.

"Really?" David answered with a mocking tone. "And what are you willing to talk about? The murder? Your career? Even better . . . the weather?"

"Us, Scribe. Let's talk about *us*," I said. "I'm even happy to save you the hassle of having to ask the uncomfortable questions yourself, not that that's ever been a deterrent for you."

"What uncomfortable questions?" He was feigning disinterest but the sharp line of his jaw indicated that he was engaged.

"The ones you're dying to ask about my relationship with Victor, which I'm only discussing with you because you and I have more of a relationship right now than him and me." There, I said it.

"Meaning?" Of course he wasn't happy with a simple insinuation. He wanted the full uncensored account.

"What me and Victor share is a relationship of convenience, and not much more than that."

"Still not clear," he said. The roguish grin tugging at his lips wasn't helping me feel more at ease.

"Do I *really* need to spell it out for you?"

"Only if you feel like doing it," he said. Of course, he was big on the journalistic principles of stating facts and being clear and precise. He was also extremely nosey.

"Only because it's *you*, and I hope my honesty is appreciated," I said. By then, I was hot and blushing.

"It is," he said.

"What I meant is that it's not like we're still fucking or anything."

"Really?" David said in a tone of half surprise, half pretended indifference, and all smugness.

"I've got that covered with you," I said, looking him straight in the eye. *Your turn, Scribe.*

"Not just with me." Was he deflecting? "Judging by your frequent use of toys."

He was just playing.

"You caught me a couple of times," I admitted, referring to some of those night visits between the two of us.

It could have been that we were still tipsy or that the sex talk was turning us on, but our stares alone could have ignited the place on fire.

"I'd say I caught you more than a *couple of times*," he said. "But never with him. Which forces me to ask, why are you still with him?"

His question was received with the same shock as a bucket of iced water thrown over my head.

"None of your fucking business," I said, teeth gritted. If a second ago we were this close to ripping each other's clothes off in plain daylight in the middle of Hill Street, right now I was about to murder him with complete disregard for the number of witnesses present.

"Sorry. Sometimes the reporter gets the better part of me. You're right. It's none of my fucking business. Are we back at being friends?"

"Have we ever been friends? *Just* friends, I mean." I may have been a bit bothered by his use of the f-word.

"Weren't we *just friends* when we were at college?" he asked.

"I was pining for you for like two years, so definitely not *just friends*." Why I had decided that was the right moment to admit something I'd never before told him, I don't know.

"My pining was longer and more anguished than that," he said, and my heart skipped a beat. Who knew this conversation would turn into something so revealing?

We were staring at each other again with a unique intensity.

I saw what looked like a father and his two small children coming our way, carrying loaded trays, but the adult in the group changed his mind midway to the table next to us and chose to sit with the kids at the farthest corner from us in the restaurant's tiny patio. The Motion Picture Association would have ranked the gazes between me and David NC-17 even if we were both fully clothed.

"Do you want to ask me anything else about the affair I never had or wanted to have with Gloria Kingsley?" I truly appreciated how definitive those words sounded.

"Nope, I'm good," I said and, for the first time in a long time, I was perfectly content.

21

"Any chance you'd let me shower at your place?" I asked David as I finished parking my ticketed car at my usual spot at the Eastern Columbia's parking area. I suspected that my water heater would still not be working.

"Do you want company?" he offered, and I let my eyes accept.

The day had started with my mother waking me up abruptly. I then had to read an extremely untalented piece of journalism, I had pissed off my dad, faced the cops, and was chased down by a lunatic. But it was finally shaping up to be a promising journey.

Perhaps we should have had that damn conversation before. We'd been all mellow vibes and heated stares since our lunch chat and on our way from the eatery.

I allowed myself to anticipate *everything* I wanted to do to David in the shower, and becoming extremely aware of the tingling sensation between my legs. But then I saw the car, and dread washed over my body.

"Aargh!" I cried out.

"Elena, ¿qué pasa?" David asked, concerned, looking around us.

"I'd bet my Critics Choice Association Super Awards nomination that's Dashing Henry's car," I said, referring to the only accolade I'd received in my entire career as I signaled a car of the same distinct model and color as the one Marky/Troubelmakr had described as Dashing Henry's. It was parked in the visitor's area of our building's garage.

"And you're despising it because . . . ?"

"Because now we'll have to find a way to break into it and see if there's anything that helps us in this investigation." I sighed. "And that's probably going to take us at least half the afternoon and distract us from our previous and much more appetizing endeavors."

David's jaw dropped. "You think we should break into it?" He had already forgotten about our shower arrangements and had journalistic thrill written all over his face. "Elena, I'm not saying we shouldn't shower together. I'm just saying, the day is still young." His reassuring words may have done something to appease me, but his grin stirred that something between my legs again.

"Is there anything else to do other than break into the car?" I said. "Apart from calling the cops, I mean."

"Which we said we wouldn't do," David completed my thoughts. "But you know a car break-in is a crime, right?"

"Hmm. With a good lawyer, we could probably be charged with a misdemeanor and not a felony," I said. And I knew that not because of my identity as a lawyer's daughter but as a crime screenwriter.

"Still sounds awful to me," he said.

"The alternative is letting the cops find this thing first."

"This is a very bad idea," David continued arguing, but I

thought he was starting to contemplate the scenario seriously.

"We could just pretend I never saw that humongously big car and return to our initial afternoon plans," I said, but even if that was what I wanted to do, I knew that wasn't the smartest decision.

"Do you even know how to break into a car?" David asked, and I guess he'd reached the same conclusion I had.

"Should we Google it?"

"You Google, I'll YouTube it," he said, and we both took our cell phones and approached the task at hand in the most digitally native way possible.

...

Half an hour after having watched an extremely informative video from an online roadside assistance business owner, and after a trip to the hardware store, we were back in the garage with an inflatable pry bar and a reach tool with a flexible tip. Following the instructions from the roadside assistance guru, I introduced the airbag bar between Henry's car frame and the passenger door and inflated it, prying the door about half an inch open. David then used the reach tool and, after a few failed attempts, managed to pull the door handle and open the car's passenger door.

The alarm started blasting.

"We should have thought this through a bit better, perhaps?" David asked. The possibility of the car having an alarm system hadn't even crossed our minds.

"I'd say we have two minutes until George comes snooping around from the tenth floor or someone else gets here." I pursed my lips.

"Let's make it count," David said.

"Has that security camera always been there?" I asked over the alarm noise when I saw the recording device above our heads.

And perhaps I should tell you here that the pry bar and the reach tool weren't the only things we'd bought, with cash, at the not-necessarily-nearest hardware store. We were also wearing gloves, head masks, and some hilarious-looking hooded white jumpsuits. They brought me memories of *Breaking Bad*, but mostly I hoped they would cover our clothes and most of the details that would make me or David recognizable, should someone see us breaking into Henry's car. That was the only reason we weren't running away already from the sound of the car alarm.

"I think the security team only had that one installed a few days ago," David yelled so I could hear him. He was going through the contents of the glove compartment, which were sparse: owner's manual and car registration. "The car registration says Atticus Mortimer. Are we sure we didn't break into the wrong car?"

"Stop panicking, that's his assumed name." David raised an eyebrow in confusion. "It's the fake name he used to book appointments or check into hotels *if* he didn't feel like being bothered."

Everyone at *LA Misconducts* knew Henry had an alternative name for certain occasions. David shrugged and kept searching, apparently satisfied with my explanation.

"No food wrappers, no paper cups, not even a used tissue. This guy must get the car detailed every week," he said, crouching to see if there was something on the floor of the vehicle.

I checked the non-contents of the trunk.

"It's almost as if he didn't live in Southern California," I added. "No beach blanket, no spare jacket for the chilly summer days, no reusable bags for grocery store runs!"

"Yeah, as if he did his own grocery shopping. Should we call it a day and preventively call our lawyer?"

"He wouldn't want to know about this," I said. "Plausible deniability and all that."

David snorted. "Not sure that's what plausible deniability means."

"Are we really arguing about words *now*?" I couldn't believe I had been thinking about giving us another try and having a more committed and even conventional relationship with him when he could be so insufferably meticulous. "What the fuck is that?" I said, pointing to a cartoon-looking cat hanging from the car's rearview mirror.

"One of those cutesy car mirror charm thingies?" David asked.

"The hell it is. Henry hadn't been cute a day in his life. Plus, he hated animals—even cats. Grab that, we're taking it," I said decisively. "And we're leaving."

...

"I'll take that shower now, even if it's without you," I told David.

We were entering the main vestibule of the Eastern Columbia after having left the garage via its car ramp, shedding our camouflage attire, and dumping it in a trash can three blocks from there.

"I'll join before you know it," David said. "But something occurred to me while we were having our undercover adventure at the garage, and I don't think it can wait."

"Is that what we're calling it? *Undercover adventure at the garage.*"

"It has a better ring than *breaking and entering*," he said.

"Look who's here? You two talk to each other now?" I recognized the rich, timbered voice immediately. George stood in my and David's way.

Ugh.

"You," I said, sending a killing stare George's way. The only reason I hadn't seen my neighbor approaching was that my gaze had been entirely fixed on David.

"Hey, George. How's it going?" David greeted him with his charming personality fully engaged.

"Are you seriously being nice to him?" I asked, pointing at George with disdain.

"Elena, it was an anonymous source. We can't assume," David said patiently.

"Oh my god! I can't believe you right now! You are so infuriatingly . . . you!"

David smirked, and that only made me angrier. "So infuriatingly me?"

"So you two are definitely *talking* and *humping* now then," George said with a tone of pure insinuation. He looked as if David and I were the latest, spiciest installment of *Love Is Blind, Too Hot to Handle* or whatever reality dating gameshow he favored. "Have you heard there's a car in the garage with the alarm sounding? They think it may be Dashing Henry's, only it's registered under a fake name and the cops missed it when they first found the body," added George sotto voce. Without another word, he left in the direction of the garage.

"Have you noticed George keeps finding out about everything before everyone else?" I asked David, still mad at him for showing so much niceness with George.

"Yes, so?"

"Don't you find that suspicious?"

We looked at each other, letting our eyes have the rest of the conversation. Could the chatterbox be the person responsible for Henry's death? It would explain his ability to know everything before anyone else.

"Nah!" we both said in unison. George hardly seemed like a potential killer.

22

I left David to whatever he wanted to do and took the elevator straight to the second floor. I didn't even ask him what had occurred to him while we were at Henry's car. I didn't care.

I opened his apartment with my own keys, made my way inside, feeling very much at home, and started stripping. I knew he wouldn't mind finding my clothes littered all around the place when he came back—or he shouldn't, anyway. And even if he took his time doing I didn't exactly know what, chances were I'd still be in the shower when he returned. Not because I was going to be waiting for him, but because I needed a long, relaxing, hot shower so badly.

I went to David's bathroom wearing my most daring Commando mid-rise thong and Agent Provocateur sheer bra and was about to start the shower when I saw an incoming call. I didn't turn the faucet on because I knew the conversation would take a while. I also knew that I *had to* answer.

I couldn't catch a break, could I?

"Victor," I answered, trying to sound normal, perhaps

even cheerful. Have I already mentioned that I am the absolute worst? Perhaps you had deduced it even if I haven't told you.

"Elena," he said. Did I also have to do the heavy lifting with this conversation? You bet I did.

Several reaction lines popped in my mind: *I guess you read the article in the* Voice, *I'm sorry I didn't pick up before, I've been meaning to call you all day.* This time I think I found the one combination of words that made the most sense.

"I'm sorry," I said, and I sounded sincere because I was. I should have broken up with Victor weeks before. And, since I pledged truthfulness to you, I'll admit that I was, perhaps, using him to portray an image—that of an independent woman who had it all, including an aspiring job as a screenwriter on the brink of breaking through, and a gorgeous boyfriend. But I was broadcasting that image, the one that encompassed the highly enviable boyfriend, mainly to one viewer who also happened to be my neighbor. And by that, I don't mean fucking chatterbox George.

I know the whole thing of pretending you're above everything and are self-sufficient while still wanting to impress your ex all the time must be the worst paradox ever.

But I tried to stop thinking about me, for once, and put my mind to the task at hand. Nobody deserved to find out via link, the way Victor had, that their romantic partner was having a dalliance with their ex. Not even if their relationship is a non-exclusive one. I should have been the one to tell Victor.

"So it's true then," he said. "Because the article was so badly written, and it misrepresented your situation in such a way that I wasn't quite sure."

And there it was, the reason I'd never gotten to breaking up with Victor, other than my selfish will to make David jealous every single day of his existence. I liked Victor—and he got me. He was also a nice person. And, during those few first months that I was into him, he'd been quite the decent —sometimes even remarkable—lay.

"I guess I should have realized something was amiss," he continued.

"Is it bad if I do the whole, *It's not you, it's most definitely me* thing?" I asked.

He sighed. "Are you breaking up with me then?"

"Aren't *you* breaking up with me?"

"I'm going to be completely honest with you. If you'd picked up the phone when I called this morning, I would probably have done just that," Victor said, but he sounded calm and measured. "I was enraged."

"I get it."

"But we have an open relationship," he conceded.

"So you can't complain . . ." I regretted those words the moment they left my mouth. But, by now, you know I am truly the worst.

"Elena, sometimes I think you have the emotional intelligence of a five-year-old," Victor said. "But I like you nonetheless, and I'm a believer in mending things. I feel we had the perfect partnership. I'm not saying we shouldn't talk about it. A few details could be ironed out going forward."

Ironed out? Who the hell uses that expression when talking about a relationship? A politician, that's who. Also, as you may have grasped, I'm not big into ironing—literal meaning or otherwise.

"We did have a great partnership, but it felt more like a business than a romance, no?" I argued. "You needed a plus one for a work event, I'd go and try my best at innocuous small talk. And then we'd leave the event, you'd go to your place, and I'd go to mine."

"Well, nobody is perfect," Victor said.

"Are you quoting *Some Like It Hot* to me?"

"Would it help my case if I said I was?"

I mean, yes. But I couldn't keep doing the whole triangle thing. It wasn't fair to him, and it wasn't fair to me. Because, let's keep things real, I was doubting my feelings about Victor, but subconsciously I knew what I felt about David. And it didn't even come close.

"Can you promise we'll be friends?" I asked.

"Ouch. Not even Billy Wilder could help me."

"I was always more of a Hitchcock person—though it's hard to ignore the stories about how he treated his actresses."

"Of course."

"But can we be friends?" I insisted.

"If that's all you want to be, we'll be friends," he promised, and I knew he'd find a way of keeping his word. If for no other reason than I was still his boss's daughter and someone incredibly well connected in Los Angeles. "Elena, be careful though. I've heard things. You know I'm not a gossip, and I know nothing about your personal relationship with David. But are you sure he's telling you everything?"

"What do you mean?"

Victor paused, then said, "There are rumors."

"He didn't kill Dashing Henry," I said, sounding perhaps a bit too frustrated.

"I wasn't referring to *those* rumors."

"What rumors were you talking about then?"

"The ones about a job offer, tentative to his ability to remain independent."

"He's always been independent." I dismissed Victor's words, his warning.

"In your view, perhaps. But there are people who think

being linked to the mayor's daughter disqualifies him. But these are just rumors, don't put too much weight on them. I'm more worried about him being a killer."

I scoffed. "He's not a killer!"

"I gather you haven't read the latest article?"

"Which one would that be now?"

"Sending the link right now," Victor said. "Take care," he added, and I know he meant it.

We finished saying goodbyes with the same fondness we'd always shared for each other and, before opening the link he'd sent me and simply moving forward to a new event on an extremely eventful day, I allowed myself to think about us. I cherished the time we'd shared.

We'd met almost a year before when he'd just moved to Los Angeles. My mother introduced us at some city hall party. He was her newest recruit. He was originally from Boston, and the fact that he was a stranger in a new city attracted me to him instantly, endeared me to him. Well, the fact that he looked outrageously sexy in a suit may have helped as well. And I say that fully aware that suits and blonds had never ticked anything for me before.

We managed to get drunk on the free booze at the party. Technically, he was off the clock and didn't start working for the city until two days later, and I'm simply an incredibly bad influence. We told each other our life stories—a sanitized version of them, at least—and we ended up on a run to a pharmacy in need of condoms and from there straight to his place. I'd never been one to fuck on a first date, let alone the day I met someone. But it felt the most natural—and urgent—thing to do with him.

It fizzled out extremely fast after that though, and we soon found ourselves in a comfortable relationship based on frequent outings, infrequent chats about the same interests, and even more infrequent intimacy.

My phone buzzed then because I still hadn't checked the message Victor had sent me with the link. I was brought back to that Friday in February where I had to add a breakup to the long list of things happening in a single day. I remedied my inattention to my phone and opened the link to the article Victor had shared with me.

Investigative Reporter David Ramos Looks Guiltier by the Minute

The LAPD has found new evidence that links former *LA Gazette* contributor David Ramos with the death of celebrated *LA Misconducts* actor Dashing Henry. Ramos was seen this morning at the Downtown police station with Mayor Aurora Valls's oldest daughter, the perennially unemployed screenwriter and wild child Elena Freire Valls.

By Gloria Fucking Kingsley

We've already told you about *LA Misconducts* illustrious actor Dashing Henry's fatal death in a hit-and-run that went terribly wrong. His body was found yesterday at the garage of the Downtown art deco apartment building Eastern Columbia.

Today new evidence arises connecting the death of the actor to the so-called investigative reporter David Ramos. Only a few hours ago, the city beat journalist was first suspected of having been the one driving and dispensing the final blow to Henry. Now the evidence against Ramos keeps piling up in a difficult-to-ignore way.

Sources familiar with the investigation say Henry's autopsy results have shown high amounts of alcohol overdose. Even if the autopsy wasn't able to determine the exact type of substance Henry drank—due to how quickly alcohol metabolizes in the body—the LAPD has hired the services of an expert forensic odor profiler.

What the actual fuck! Not in my wildest, most imaginative moments as a screenwriter would I have thought about adding a character who was a smell expert! I was hooked by the turn of events, and I continued reading.

The smell expert was brought in by the lead LAPD investigators to determine if there were any connections between the evidence found at the crime scene and a potential suspect. Law enforcement sources who wish to remain anonymous say the forensic odor profiler was able to identify the intoxicating beverage Henry had drunk before his death as Fernet-Branca Liqueur.

Fernet-Branca has a characteristic licorice-like odor and around 75% of its world production is consumed in Argentina.

Ramos, who is of Argentine descent, is a self-proclaimed Fernet-Branca lover. The reporter has openly written about his taste for this spirit in several of his posts on social media, and the police believe this furthers their case against him. They believe Ramos would have made Henry badly intoxicated before running him over. They should be ready to make an arrest in the next 24 hours if Ramos stops running interference.

The journalist was at the LAPD Downtown station on Friday morning to recant his previous statement where he'd lied and said he'd been alone all night on Wednesday, the night the killing of Henry took place. Ramos was joined at the station by intermittent girlfriend Elena Freire Valls and their lawyer, Mateo Freire, who also is Freire Valls's father and is married to Los Angeles mayor, Aurora Valls.

A Now Tarnished, Once Promising Journalistic Career

But facing being charged with murder is not the only issue that should be a source of preoccupation for Ramos at the moment as the journalist may also be confronted with questions about his reporting.

There have been insinuations that Ramos could have concocted the allegations made against Henry when he first published a series of damning articles about the actor six months ago. Even if we're still gathering evidence to corroborate it, Ramos is suspected to also have fabricated some of the sources on his articles that were meant to end Henry's career.

That's where I stopped reading. As if Gloria Fucking Kingsley could pretend she'd ever cared about the appropriate way of gathering evidence while writing an article.

It was preposterous that she was insinuating David had fabricated any evidence or sources in his reporting against Dashing Henry.

I was so enraged that I did the only logical thing. I called my dad. My hands trembled as I dialed his contact.

"Did you see the article?" I asked when he picked up the phone, trying to breathe slowly, my heart rate spiking.

"I have no idea what you're talking about, and good afternoon to you too. How are you doing?"

"Not so great. Just read another article in the *Voice*. This one is saying that David made up the evidence against Henry to ruin his career." My tone was elevated, and I was hyperventilating. But my dad had a way of calming me. He'd always had.

"That's preposterous!" he said.

"Exactly my thoughts." Long inhale in, long exhale out. "Papá, call the cops and tell them I'm willing to talk to them in case they're giving any credibility to that article. David didn't kill Henry in fear that he was going to uncover him as a fake reporter who made up sources. I can tell the cops exactly what Henry tried with me and how he was unequivocally a predator. I can talk to them about how David's article probably helped a lot of people by stopping him."

"Are you sure about talking to the police?"

"Completely. Haven't been more sure about anything in my life. Should have told David years ago, all of it. If I'd been a source in his article, he could have published it months before. The pervert probably tried and succeeded in assaulting and harassing other people during that time, and I could have helped."

"Elena, you know why you did what you did," my dad reminded me.

"Yes, and there's not been a day when I haven't regretted it." It was true. I breathed deeply again, but I felt better just by saying what I did. "Reach out to the cops. Tell them I'm ready to offer my testimony about David. And Papá, I'm gonna talk to him."

"I'm not going to tell you not to do it, cariño. You should have probably done it months ago." Dad showed his wisdom once again. "You may not want to tell your mom about it, though."

"I don't care what she thinks."

"Are you sure about that?"

My dad had a point, but I wasn't keeping quiet any longer. I sent him a hug and hung up.

Now where the hell was David.

23

Dashing Henry's death, the onslaught of articles, the chats with my dad ... They were all bringing it back.

It had been an evening more than two years before. I was on the set of *LA Misconducts* as the first script for the show with the "Written by Elena Freire Valls" credit was being shot.

I was ecstatic. I didn't mind the late hour, the overtime, the bad food, or even the honey wagon—we were shooting a street sequence. I was pumped, happy, and proud.

We'd been shooting a sequence where Henry's character was walking around the downtown area of Los Angeles and looking for an old acquaintance. He found him and tried to get some information out of him. It was a straightforward enough sequence. Henry had probably shot thousands similar to that one. If nothing else, *LA Misconducts* was a formulaic show. We were told repeatedly by the network execs that that's what made the show work. People wanted the same rehashed recipe week after week. The predictability brought them comfort. There were enough unpredictable things in life already. And I could relate to that.

And yet, despite the familiarity of the scene, Henry was having problems delivering the dialogue. He was getting frustrated too.

After shooting the same lines over eight times and not getting a definitive take, the director was getting frustrated as well. We broke for lunch, which was technically dinner but you would call it lunch, even if it was 7 p.m., because of showbiz lingo and union regulations.

The director suggested cutting some stuff out of the script so the sequence would be similar but would have Henry go over fewer lines. I agreed. Henry suggested he and I could work it over lunch at his trailer—of course he had a trailer while everyone else was eating under a wall-less tent the production team had put up a few hours before. To be honest, I think the writers had a trailer too, but I hadn't been able to find it.

Henry also had his own catered food, so I thought I may find something tastier there than at catering. I was wrong.

Henry was going through a hard paleo phase, and the options at his trailer were limited to almost completely raw steak with an insignificant handful of fresh berries, nuts, and arugula leaves with no dressing.

That was probably the beginning of my vegan ways. The red meat made most of the plate, and I'd never been one for beef without lots of starchy and vegetable sides. But the food wouldn't end up being the worst part of the evening.

We went over Henry's lines again. I even offered to run the lines with him if he wanted. He half laughed at me, half got offended. Bear in mind that I was a baby staff writer talking to a two-time Emmy veteran. I gathered that screenwriters don't normally offer to run lines with actors—and they don't.

I proposed to trim a couple of things that would leave the script looking almost the same. He dismissed me. That's when I realized he hadn't asked me there to talk shop and fix a few lines.

We were seated at the three-seat sofa in his trailer. I had the pages on my lap and only then I realized how minuscule the whole setup was. He drew nearer, sitting impossibly close to me.

"Why don't we put this aside for a minute?" he said, grabbing the script from my hands, touching them in the process, and leaving the pages on a nearby table.

My body jolted at the contact, in a bad way. He was too close to me. His breath smelled of burnt coffee and dead cow. I could count the pores on his nose. I was paralyzed with something that still, to this day, is difficult to describe —horror, fear, shock, surprise at what was happening and how bad I was at dealing with the situation.

One of his hands was on my knee, and I knew he was not going to keep it there but would make advances toward my thigh. His face got so close that his pores were gigantic even with full TV make-up on. Wasn't he supposed to have a good dermatologist? Some of the best skin doctors in the country practiced in Los Angeles, and Henry had enough money to employ one full time. Can you believe the idiocy of what I was thinking?

Now I realize that shock had me frozen and thinking absurdities. For months after, I just felt stupid—and guilty.

He could have gotten away with kissing me because of how much of a paralyzed gazelle in the headlights I was in that moment. He touched my hair with his free hand and that felt so intimate—and so wrong—that I finally snapped out of it.

I put a hand on his chest and pushed him away, catching him off guard. I stood quickly.

I didn't even think and went straight for the door. I started running once I was out of the trailer and didn't stop until I got to video village. The director and some of the camera crew were eating there, but their backs were to me and they didn't see me arriving in a rush.

I was trembling. What would have happened if the door in Henry's trailer hadn't been so close? If it had been locked? If I hadn't been able to leave so quickly?

"Elena, we haven't finished fixing the script."

I heard Henry's voice behind me and winced. The hair on my arms stood on end in revulsion.

"Yes, we have," I said, turning around, putting more distance between the two of us. I said those words with as much determination as I could muster given the circumstances.

"Are you sure? I wouldn't want to have to call Fred and tell him you did a poor job," Henry said. He was a powerful person who could probably have me fired, and I panicked.

Then I reminded myself that even if Henry wanted to ruin me, I wasn't nobody. I had lots of friends and connections from college who all worked in the industry. Try me. I would find another job. Also, not in a million years was I going to go back to that creep's trailer.

"I'm sure," I said, and I may have even sounded smug if I hadn't still been trembling.

"Suit yourself, but Fred won't like hearing about it."

Amelia got there then. She had a late call time as her character was supposed to appear only briefly in that sequence.

"Dashing, quit frightening the writers, will you?" she said in a joking tone, and I think we probably started our friendship then and there.

Amelia and I talked about this months after it happened. At the time, she didn't suspect anything. Henry had never tried anything with her. He was smart. It wasn't until Amelia's then girlfriend, now wife, Brenda, who was a production assistant at the show, told her that Henry had attempted shoving her into a closet and kissing her that Amelia started putting things together about that day with me. She wondered what other things she may have missed, and she felt guilty about it too, even if she wasn't the one to blame.

Dashing went back to his trailer after Amelia scolded him that night. I gave her a relieved smile and went to make a much-needed phone call. I called David first. But when he didn't pick up on the third try, I remembered he was supposed to be meeting a source for a story he was doing on corruption at city hall. That article would eventually mean the beginning of the end of the former mayor.

My sister was too young to burden her with the dirty story I was carrying, so I made the next logical call: my dad.

He was on the set in twenty minutes. I'm still not sure how he managed such a speedy commute from Beverly Hills. He played the role of the entertainment lawyer over-joyed with his daughter's career to perfection that day on set. I felt safe having him there. He's been denying it to this day, but I know he talked to Henry at one moment or another that night. The actor never tried anything else with me. He didn't even look my way or smile at me more than necessary. Fred never mentioned any dissatisfied call from him.

When my dad found out that David was going to get

home late that night, he decided to drive me to the Freire Valls family home instead of the place I shared with David. I spent the night in my old room. Dad even arranged for someone to drive my car there.

I'm spoiled if nothing else. I get in trouble and call Dad, and he rushes in and fixes everything.

He hugged me and comforted me. But he made one request: not to tell David. My mother was going to run for mayor. I'd suspected it but nothing had been officially announced yet, not even at the family level, and apparently we couldn't risk David trying to advance his career by writing about the next LA mayor's daughter as the victim of Dashing Henry's predatory practices.

And I, for some idiotic reason—basically because I was feeling unempowered and weak—promised not to tell the man I loved, the one person I didn't have any secrets with, the one thing I most needed to get off my chest.

Insecure Elena was born that day.

24

Friday, February 23rd

After the chat with my dad that Friday of February, two days after Henry's death, I did the only thing that made sense and called David.

He picked up right away, and I couldn't avoid thinking that some things had dramatically changed for the better after we'd separated.

"Where are you?" I asked

"Miss me already?" he answered, his tone playful.

"I need to see you." I nibbled nervously at my nails and hangnails and paced in David's bedroom area, phone tucked between my ear and my shoulder.

"Be there in literally two minutes," he said, flirtation still in his tone, but I'm not sure if he added anything else as I dropped my phone then and accidentally kicked it under the bed.

I crouched to reach under the bed and get it, and that's when I found something else there. Something troublesome.

"What the actual fuck?"

...

Exactly one minute and forty-seven seconds later, David opened the door of his apartment. I was still in my sexy underwear, seated on David's most comfortable chair. A chair, I should probably add, we'd been favoring as our favorite place for sex for the last couple weeks or so. We went through phases.

All this to say that he read the room the wrong way. He came in, saw me, smiled, and took his T-shirt off. Two days and I have already written him without a T-shirt twice. This is starting to look like one of those TV shows with a hunky protagonist where they always look for an excuse to have him shirtless in every single episode. Not that there's anything wrong with that.

"Back even before you noticed I was gone," he said, kneeling in front of me and kissing my neck in a way that made the next part so much harder. "Ready to enjoy that bath?"

"I think we should leave sex for later," I said.

He stopped kissing me right away and sat on the floor in front of me, but he was obviously confused. "Are you feeling okay?"

I was having way too many adrenaline-fueled experiences, but my feelings hadn't changed one bit from the previous day. All I wanted was a comforting shower, a fabulous fuck, and a restorative siesta. Really. I am this simple.

I guess by now you've realized I feel confident in my semi-permanent state of horniness. David for sure was aware of it, hence his confusion. But I needed to talk to him first.

"Sadly, I'm feeling okay. I don't mean that I feel sad, because I feel fine. I mean that it's sad to feel fine and still have to say no to sex—for now."

"For now." He took it as the promise it was. "Something happened?"

"Not even sure where to start," I admitted. "Why don't you tell me where you've been."

"Downstairs with the security guy going over the CCTV footage from the night Henry died. There's probably some stuff there, but that's not important right now," David said. "We can leave that for later. What's wrong? Obviously something happened."

"Okay, I'm gonna do it chronologically because it's how it happened and—regardless of what I do sometimes when I try to be a fancy screenwriter—chronological order is the best way to tell a story."

"Agreed."

"There's a new article. Gloria Fucking Kingsley says there's new evidence against you because Henry was intoxicated on Fernet when he died, and it had to be you getting him drunk because who else drinks Fernet?"

David looked taken aback. "Lots of people."

"I literally know no one else, but not the point. She's insinuating your reporting on Dashing was fake and you invented witnesses or something."

I saw David's face going up in flames and, in hindsight, I should have been a bit more delicate. But then again, I was a woman on the brink of a nervous breakdown.

"Don't worry, I've got you," I told him, and I wanted him to know that I meant it. "I've already talked to my lawyer and told him I'll talk to the cops and tell them you didn't invent anything about Henry because . . ." My voice broke, and David's expression shifted to one of concern. He came up on his knees again and got closer to me. "Because he also tried it with me."

There were a few seconds when he processed everything. And then he demanded to know more, so I told him about the night on the set of *LA Misconducts*, Henry touching me and threatening to ruin my career, and my dad coming to the rescue of the damsel in distress and fixing everything.

"Are you okay?" he asked.

I nodded. "I am now."

My throat was in a knot, and I started crying then. He hugged me, and it was warm and comforting and sweet, and his naked skin smelled so good that I wanted to remain there forever.

"Why didn't you tell me?" he asked then, and I knew that was going to be the hard part.

"Dad made me promise not to," I said, still inhaling David's smell. I didn't want to let go of his body, of that hug, but I knew I had to. I owed him an explanation, an apology. I just hoped he'd let me hug him like that again.

"Why didn't you tell me anyway?" he asked. "Oh god! You thought I was going to use you and write about it even if you didn't consent. Elena, I would never!"

"I know." I wanted to start crying again but didn't allow myself to.

"Then why didn't you tell me?" He was angry, and I can't blame him.

"Because I'm a fucking idiot, and I was hoping you would realize something had happened to me!" There, I said it and I was angry too.

David exhaled sharply, his face etched with pain.

"How was I supposed to realize? You didn't tell me anything!"

"I don't know! But you could have!"

"Are you being serious right now?" We may have been screaming a bit by then.

That's when the doorbell buzzed, and we heard Detective Clooney's voice on the other side of the door.

"Mr. Ramos, Ms. Freire Valls, I need to speak with you."

25

"You two don't lose any time, huh?" said Clooney when David opened the door.

He was still shirtless. I was wearing his T-shirt over my underwear, and Clooney noticed it right away. I mean, I guess you didn't have to be the most sagacious detective to realize neither of us was completely clad.

"I wish. This is really not what it looks like. It could be, but it isn't. By the end, we were sort of having an argument," I said, more to myself than for Clooney's sake.

"Yeah, I could hear you from the landing. These walls *are* thin."

"To what do we owe the pleasure of your company, officer?" David gracefully intervened. "We really need to go back to our argument."

"One thing is clear, you two are funny. Possible murderers and, at the latest, you're clearly hiding *something*. But funny nonetheless," Clooney said with a chuckle.

"We strive for entertainment," I said, acidly.

"You two wouldn't by any chance know something about a car in the garage owned by Dashing Henry?"

"George just told us something about a car being found at the garage, yes." I was opting for the deflection technique until it was no longer possible.

"It's been broken into. Anything you may know about that?"

I crossed my arms. "George also told us about it. Still not sure how he's always two steps ahead of you."

"Funny, again," Clooney said, but I knew this time he wasn't actually thinking that. "You wouldn't happen to see or know who broke into the car, right?"

"Does it look like we could have seen anything in this condition?" I gestured to my and David's states of disrobement.

Clooney was having none of it. "Answer my question, please."

"Is this turning into another interrogation, Detective?" I said. Once deflection was no longer possible, you never lied. You did something better. "Because we can continue this conversation, but we'll have to wait for our lawyer."

"I see how you're playing this." His smile didn't meet his eyes. "You know this doesn't look good for you both, right? It's almost as if you're hiding something, *again*."

"On the contrary. But I'm a lawyer's daughter and I do what my dad has always told me to do: I call him when I feel something is not quite right." That sentence rang so true right then.

"Your dad, I mean your lawyer, called to let us now that you were prepared to make a statement in case we decided to consider Mr. Ramos's reporting of the deceased in relation to the murder investigation," Clooney said, and it was almost as if he knew or intuited that David didn't know about Henry's attempt with me. I was glad I'd already told him.

"And I'm prepared to do it. Tell me when and where, and I'll be there—with my lawyer," I said. "Or I can make him come now if you want."

"That won't be necessary at the moment, but you two keep reachable," he told us.

"We will," David said. With that, we bid our goodbyes to the cop and closed the door.

I was going to say something the moment Clooney was no longer in sight, but David brought his index finger to my mouth and his other index finger to his in what was probably the sexiest way of telling someone to shut up.

He looked through the peephole and, once he made sure Clooney was in the elevator and out of earshot, he took his finger from my lips. I missed his touch instantly.

"You really want to talk to the cops about Henry? About what he did to you?" David started.

"I want them to know you didn't have any reason to kill Henry because he'd sued you for libel, and the charge had no foundation."

"Brenda would vouch for me. She's one of my first on-the-record sources. There's no need for you to get involved."

"I want to get involved. I've not been involved for way too much time," I said. "You know reading that article sent me straight to your place that night six months ago with only one idea in mind, right?"

"I had an inkling that had something to do with it." He smiled. "The thing is, I was barely able to publish it."

I felt guilty once again. "I know, because no one wanted to talk to you."

"Finding sources was hard, but that's always the case with a story like this," David said, putting me a little bit at ease. "But one of the *LA Misconducts* producers tried everything in his power to prevent me from getting the story out. I think he's the one who ultimately managed to get me fired. Even after the article was published, he maintained it was total fabrication and that Henry was a model citizen and a victim."

"What producer?" I suddenly realized. "Do you remember his name? Could that be Archie Eisenberg?"

"It could, I guess." David's brow furrowed in thought. "Name sounds familiar. But I'm not sure, to be honest. I'm usually good with names when I'm working on a story but forget them the moment it gets published."

"He may have gotten you fired, and you don't remember his name?" I've never understood David's ability to be cool with everything and everyone. But not holding a grudge against the person who cost him his job was even more inexplicable to me.

"I don't believe in holding on to negativity," he said.

"I don't think you realize how boho, Californian, tree-hugger that sounds!"

"Is that a bad thing?" he asked, a knowing smirk on his face.

"I'm sorry I didn't tell you what happened before," I told him then. I needed to come completely clean with him.

"I'm sorry you couldn't trust that I wouldn't put you before my work," he said. "That wouldn't happen. You know, right?"

"I do now."

We stared at each other for so long. I felt butterflies flutter in my stomach and had the feeling of being a silly twenty-something-year-old flirting with her best friend again.

"This is new," I said, referring to the blue-inked tattoo on the left side of his torso. Of course, I'd seen the body art depicting a bird of paradise flower before, but I never was able to inquire about it because of our self-imposed silence pact.

"I got it when you left me," he said, eyes still fixed on mine, electricity crackling in the air between us.

"I didn't leave you. We decided to part ways," I said, stubborn as always.

He shook his head slightly. "We'll agree to disagree."

"In any case"—I dismissed a squabble that wasn't going to be settled easily—"I like it." I went to trace the lines of his tattoo, but I knew exactly what that would trigger. And we had a lot on our fucking plates.

So, against my best and most hedonist feelings, I extricated my fingers.

"There's something else we need to talk about," I said.

His eyes widened. "Tell me nothing else happened to you."

"No, no, no," I appeased him. "It's something else about the case."

"The case?" he said, one of his eyebrows arching in amusement.

"You know, this murder we're trying to solve to clear your name and so you can write an article or two about it and win a Pulitzer or something."

"That's what we've been doing these past two days? Trying to get me a Pulitzer?" he said, chuckling.

"We've also attempted to get the cops off your back," I said. "And we've been using this whole thing as an excuse to flirt like crazy and spend time together."

He grinned triumphantly. "So you're admitting it," he said, relief plain in his voice.

"Of course, I'm admitting it. The only reason we're not fucking over that chair or in the shower right now is because we're in even more shit than you realize."

"You're going to need to back that up with some serious facts because it sounded like a paltry excuse."

"Seriously, since when do I find excuses *not* to fuck you? Come," I said and grabbed his hand, walking us toward the bed. I crouched and showed him my most recent preoccupation underneath the bedframe. "See for yourself."

26

"What is an expensive watch I've never owned doing under my bed?" When David reached to bring the watch closer, I slapped his hand.

"Don't! That's a Patek Philippe," I said. "And I'd bet my membership in the Procedural Writers Association of America that it's the watch Dashing Henry was wearing when he was killed."

"Elena, I didn't kill him," David said.

I threw my hands up in exasperation. "How many times do I need to tell you that *I know*."

"I don't know how that watch got there, but I'd never seen it before in my life," David said.

"Ei, I'm on your side. I know you didn't kill Henry. And the reason I do is not only because you were thoroughly thinking of all the ways to make me scream when the murder took place, but because I *know* you."

"But how did *that* get here?"

"My theory is, whoever killed Henry wants to pin this on

you and they took the opportunity of planting the watch here when you weren't home."

"But how did they get here? I haven't noticed anything missing or out of place . . . other than the mess you tend to make."

"Who else has keys to this place?" I said, ignoring his comment about my chaotic tendencies.

"The landlord, I guess. You, obviously. My parents. My sister also has a copy." He ticked each of us off on his fingers. "I think she may have gotten another spare copy for a cousin who was visiting and stayed here when I was on vacation last summer."

"During the trip to Greece?" I asked.

"How do you know I went to Greece?" I wasn't going to answer. I had basically told him I was mad about him. I wasn't going to admit I had found a way of following his moves and learning whether he traveled solo, with friends, or with company of the romantic type. To my knowledge, it had always been the first two options for the last year. When he saw I wasn't going to come clean about my knowledge regarding his Greek vacation, he said, "No, the trip to Puerto Rico."

Between you and me, I extracted the information from a common friend who loves gossip. It wasn't even that hard to get.

"Anyone else have keys?"

"I sometimes hire a professional crew to clean," he said sheepishly. I knew he had difficulties admitting he could be a bit bougie himself sometimes. "They're better at doing the stove and the windows. Oh, and I've always kept a spare copy in all the newsrooms I've worked in. You know, an emergency key."

"And you put those emergency keys in locked drawers or something?"

"What would be the point of having an emergency key in a locked drawer?" he asked. "Knowing me, I would have misplaced the key to the drawer."

"Good point. And those spare keys in newsrooms . . . Did you ever get them back when you stopped contributing for said outlets?" I suspected I knew the answer to that.

"I don't think so. I should though. I left my good flannel jacket at the *Gazette* and still haven't got it back."

"So let's see if I'm clear, because I felt special when you gave me a key to your place, but pretty much half of LA and an out-of-town cousin also have one."

"You're the only person I gave a key to who I wanted to visit me in the middle of the night, but I guess you have a point." He grabbed his T-shirt, the one I was wearing, and tugged at the hem, pulling me toward him.

We needed to stop with the flirtatiousness and start thinking clearly. But I wasn't sure we were going to manage it.

"Okay, the sexual tension is killing me," I purred. "And killing you."

"You got me," he admitted.

"Let's get this out of our systems. Let's have one, maybe two, quick fucks. And then we can think straight. You can tell me about the CCTV, we can decide what to do with that watch, you can start doing some writing, I can come up with a good pitch for my agent. We're not getting anything done because of this constant need to fuck each other numb."

You may think it was odd that we were thinking about sex after finding out David was framed for murder. And, in hindsight, it didn't make much emotional sense. But somehow finally coming clean with David and telling him everything that had happened, and that had kept us apart, had brought us even closer. I *needed* to feel the connection you can only find with sex.

"Quick," David said, and I knew he thought my idea was brilliant even if it was possibly the most irresponsible thing we'd ever done. More irresponsible than the time we broke into UCLA's Powell Library one night after closing hours because we were high and felt like being surrounded by books.

"Quick," I said.

Within seconds, I was no longer wearing his T-shirt or *any* T-shirt. I had dispensed with David's zipper and was halfway under his boxer briefs. We met in a clash of lips, teeth, and desire, and he'd pinned me against the wall, one of his legs making its way between mine.

I've never been so horny in my entire life and, again, I'm used to the wanton sentiment.

"We said quick," I told David in a moan, as he was torturing me with expert, meticulous care and getting himself even more acquainted with every single spot on my nape.

"There's no rush," he said, biting my earlobe and drawing out a throaty pant from me. And he had a point. Everything could wait, I guess.

I'm sorry if, like me, you thought *this* was the moment when I finally managed that phenomenal fuck I'd been craving. Fate was mistreating me in the worst, most devious ways.

I'd dropped David's jeans and underwear to the floor, and he was diligently taking care of my bra when an alarm blasted.

"¿Qué está pasando? David said, taking his lips from my clavicle to begrudge. "Not another non-fire."

But the alarm sounded different from what we'd heard the day before.

"No, that's my Bat-Signal." I sighed, resting my head on his naked chest , and I can't really emphasize how resigned I sounded—and felt.

"Your *what*?" David said, and he was carefully reclasping the lingerie he'd just unfastened.

"My Bat-Signal," I repeated. "My mother made me promise to carry this electronic device with me everywhere. If it sounds, it theoretically means there's been a security breach of some kind, and the family needs to regroup because there can be a potentially dangerous situation."

"You sound eerily calm for a potentially dangerous situation."

I paused, realizing that Gloria Fucking Kingsley had made public the place where I lived in her pretend reporting. But I dismissed the possibility of a real threat against me. Statistically, this was another sort of situation. "Are you acting like that because she interrupted us?" David asked me, still confused.

"Yes. Plus, my mother abuses this thing whenever she feels like summoning me." I searched the clothes I'd left on David's floor and found the sound-emitting device in one of my jean pockets. I made the sound stop. "We should probably get dressed. They'll be picking me up in less than five minutes."

27

"What would the non-emergency be this time?" I asked my mother as her security team escorted me inside her office at city hall.

She dismissed the man and woman who'd picked me up at my place less than ten minutes before and only talked once they had left the room.

"Elena, you look terrible. What happened to you?" Of course, she'd be the one to realize that I hadn't seen shampoo, body wash, or a hair dryer in days. She never missed anything.

"Ah, you know, the life of the in-between-gigs screenwriter who gets interrogated by the police," I said, trying to sound cool.

"I wouldn't know, actually." She was nothing if not proper. "And this wasn't a *summons*."

"Really? You don't want to advise me on my attire for next week's dinner thingy with the San Francisco people, or remind me not to smoke pot in public? I switched to edibles anyway."

"I wish you stayed away from that stuff altogether."

"Why? It's fucking legal in California!"

"Elena, language. And I didn't make you come here to talk about your questionable lifestyle choices." I wanted to say she'd just admitted that she had indeed summoned me, but she continued, "But to talk about your questionable choices in men."

My face must have said pretty transparently, *What the actual fuck?* because she explained herself.

"It's come to my attention that Victor and you are no longer an item," she said, choosing to use a euphemism as usual.

"You politicians are even faster at gossip than writers. *Technically*, we haven't been an item for months. Today we just broke up."

"And I can infer that means you resumed your entanglement with the reporter?"

"Again, if we get technical, the *entanglement* was resumed months ago. When he published an article exposing the man who had attempted to coerce me into sexual favors. And after we'd broken up because I was told not to tell him about that man so that I wouldn't jeopardize your career." I may have sounded a tad bitter.

My mother shook her head. "Elena, it's unbecoming of you to talk about these things."

"Oh my god! You're the fucking worst!"

"Don't be a silly child, and don't blame me for your relationship failures. Are we done with the tantrum?"

"Tell me what you wanted when you summoned me here," I said, as I was still standing in the middle of her office, my arms crossed in an almost defensive stance.

"I wanted to warn you that your reporter may be about to get arrested. You see, I do love and care about my daughter even if she feels like I'm the worst mother on earth."

"Not the worst. Just not as great as you used to be."

"Before I became a politician and had to put some of my needs before yours, you mean?" She was better at this game than I was. "Can we leave your mommy issues aside? I just told you the reporter is going to get arrested. Who's being selfish now?"

Touché.

"Does Dad know about the arrest?" I pretended I hadn't heard that last part.

"I'll brief him on the subject when we finish our meeting." The woman felt absolutely no embarrassment for using the verb *brief* when referring to a chat with her husband or the noun *meeting* while talking about seeing her older daughter. I wondered if she *conferred* with Marta.

"Why are the cops arresting David?" I finally managed to say. "He didn't kill Henry."

"They're not charging him with murder at the moment," my mother said. "But your whole dramatic gesture of coming clean about Henry's attempt with you has them thinking David had even more motive than they initially thought to get rid of Henry. They're now thinking it may have been a crime of passion to avenge your virtue."

Rage caught in my throat. "That's ridiculous!"

"Ridiculous or not, that's why you should have stayed quiet. Nothing good ever comes from stirring up trouble," my mother said, and I hated when she was right. "They also have CCTV that seems to prove he broke into Henry's car."

"Seriously? If they have him on CCTV, they have me as well. And you don't look even mildly surprised that I'm telling you this."

"They're only interested in him—at this point," she said.

"But Elena, stop doing silly things. There's only so much I can do to keep you out of this."

I wasn't sure whether to thank her for putting pressure on the LAPD so that they would leave me alone, get mad because she hadn't done the same for David, be grateful because at least she'd warned me about David being arrested and I could warn him . . .

"I'll do my best not to disappoint you," I said. When in doubt, I always opted for irreverence.

"Your efforts are always appreciated," she said. She wasn't being sarcastic. "And, Elena, perhaps you should talk to that reporter of yours."

"His name is David, as you know perfectly well since you forced me to have him over at your house several times when we were together."

"*Were* together? Are you not together now then?"

"Never mind," I said, rolling my eyes. "What should me and David talk about, according to you?"

"His job offer," my mother said.

I blinked, clearly not knowing what she was talking about.

One good thing about Aurora Valls: She didn't beat you when you were down—unless you were her political opponent—or when you were doubting whether your lover was hiding something from you. So she didn't say anything else about the subject. But my mother was now the second person at city hall to warn me about a job offer that had apparently been extended to David that I knew nothing about.

"Will that be all?" I changed subjects.

"You can be dismissed, but your dad asked me to remind you that you promised to join us for brunch on Sunday." I probably uttered my chagrin too vocally because she added,

"We're going to the Four Seasons."

That changed things. Brunch at the five-star hotel features a buffet stuffed with unlimited heirloom tomato salad, avocado toast, squash blossom pizza, and—my favorite—matcha-based margaritas. And I wasn't going to pick up the check.

"Yeah, I'll be there," I said. There was nothing I liked more than being drunk on antioxidant green powder and tequila on a sunny Sunday afternoon.

...

I called David straight from city hall, right outside my mother's office doors.

"I need you to get out of your apartment immediately," I told him when he picked up the phone. "Grab your computer, maybe a change of clothes, and get in the car."

"What are you talking about?" He didn't sound happy.

"The police are going to arrest you, and it's better if they don't find you right away. That gives us some more time."

"Some more time to solve the case?" he asked, still unconvinced.

"Exactly, and to get you that Pulitzer." I then realized that my plan, which had been concocted on the spot, had a very big flaw. "Oh shit!"

"What else is wrong?"

"If the cops get a warrant, they'll search your place and find—"

"Don't worry about that. That's been handled."

"Oh my god, you sounded exactly like Olivia Pope in *Scandal*. It gave me chills!"

He huffed out a laugh. "No clue what or who you're talking about."

"It's impossible to pay you a compliment with your pop culture illiteracy," I complained. "I compared you to someone *very* sexy."

"I see. I like that," he told me, and the way he said those words, I *knew* he liked being called sexy. "I should probably let you go as it looks like I'm on the run."

"We were flirting and not focusing on the case again, right?"

"Yeah, we were—we are."

"Okay, bye!" I said. "Wait! It's better if you take my car instead of yours. There's a spare key card at my place. It's inside the bowl at the entrance where I put all the random crap."

"I don't like your car," he protested.

"Liar. Also, I don't care," I said. "The police will probably be looking for yours. And David, can you pick me up at city hall? My mother didn't see it necessary to provide me with a ride back home."

28

"Let's see that CCTV footage," David said, taking a USB drive from his pocket and connecting it to his laptop.

We were both at my sister's place, a.k.a. my parents' pool house. She was going to be held up between classes and an internship at the Academy of Motion Picture Arts and Sciences. But she'd offered her place when I called her and told her I needed to lie low with David for a while. I was quick to accept.

"Did the Eastern Columbia's security people give you a copy of the CCTV from the night of the murder?" I asked him, impressed.

"Miguel did, yes," David answered.

I shouldn't have been surprised. "Of course, you're on a first name basis with them."

"Just with Miguel, the other one is relatively new," he said.

"And they still haven't warmed up to your charms, have they?" I teased him.

"My many charms are what got us this CCTV material," he said.

"Have you already watched it?" I asked as he opened the video file.

"Not really. I was going to do it at the security office, but then you called me and I went upstairs. I took the drive with me."

There was silence then as we both knew why I had called him urgently.

We started watching the video. It contained a wide shot of the entrance ramp to the parking at the Eastern Columbia. There was a date stamp watermarked on the video that read *02/19/2024*—the night of Henry's death. David fast-forwarded until around nine that night, and we simply watched. I recognized my car making its way into the building. Around ten minutes later, we saw the Mercedes-Benz we'd broken into that afternoon—Henry's car. Close behind it followed a silver Toyota Prius.

"Stop the frame!" I said to David. "Let's *CSI* the shit out of this."

"And how would we go about this? The only software I have on this computer is for grammar correction," he said.

"Seriously? This is the pop culture joke you actually get?" He smirked at me. "Can your grammar software enhance that image?"

"No, but I also have an image editing tool here somewhere," he conceded. "Since now I need to write but also most times they expect me to provide the pictures illustrating my articles."

David screenshotted the video image and zoomed in to the Prius. The driver was indistinguishable and the car's license number too pixelated, but there was a bumper sticker—it was green with a red star-shaped motive. I had perhaps seen something similar, but I couldn't recall where.

"See, it pays to be a multifaceted journalist," I told David after the sticker discovery.

"The only thing this proves is that *that* is not my Prius," David said. His own vehicle of the same model was white and had a Freedom of the Press sticker in black and white and a UCLA Alumni license plate frame. "But we still have no clue who the mystery Prius driver is."

David's phone rang then and my dad's name appeared on the screen. David picked up right away.

"Mateo," David said, his voice polite and strained. "I see, can you give me a few more hours?"

Whatever my dad told him didn't seem to make David too happy.

"Okay, let's do that. Thanks, chao," he said and hung up. "Your dad says the cops went searching for me and weren't happy when they didn't find me home. They have a warrant, so they may be making a complete mess of my apartment. And I just had it deep cleaned!"

"You're worried about the mess? What if the killer planted something else at your place?" I panicked. "You said you took care of the watch, right?"

"I did, and I'm also quite certain there's nothing else."

"Can I ask you how you handled it?" Curiosity was killing me.

"Does your Olivia Pope character always tell all her tricks?"

Aw, he remembered. "It's not my Olivia Pope, it's Shonda Rhimes's. And no, she doesn't."

"Let's keep the mystery here as well," he said. "I'm not sure what I did is completely legal, and I prefer to keep you out of it."

"But you trust me?" I needed to know.

"There's no one I trust more. You're also the last person I'd like to see dragged into this ugly legal business any further." I felt a thrilling pang in my stomach. "Your dad told me the cops tried locating me by finding my phone. I left it at home, so they didn't get very far. I'm using a burner," he said when I looked confused.

"Oh my god, you're like a professional law-avoiding citizen!" I quipped.

"Being an investigative reporter helped me know how to remain hidden and, of course," he leaned over, whispering in my ear, "having you as a lover also helps."

"You should thank my mother," I joked, but I savored his use of the word *lover*. I liked it so much better than girlfriend, girl, significant other, and the other qualifiers we've used in the past for one another that sounded so childish and ordinary now somehow.

"It looks like I'll have to thank both your parents," David said. "The cops reached out to your dad when they couldn't find me. He told them I was in the middle of an article assignment and momentarily incommunicado."

"Which is technically true," I said.

"He does have a way of describing almost-facts in a creative way," David admitted. "I should surrender in the next twenty-four hours or things will get ugly, though."

"Ugly?"

"Legally, I'll be a wanted man."

I was going to go the irreverent way and say that non-legally speaking he very much was a wanted man already, but then I realized the gravity of the situation and forced my hyperactive libido to sober up a little.

"I see. We have twenty-four hours," I said.

"By the way, where did you put the charm?"

"What charm? My charm is fully on," I said, as my libido could hardly be tamed even if I tried.

"I meant Henry's charm," David said, smiling. He was enjoying my confusion.

"He lacked any of it," I snapped.

"I meant the cat thingy we found in his car," David explained.

"Ah! That! You took it."

"No, *you* took it."

"No, I distinctly remember *you* taking it." He was so stubborn sometimes.

He stared at me in disbelief, and I returned the incredulous gaze. We let our eyes do the talking for a few minutes the way we'd learned to communicate without words those past few months.

We were saying things like, *There was never time for that quickie. What I really want to do right now is not be looking for something that you misplaced. Damn it, we're not even home!* and *I still haven't made you scream like you asked me, but I've been thinking about it non-stop.*

All the non-verbal sexy banter and unresolved heat was keying me up. I tried shrugging it off and put my hands in my pockets. And inside one of the back pockets of my jeans, I found a plasticky object that I didn't recognize to the touch.

"What the hell?" I took the unknown object from my pocket and, obviously, it was Henry's fucking cat charm. Apparently, I didn't so distinctly remember telling David I'd keep the charm after he offered to because I thought he'd probably lose it.

I know he was tired, preoccupied about his police troubles, fearful for the next accusatory article that would get published against him, hungry, and at least as horny as I was. But, for the first time that day, he looked perfectly satisfied.

He didn't say, *See, I told you*. His eyes were doing all the talking.

"Quit with the smug face. It doesn't suit you," I told him.

"Liar. You've told me my jaw gets sharper when I look smug, and I know for a fact that you find that very sexy," he said, his fucking jawline irresistibly accentuated.

Bastard. He knew me too fucking well.

"Okay, I had the cat. So what?"

"I don't think it's just a charm," he said, holding out his hand. "I realized this when I was at the security office with Miguel and wanted a copy of the CCTV footage. He opened a drawer full of USB drives. Some of them were colorful and in the shape of cartoon characters."

"You mean . . ." I gave the cat to David. I was a universally known clumsy person with butterfingers and the ability to break *anything*.

"I mean . . ." he said, pulling the cat into two pieces easily.

One of them showed a USB-C connection.

29

It was after ten at night. David had managed to cook us some vegan tacos, making use of the many ingredients inside my sister's fridge. I was surprised to see she even had anything more than the coffee beans and almond milk necessary for the morning coffee she took before heading to the main house for actual breakfast.

I texted her to inquire about it.

> Fridge is full of yummy things. Hope you don't mind we cooked some dinner.

> Also, where are you?

She replied right away.

MARTA

> Of course the fridge is full. I told the house staff to pack it with plenty of vegan options when you told me you'd be there.

I rolled my eyes. For me, the family money still came like a difficult thing to believe. For her, it was second nature. It had been a more significant part of her life, so it only made sense.

MARTA

> It's Friday night and, unlike you, I'm young.

> I'm out with some friends. Don't wait up

"Do you know if Marta is seeing someone?" I asked David.

"Seeing?" He looked up from his computer screen where he was still trying to figure out how to open the zip file inside Henry's drive.

"You know . . ." I gave him a look.

"I don't actually," he said. "Why are you using euphemisms? You never do."

"Because we're talking about my younger sister. Now, do you know if she's—"

"Dating someone?"

"So *seeing* is a euphemism but *dating* isn't?"

"Elena, you're so difficult. I have no clue if your sister is . . ." He floundered.

"You can't either, huh?"

"I guess she's always felt like a little sister," he said as if he'd just realized. "Wouldn't she have told you if she was *seeing* someone?"

"Not sure, she barely tells me anything anymore," I said. "I had always been the cool older sister, but I guess now I'm the not-so-cool-anymore *old* sister."

"Okay, this needs to stop." He closed his laptop. I must have looked at him with a face that said, *Shouldn't you try a bit harder?* because he added, "My hacker friend is going to email me back, I just sent her the zip file."

"Hacker friend? You keep surprising me," I said.

"What, isn't this the kind of thing the lead in one of your scripts would do?"

I scoffed. "Don't get cocky. The lead in this particular script is me."

"I see."

"What needs to stop though?" I asked, genuinely intrigued.

"Your insecure phase. You thinking that I cheated on you, that your sister no longer finds you cool. When did this nonsense start?"

I bit my lip. "Pretty sure it was the day Henry tried something with me, and I reacted in the worst possible way. I'm still not sure what would have happened if he hadn't touched my hair, and I sort of magically snapped out of it. I was paralyzed. And I kept like that for months."

"And I didn't even realize," he said softly, the resentment I hadn't shown him present in his voice. "Or I did see you were more reserved, inward, and subdued. I just thought it was stress."

"Let's not hold grudges about the past," I said. "I think these months have helped me regain some of my past foolish self-assuredness."

"I'm glad to hear that because foolish, self-assured Elena is my favorite one." He moved closer and tucked a strand of my hair behind my ear the way he used to do before we broke up and the irreconcilable differences started piling against us. I *knew* he was about to kiss me.

You may think I'm abusing certain dramatic effects like always interrupting my scenes with David when things get heated or are about to get there. Sadly, this is exactly how it all happened, and David's burner phone started buzzing then.

"Hacker friend," he told me, his eyes apologetic, then answered the call. "Emma, did you get something?"

I didn't know if it was because we finally talked, because he'd so much as told me he didn't care romantically for anyone else, or what, but I didn't feel the least bit of jealousy about that Emma hacker calling him, regardless of how cool she sounded. I was curious about how they'd met and how Emma had become a hacker, but I was returning to the unpreoccupied, never jealous, never envious, never insecure person I'd always been. And I was happy about that.

David hung up.

"How important would you say his career was for Dashing Henry?" David asked, and I could see him already thinking.

"The most important thing in his life," I answered, unequivocally.

"Why are you so sure?" David was in reporter mode.

"Because I knew him, and he was a narcissistic prick who only perked up whenever he was being accosted for an autograph or nominated for an award. And he was vile if he wasn't the one winning that award," I explained.

"So he wasn't big on the whole *just being nominated is an honor* thing," David said.

"He couldn't care less about honor."

"But there must have been something else in his life, no?"

"He had no family, no friends. He attended award ceremonies with his manager as his plus one," I said. "He had no hobbies. He wasn't into reading, fishing, puzzles, or freaking knitting. The only thing he liked watching on TV were reruns of his own shows."

"So *LA Misconducts* was his life?"

"Pretty much. He'd tried dabbling in movies but hadn't

been successful. He wasn't that great of an actor, to be honest. He was famously cranky whenever the show went on hiatus between seasons. He even hated the holiday break every winter."

"And he was going to get fired from *LA Misconducts*?" David was confirming a piece of information I had given him the day before.

"He had *already* been fired," I said. "You can talk to my agent. I'm sure she'll be thrilled to give you all the juicy details if you quote her as an anonymous source. She loves babbling. What did the hacker tell you?" I finally asked. I wanted to know what had prompted those questions.

"That Henry was the one who leaked his own doctored emails," David said. "Apparently the zip file on the pen drive contained a copy of them."

"Was he also behind the fake email address in your name?" I suddenly realized.

"Not only that," David said, "it looks like I won't have to worry about YouReallyDontKnowWhatsOutThere.com publishing anything else about me."

"I told you so," I said, rolling my eyes.

"No, the reason I won't have to worry about it is because Emma was able to trace the blog back to Henry. He was the one who published the post saying I had sent him a series of emails and asked him to go to the Eastern Columbia the night he died. He'd scheduled that post, and it was published even if he was already dead. If you think about it, the piece didn't mention anywhere that he'd been run over by a car, just that I had lured him to my place and something nefarious had happened to him there."

"Okay, so?" I knew David was making some kind of connection I was missing.

"So, I think he was a desperate man. His lawyer had told

him the libel accusations against me were moot and had left him. He wasn't going to be able to prove that I'd fabricated anything against him. He'd just been fired. His team, the only people in his life, were deserting him. He had nothing left."

"Not sure I'm following you." And I really wasn't. "You're saying he realized that his career was over."

"Hence, his life was over," David added.

"And since there was nothing else, he tried getting you accused of his murder, but it was him who took his own life?" I couldn't avoid the tone of doubt in those last words.

"Yeah, hearing you saying it out loud, I realize that it sounds a bit ridiculous," David admitted. "I mean, Henry was an egomaniac and career-obsessed enough, but to the point of suicide? Plus, he was probably aware that there's nothing Hollywood loves more than a good comeback story."

"As the Hollywood expert here, allow me to say there are comeback stories and *comeback stories*. When you throw sexual assault into the mix, like in his case, the options for redemption start getting thinner."

"He hadn't been convicted of anything," David tried reasoning.

"True," I said. Most of the complaints made against Henry had been for aggressive sexual advances and coercion like the ones he'd made with me or Brenda. But at least one of his victims had accused him of aggravated assault. That case had been settled for an undisclosed amount outside of court though, and the other party involved had doubtless signed an NDA. "We're not really contemplating the possibility of him being the one who ran himself over with a car though, right?"

"The whole thing sounds a bit preposterous. How do

you even run yourself over with a car?" David rubbed the back of his neck.

"Preposterous or not, he'd tried implicating you," I said. "The whole thing with him being at our building and being drunk on Fernet. I'm sure he made himself drink that stuff."

"It's good stuff," David insisted.

"In any case, the plot thickens."

"And it's definitely time for me to get an actual assignment."

30

David was talking to his editor on the phone and I realized—I guess I actually reiterated my realization—that metro editors and writers seem to work all hours of the day and night. Who answers their phone after 11 p.m. on a Friday? Not me. Hell, if it's a Friday I won't reply to any call or email received after 11 *a.m.*, in case said form of communication has anything to do with a work assignment and you're about to ruin my lazy weekend plans.

But I digress. While David was on the phone, I kept going over what he'd just said, and it started making a bit more sense.

We didn't have a lot of details about Henry's personal life. Maybe he was sick, maybe even terminally ill, and he'd decided to die in a dramatic way, taking David with him in the process. David was, after all, the man who'd precipitated the end of his kingdom in *LA Misconducts*. Maybe Henry had money problems of some kind: gaming debts, too many vacation-home loans to pay now that he was going to be without a steady job, a balloon mortgage to cover the cost of his private jet. Who knew what was going on with him?

What if he had finally had a revelation and realized his days as a two-time Emmy winner and star of *LA Misconducts* were over for good? He was now a has-been, a canceled actor who'd never be hired again—not even in a cough-suppressant syrup commercial. Not after Archie Eisenberg made sure all his peers in Hollywood knew what kind of a depraved sexual bully Henry was.

But even if he was struggling with his mental health, even if he was contemplating suicide, that still didn't explain how he died. The whole story was so convoluted. Did he write a series of accusatory emails against David, go to his place, drink a bunch of Fernet, and then pay someone else to run him over at our building?

That's it! I thought. It had to have been an accident. He'd probably paid someone to follow him and hit him with the car, just to break a leg or something and pretend it had been David, but in the end the ruse had been fatal.

"I think I know what happened to Henry," I told David as he wrapped up the call with his editor.

"You can tell me about it when we start drafting this. It may fit into the story," David said.

"Got the assignment, then?" I asked.

"Sure did!" He looked happy. He always did when he had a new journalistic assignment. It was only after he'd been working on a story for many *many* hours, had sent revisions to his editor at least twice, argued with said editor about a specific paragraph, and then argued some more about what the nut graph of the article really was, that he looked ready to quit.

"Wait, this is not for the *Voice*, right?" I asked. After those damning Gloria Fucking Kingsley articles, I didn't want to hear anything about them.

"This will run on the *Gazette*," David explained.

"The bastards at the *Voice* don't deserve you," I said, and I meant it.

"I'm also not sure they would want anything to do with me. I told the editor at the *Gazette* that I'd been working with you and would like to give you attribution in the article, and he saw no problem. With the *Voice*, it would have been a whole issue," he said. He seemed slightly flustered.

"They don't like two people working on a story together or what?" I asked. His profession was so bizarre. In mine, as a rule of thumb and unless you were Taylor Sheridan, the more writers the merrier.

"They don't like *you*, specifically," David said, and he was being a bit weird.

"Because I'm not that kind of writer and dabble in fiction more than fact?" I asked in the most oblivious way possible. Why did I have a bad feeling all of a sudden?

"Because of your link to city hall," he said, and it suddenly all clicked. Victor's warning about a job offer for David tentative on his ability to remain independent. My mother's own mention of said job offer. And my astounding capacity to ignore both of them until that very moment.

"I have a link to city hall that makes me partial, not neutral. Does it also taint you?" I asked him, bitterly.

"It doesn't taint me!" he protested.

"The *Voice* thinks it does," I said. "Was it them who offered you a job?"

"How do you know?" he asked.

"Because I for sure am fucking tainted," I said. Actually, if I'm being precise, I yelled it. My bad feeling had officially turned into anger against my fucking ex. Who, by the way, should have remained an ex, and nothing but that, but I had somehow managed to upgrade to an ex-with-many-benefits-and-relationship-prospects because I'm an idiot.

"Nothing escapes the network of spies at city hall, I guess," David said.

"I mean, you're making it sound as if my mother was the smart bald character in *Game of Thrones*, but basically yes, nothing escapes it." The fact that I could be joking about a TV show at the moment should give you a lot of information regarding the kind of person I am. I was still beside myself. "Did the *Voice* make you a job offer?"

He drew in a long breath. "They did, on Wednesday."

"Why didn't you tell me?" I needed to know the reasons behind his treacherous behavior.

"I specifically remember us not being on talking terms then," he said.

"And I specifically remember us starting to talk at some point the following day, which was also yesterday. You've had plenty of occasions since then," I said.

"I tried talking to you and then a murder happened!"

"No, no, no." I held up a finger. "Don't twist reality on me. A murder happened, and that trauma led us to talk again."

"Could you please stop breaking down our lives as if they were the scenes in one of your scripts?" He had the gall to tell me.

"And could you stop stalling? Why didn't you tell me that the newspaper of your dreams, the place you've been wanting to work at since you were a kid, was offering you a staff position? Not a contractor one but one with silly perks, health insurance, and a good salary."

"Decent salary," he corrected.

"But health insurance?" I needed to double-check.

"Health insurance," he confirmed.

"So why didn't you share the good news?" My bad feeling was starting to morph and causing me to go from anger to fear. He didn't share the news because he was going to leave me.

"Because it wasn't actually good news," he finally said. And when he did, I could almost see the relief on his face.

"You're going to have to keep talking because I'm not getting it," I said. I needed to hear him saying it.

"I was told in so many words that the only reason a position was now being offered to me was the fact that I had been *separated* from you for an extended period of time."

"Because I'm tainted," I said.

"Because of your link to city hall," he explained. "A metro reporter can't be entangled with city hall."

"That's ridiculous. Lots of journalists have conflicts of interest. That's what author pages are for. You disclose all the reasons why you shouldn't be objective and write about what you're writing about nonetheless. Didn't you tell them that?"

"I didn't because when the offer was extended to me, you and I weren't *technically* having a"—I could see him thinking and measuring each one of his words—"common relationship."

"Are you kidding me? We were fucking on a daily or bi-daily basis." I fumed. "It doesn't get more common than that."

"You weren't talking to me, and you were seeing someone else in an official capacity."

I could hear my heart beating so hard, I was sure it would burst from my chest.

"So what, you were going to break up with me? Are you breaking up with me?"

"Elena, I don't know what I was going to do," he said. "I couldn't break up with you because we were nothing. I couldn't even have a conversation about it with you. You'd made sure of that. But I also didn't want to give up whatever crumbs of a connection we had."

"But you thought about it," I said. "Oh my god! I've been so stupid. All this time, I thought you were as mad at the *Voice* as I was because they published that awful article. But it wasn't that. You couldn't care less about what they were saying about me, about you, even. You were mad because you realized they'd found out about us, and they would no longer want you in their ranks!"

"You're making it sound very calculating on my part. I'm not as obsessed with my career." I probably gave him the vilest of looks. "Don't get mad at me because I love my job. You do too!"

"But no one at my job tells me who I can and cannot fuck!"

"Elena, conflict of interest policies are common at all workplaces. You just don't have to observe one because you don't have a job," he said, and he only realized the blow he'd just dealt me after he saw my face.

The man I had adored, and who I somehow had allowed back in my life, also believed that I was nothing but a silly, jobless nepo baby. One who deluded herself into thinking she was a screenwriter even when everyone else knew that, at present, she was simply a professional procrastinator.

I recall him trying to apologize. I just didn't pay him any more attention. He even followed me around the place and probably tried dissuading me from leaving, but I grabbed my cell phone, got out, jumped in the car, and headed home.

31

I know I shouldn't have been behind the wheel considering I was angry and in shock—and that my abilities as a driver are already somewhat impaired on a good day because I get easily distracted. It's possible that I was also crying, but I would prefer not to acknowledge it. While my head was still going over the argument I just had with David, I decided not to take the freeway and to let the car do most of the steering.

Breaking up with two boyfriends on the same day had been mentally but also physically exhausting. Then again, that's what you get when you're a morally dubious woman, I guess. One who keeps two men on the side. I'm sure Marky Fitzsimmons would tell me that served me right for my impropriety and sluttery.

I realized then that David had lied to the police about being alone the night Henry died not because he wanted to spare me an uncomfortable conversation with Victor but to prevent his editors at the *Voice* from knowing about us. He was going to end the relationship, if you could call it that. That's why he left my place early on Wednesday night, why he was so adamant about talking to me on Thursday. And yet, he hadn't had the courage to say it: *I can't keep seeing you. I don't want to continue this. My job is more important.*

And all the while I'd been worried, I'd been doing everything to help him, using my family to help him, imagining he also wanted to talk things over and to be together *together*. I was so stupid. Naïve. Dense. Slow. Credulous. Witless.

I was still mentally listing synonyms of my imbecility when I jumped into the elevator at the Eastern Columbia. At least I'd stopped crying by then. Not that I'd actually been crying or anything. As a rule of thumb, the Freire Valls clan doesn't do crying, no matter the occasion.

"We finally meet."

A voice took me out of my inner misery. I hadn't even realized someone else had gotten inside the elevator before the doors closed. He was a bit taller than me and around my age, with tousled dark hair and an air that reminded me of Andrew Scott—a.k.a. Hot Priest of *Fleabag* fame. He was wearing medical scrubs and a smile.

"Finally?" I asked, confused. I had no clue who he was.

"I'm Andrew," he said, accentuating his smile. I decided to privately refer to him as Hot Neighbor. "Apartment 10D?"

"Oh! Ah!" I said. "I'm in 10B, Elena."

"Yes, I know," Andrew said. "I met your boyfriend the other day."

"Not my boyfriend," I protested but felt bad. Andrew seemed nice. It wasn't his fault that at present I hated all men, but especially my not-boyfriend David.

"I see," he said, and he looked a bit uncomfortable. "Have you talked to the police by any chance?"

"The police?" I asked, confused.

"Yes, about the murder in the building," he explained. "I

work nights, you see. Not today but most nights. And during the day I just take an Ambien, throw some earplugs and an eye mask on, and I'm zoned out. I think they've been trying to talk to me. They left a card, some Detective Clooney or something. I was wondering if they're making the rounds or I'm a suspect." He laughed nervously.

"I think they just want to clear my not-boyfriend's alibi," I explained. "He told them he saw you on Wednesday night when he left my place."

"When? This Wednesday?"

"Yes, the night of the murder in the building."

Andrew frowned. "But I never saw him on Wednesday!"

"You just told me you met him the other day," I said.

"I meant last week."

The doors to the elevator opened then as we'd reached the tenth floor. Andrew exited and tried a nod as a way of saying *goodbye* and *sorry I can't corroborate your not-boyfriend's alibi*. He headed into his apartment. I remained immobile in front of my own door for a few minutes before I was able to snap out of it and open the door.

Considering this story has only one POV—mine—you may be wondering whether everything I tell you is accurate or if I'm missing anything. Do you feel tempted to think David is guilty, seeing all the things lining up against him? Don't. You don't want to get distracted by the red herrings. But then again, could I be the one fooling myself about him?

32

Two Nights Before

The Shonda Rhimes talk at the TV Academy had been totally worth the drive to the Valley. The dinner with colleagues, not so much. Who suggests a sushi place when one of the members in your party is vegan? And my former colleague Greg needed to start doing something with that unruly haircut of his. But then again, so did I.

I'd just parked at home and had taken the elevator at the parking level of the Eastern Columbia. I was checking my overgrown hair in the mirror inside the elevator and thinking I should make an appointment with my hairdresser before my mother would accuse me of being unkempt *again* when the elevator stopped at ground level.

Aargh! I had no desire to make small talk with any neighbor at the moment.

When the doors of the elevator opened and I saw him waiting at the building's main vestibule, he didn't say a word, didn't even acknowledge me. But his eyes told me, *I'll take the stairs.*

The doors to the elevator closed again and I made my way to the tenth floor alone, thinking about him. Was he working out more? Had I seen him running more often? Had he gotten new clothes fit for rebels? He looked so damn sexy.

I got into my place, left the keys inside the crap bowl at the entrance, checked the time, and realized it was still early.

I smiled, dimmed the lights to a mood-affecting glow, set the sound system to play Mitski's "First Love/Late Spring," and started undressing slowly and playfully.

I opened the pleasure box, popped a cannabis-infused, chocolate-covered blueberry, and chose a toy.

I settled on the sofa and let my mind drift to thoughts of sexy half-undressed people and romps on the beach. I was on the edge of a much-needed release at the end of a long, testing day when I heard the front door open.

I guess I probably smiled again. Wider.

Am I interrupting something? his eyes said.

Please join, mine told him.

He took his T-shirt off first and even in the nonexistent light, I could see the lines of that tattoo of his that I was so surprised to discover six months before when our wordless, sex-filled game had started.

He's definitely putting in more hours at the yoga studio. Or did he ditch yoga for some CrossFit? But I didn't let those words reach my eyes. He didn't need to know I liked this toned version of him so much more or how much I was obsessing over him even when we weren't together.

I kept watching while he continued undressing. In the spirit of full disclosure, I wasn't only watching. My toy was still humming earnestly. And yes, there are few things more arousing than watching your lover stripping while you are getting yourself off.

You know George complained about us being loud that night? My neighbor is a gossipmonger, and I can't stand the sight of him—mainly because he always wants to talk to me. But he was telling the truth.

David approached from behind and I made room for his body. I kneeled on the sofa and, when his thighs surrounded my legs, I sat on his lap. His cock pressed against my ass.

He teased my neck with his teeth. The skin of his chest was lighting my back on fire. The heel of his left hand pushed against my breast and crushed my throbbing nipple.

He somehow managed to take control of the vibrator between my legs and pushed it hard against my clit. I shuddered in pleasure. He was so acquainted with all the gadgets in my collection, he knew exactly how to work that particular one for maximum efficiency. But I was close again and I didn't want to be the one doing all the screaming this time.

My arm left the contour of David's strong thigh for one moment and pointed to the one place in my living room where we both knew I kept condoms.

He chuckled, and I could feel his breathing in my whole body. But I wasn't being lazy like he seemed to imply. His arms were simply longer. His chest left my back for one fraction of a second while he reached for the pleasure box on top of the coffee table.

I missed his body dearly.

He was soon back. I heard the foil package opening. And when I felt him inside me, I sighed in relief. Everything felt right.

I'm not sure how long the loudness lasted. I just know I

wasn't the only one to scream. We were still on the sofa, gasping for breath and interrogating each other's eyes about what we could do to each other next when we were distracted by a screeching noise outside. It sounded like a car speeding on Broadway, leaving a trail of burnt tire rubber on the pavement.

The imitation midcentury digital clock on top of my media console flickered and I saw it was 10:21 p.m. I relished yet again at the idea of it being so early and bit his lower lip.

What I didn't realize at the time was how vital that time stamp would be. I had listened to the voicemail Dashing Henry had left his lawyer. The police had told me Henry's fatal hit-and-run happened right before that, at around 10:17 p.m. That car bolting at high speed on Broadway was the killer.

Even if he looked like one, David wasn't that killer. He was a liar and the worst possible kind of ex, one who wouldn't disappear, but not the person responsible for Henry's death.

I warned you about red herrings.

33

Saturday, February 24th

It was early Saturday morning, and I was the doomedest woman in Hollywood. I was convinced I was never going to be allowed to sleep past 7 a.m. again. That's what you get when you're a bad woman who keeps two boyfriends and breaks up with them on the same day. All those thoughts were clouding my mind as my cell phone kept insistently ringing.

"Hello?" I finally managed to answer. I'd checked two things before answering it even in my heavy somnolent state: time and identity caller.

It was 6:34 a.m. on a fucking Saturday, and Beatrice was responsible for interrupting my dreams.

"Good! You're up!" she said, way too much pep in her voice for that early in the morning.

"Not really," I assured her, still lying in bed and sounding like a heavy smoker. My voice was coarse.

"If you leave now, you'll manage to get there on time-ish," she said, and she clearly didn't realize I wasn't following—or going anywhere outside of the confines of my own bed.

"And where am I supposed to be going?" The sarcasm was unmistakable in my tone. Yet she succeeded in ignoring it.

"You've been invited to join Fred Appleton during his morning hike in Griffith Park." I didn't have time to protest. "Now, don't get agitated. I'm assured it's just a one-mile loop at an easy pace, so even exercise-shy people can endure it."

I guess the implication was that I was exercise-shy and completely out of shape, and that may be *somewhat margin-ally* true. But I still got offended. And I still wasn't completely following what Beatrice was telling me. I wasn't even fully awake.

"Elena, I know it's a bit early," Beatrice conceded.

"So you realize that calling me before 10 a.m. on a Saturday is *not* normal?" Had I not been so fucking asleep, I would have also wanted her to know that it was completely uncool of her.

"Fred is moving to New York, flying there tomorrow actually. And he'd love it if you could join him for a walking meeting. He promised to honor my deadline. You still have till 5 p.m. today to decide about joining *NYC Misconducts*, but he'd love to chat with you this morning," Beatrice explained, trying to maintain a reasonable tone.

"When?" I asked, resigned.

"His daily walk starts at 7 a.m.," my agent said. When she realized I was about to revolt, she added, "Even if you decide not to work on *NYC Misconducts*, he still knows plenty of people and is a good friend to have. You may not know who your next showrunner is going to be, but I'm sure Fred could introduce you to anyone in town."

Aargh!

...

Seven minutes after hanging up with Beatrice, I was picked up by a smiling Uber driver who looked much more aware of his surroundings than I was. There was no chance I'd be driving in the state I was in. I was still wearing yesterday's clothes—no, I hadn't undressed when I got home the night before and now it came in handy because I literally had no time for anything. I was still very much unshowered, unshampooed, and un-everything. I had brushed my teeth, but that was all the effort I'd put in. The truth is, I hadn't even put much effort into that. I may have fallen asleep on the bathroom sink while brushing.

Oh, and I was pissed. With the world. With my parents for having uprooted us so many years before. I was sure I'd be a model citizen if we'd stayed in Barcelona (or at least for sure a person who showered every day. People were big into grooming in Europe, no?). I was pissed with the city of Los Angeles for having good traffic only during early mornings on weekends when I was always invariably sleeping. Pissed with Beatrice for waking me up. With Fred for being a fucking pain in the ass who couldn't take *No, I don't want to work on your TV show* for an answer. But mainly and most ardently, I was pissed with David for being a conniving, insufferable liar who'd gotten me addicted to sensational sex and had turned out to be a suspicious and sloppy non-killer and a careerist of the worst kind.

I was still fuming when the Uber driver dropped me off at the meeting point Beatrice had so generously sent to my cell phone. It was an empty parking lot in the heart of Griffith Park with nothing in sight but a presiding fig tree at its center, a neighboring golf course, and the skyline of downtown Burbank and the San Gabriel mountains in the far hazy horizon. I don't think I can reiterate enough how much the place was the middle of fucking nowhere.

I thanked my driver and left the car reluctantly.

I checked the time on my cell phone: 7:01 a.m. Fred was late. Because who is early for a 7 a.m. meeting? Not a screenwriter if you've met one in your life. We're always fashionably late, unfashionably dressed, and carrying a cup of coffee. Which reminded me: Why hadn't I stopped for some coffee?

While I was waiting for Fred, I did what any other high-functioning millennial does if faced with the horror of having to kill some time: I immersed myself in my cell phone.

I was about to open Instagram to check some videos of cute kitties to soothe my temper and then I remembered I'd left my sister's place the previous night and never bothered telling her that I wasn't going to be there when she got home. So I texted her, knowing well that she was way smarter than me and always remembered to silence her cell phone before bed. I had been violently woken up. I didn't want to do the same to a dear relative.

Fought with David yesterday. Don't ask him to tell you about it. I want you to have my version FIRST

He's a master manipulator!!

Also, he's wanted for murder but don't worry. I wouldn't have left him with you if he was guilty. I ran all the events of Wednesday night in my mind again and there's no chance he killed Henry.

I can't go over them with you because it's a bit awkward

> Btw, I'm already awake because Fred Appleton wanted to meet me for a "walking meeting" 🙄

> I hate Hollywood

I guess I'd been really immersed in the one-way message conversation with my sister because I didn't see Fred arriving, parking, and getting out of his car.

"What a beautiful morning," he told me out of nowhere, and I almost dropped my cell phone from the fright.

"Morning," I grumbled in reply as I judged his iced Erewhon latte. Out of absolute spite and pure prejudice, I assumed it had to be packed with sweeteners and not strong enough. Also, who drinks cold coffee in February?

"I was so glad to hear you wanted to join me for a walk this morning," Fred said, and I think, for the first time in years, I genuinely wished my parents would have never moved to Los Angeles. For one, I know for a fact no one has any kind of work meetings on Saturdays in Barcelona, no matter the time let alone seven in the fucking morning. But also, there I would have been able to forgo the niceties and simply say what I wanted to say: *I never wanted to be here. You requested my attendance.*

We headed for the steep dusty trail, and I realized this wasn't going to be an easy walk. And I wasn't wearing the right shoes, clothes, or attitude.

As I tried catching up with Fred's power walk cadence, which was definitively no easy pace, I made up my mind. I had it with Hollywood. I had it with California. I had it with everyone. I was moving back to Barcelona where I'd be able to sleep in on weekends and actually bathe on the beach during summer. I was so immersed in my inner ideal future life in Barcelona, I didn't hear anything Fred was telling me.

"Elena, are you feeling okay?" he finally said.

"Uh, sure." I snapped out of my Barcelonian fantasy, which wasn't as much a desire as a sort of pretend daydream. "Just incredibly sleepy. I worked until late last night and my agent called me early this morning. I had no clue this meeting was happening."

Heh, Elena Freire Valls was finally fed up and had decided to abandon her polite California ways.

"Sorry about that," Fred said, uncomfortable.

"So, you wanted to talk?" I just wanted to get over that conversation and head straight to my bed.

"Wondering if you've heard about my next project . . ."

"*NYC Misconducts*, is it?" I tried to sound a bit more civil when I remembered Fred knew a bunch of people who could potentially become my next boss or my next producer.

"Exactly. It's going to be a complete departure. A fresh new concept. A new challenge full of opportunity and creativity." I promise you I did my best not to roll my eyes. But come on! He was talking about a fucking spin-off of a procedural show that had been molded around so many other pre-existing properties already. Could we at least stop pretending that what we were talking about was original!

"And I hear you want to be completely based in New York," I said because I literally couldn't think of anything else.

"It's integral for the inception and development of the show that its team be based in Gotham City," Fred said, and I think here I did let my eyes do all the rolling they wanted.

"I see."

"I hear you're not a big fan of the Big Apple," Fred said.

Fucking Beatrice. I was surrounded by blabbermouths and gossipmongers.

"On the contrary, I love New York," I said. And that was true. I loved going there every year. I attended a bunch of Broadway shows, went to more museums than I could remember, saw some friends, walked to the extreme of exhaustion. And then I returned home and put the mufflers, scarves, and mittens back at the bottom of the closet.

"So I've been misinformed then," Fred said, and I'm aware that I was making things a little bit unpleasant with so much confrontation. But I really couldn't give a damn. And I sort of liked the sensation.

"Are you attending the SAG Awards tonight?" I finally decided to change subjects.

"Yes. Amelia is nominated for the movie that me and Archie produced with her. Are you her plus one?"

"I think I'm supposed to be her plus one for the after party." I suddenly remembered. And I guessed that at some point between then and that evening, I really needed to squeeze in that shower. Maybe even do something with my mop of hair.

"Well, let's talk tonight then," Fred said. "Beatrice said you'll be more open to talk about your future then."

How do you answer such a bunch of coded words and indirect terms?

"Let's." That's how. I guess.

"And I hear you're working on something else at the moment?" He was doing all the heavy lifting, carrying the weight of the conversation. But my mind was fried. I was tired and dragging my feet, and I really just wanted to be sleeping. Also, his fucking question reminded me of David, and that only made things worse.

"Been working on my spec," I said, but what screen-writer wasn't doing that? "And dabbling as an investigative reporter."

"Really?" Fred sounded genuinely interested, and I couldn't avoid feeling pleased about it. I can't stress enough how much constant praise and reassurance writers need all the time. We're needy.

"Well, since Dashing died in my building, as I'm sure you've read about it"—I didn't leave him the option to comment on that—"I've been investigating on the side. See if there's a movie to be written about it."

"About how he died?" Fred asked.

"And who killed him," I said. Even if I wasn't anywhere near an answer for that, Fred was also a producer and I'd be needing one at some point. So I really needed to sell the hell out of the screenplay I hadn't written—or even outlined—yet. "I mean, the story has everything: a Hollywood backdrop, a whodunnit, a controversial famous figure, and the whole true crime angle, which now is golden."

"Do you know who killed him?" Fred asked and his interest was piqued for sure.

"Getting closer," I bluffed.

As we continued with the power walk for a few more minutes, I finally breathed in relief when I recognized the parking area where we'd first started our hike. The loop from hell—and one of the most inconvenient meetings in my career—was finally about to be over. One good thing about Americans: they know how to do a proper quick sendout.

I was debating whether to ask Fred to drop me off somewhere a bit more convenient to hitch a ride from there or simply try my luck asking for an Uber to pick me up in the middle of nowhere with the advantage of having to wait for my transportation alone.

There weren't that many cars parked at the structure that time of the morning. But one of them stood out even if it shouldn't have. It was a perfectly common silver Toyota Prius. I recognized the red and green sticker right away. And Fred was heading to that car.

"Did you drive?" he asked me.

"Oh, I just Ubered." My mind was on overdrive. *Fuck, fuck, fuck.* What was I supposed to do?

"Want me to drop you off somewhere?" he offered.

Somewhere even more remote where you can chop me up never to be found by my family again because I just bluffed?

"No, thank you. I think I'll walk." Believe me, I know. Worst excuse possible. It would have worked in New York, actually. But not in LA. It was probably a two-hour walk from where we were to the Southern limit of Griffith Park. And, from there, two and a half more hours on foot to my place, plus crossing a couple of freeways. So you get the incongruity.

"Elena, not so fast. Walking from here is madness! You're not even wearing proper gear!" Fred tried stopping me, and my heart leaped into my throat. I tried to pull away, but his fingers clamped around my arm.

34

David

Allow me to hijack the narration, as Elena has been doing all the recounting so far. If this was a suspense romance book that followed the norms of the genre, you should have heard from me much earlier. I told Elena we should have opted for a dual POV and indicated the name of the narrator at the beginning of each chapter. She preferred to tell the story from her own perspective.

But it's relevant that you know what was happening while she was holding a grudge against me and finding out Fred Appleton wasn't simply the most self-preoccupied and oblivious writer in the guild. And I'm talking about a profession of egomaniacs here.

Elena left her sister's place on Friday night, and I was gutted. To be completely honest, I'd been gutted since Wednesday when an offer I couldn't refuse was extended to me and I realized I'd have to do precisely that and decline.

The hold Elena had on me was too strong, and on Wednesday night I'd left her place before either of us wanted me to because I needed to keep my mind clear and think.

The conclusion I reached was pretty straightforward: I still loved her.

So on Thursday, I was determined to break the rules of our strange pact and tell her I needed her. I was tired of only getting to have a piece of her. I wasn't sure that was my most brilliant idea. She's never reacted well to ultimatums. But I needed to try. I owed it to myself. And to her too.

Then a fucking murder took place, our world got upended, we suddenly found ourselves not only talking but working together, spending practically every minute of the day with one another—and you know the rest.

So Elena understandably got mad at me when she found out about the job offer I hadn't told her about. And she thought I was going to leave her for a job. Also, the job decided to leave me for someone else. I heard Gloria Fucking Kingsley was offered the position I no longer wanted. We may have been friends and colleagues in the past, but Gloria was starting to rub me the wrong way.

Now that I've told you that I'm a nice guy—and Elena was a bit of a drama queen who overreacted on Friday night —let's get back to the action. Elena left and I ransacked her sister's place for alcohol. It turns out a twenty-something-year-old grad student with a generous family stipend keeps quite the well-stocked cellar.

I was on my third glass of a chilled bottle of Godello from Ribeira Sacra when Marta got home, and I told her everything that had happened. We've always been good friends, and I know she likes me and would love for Elena to give me another chance. So I wasn't above trying to plead to the younger sister so that she would make my case with the older one.

"We'll call her tomorrow," Marta reassured me. "I'll tell her I need to talk to her, and I promise to represent your case in the best way possible. But it's her choice if she wants to hate your guts, and you know she's a bit stubborn."

I laughed. "A bit?"

"Okay, she's very stubborn, but I think you've drunk too much." Marta took the glass from my hand. "Let's make the sofa bed. You need to sleep. Tomorrow, you need to write that article."

"Can it wait?" The last thing I wanted was to worry about a fucking work assignment.

"Considering you told me the police are set on arresting you, I don't think the article can wait. It may be your last chance to establish your innocence in a public way." She sounded like her father. But she resembled a younger version of Elena. It was all very weird and I assumed I was probably too drunk. So I went to sleep and set the alarm for 5:30 a.m. the following day.

...

On Saturday, I woke up refreshed and reenergized. I made some coffee, making sure I was quiet enough not to wake Marta up, and started working.

I went back to every piece of evidence we had gathered. From the interview with Fitzsimmons, to the several accounts Elena had shared with me from her gossipy agent, the emails, and the CCTV videos. I was watching those one last time, trying not to yawn—you couldn't describe it as riveting or dynamic—when I saw something we had missed before and panicked.

A cell phone started buzzing on the kitchen island where I had been working. It was Marta's. She'd left it there the night before. I didn't want to pry—I'm really not as nosey as Elena has made you believe—but I saw the one sending messages to Marta was Elena, and I couldn't avoid reading them.

"Fuck!" I yelled, realizing what was happening. I knocked on Marta's bedroom door. "Marta, wake up. We need to leave. Elena has gotten herself in trouble!"

35

Previously on *Things told from Elena's POV*, Fred was trying to get me inside his car and probably make me disappear.

"I *really* need the exercise," I said as I yanked my arm out of Fred's hand and kept walking away from him at a brisk pace that had me almost panting. "My cardio fitness is ridiculous for my age. I'm turning thirty-five in a couple of months." I kept babbling while putting distance between me and Fred. "And I have decided to start with the good intentions and resolutions early for a change."

Everyone who knew me even a little could tell those were a bunch of lies. Elena Freire Valls had never started something early in her life. But it got me thinking about my thirty-fifth birthday because I was starting to doubt I was going to see my mom's sour face that day. She's disappointed in everything I haven't achieved at my age and makes sure I'm aware of it every single year.

I became conscious of the fact that this year I wouldn't get the talk about my successless, childless, marriedless, awardless, and overall unsatisfactory state from my mother.

Not because I didn't deserve it, in her opinion, but because I wouldn't be alive. My anxiety grew as fear took hold.

Fred had switched techniques and no longer tried convincing me to get in the car with him. He'd jumped into his battered Toyota Prius and was now speeding in my direction. Even without my eternally neglected glasses on, I could see the rage and determination in his face.

This was my second day in a row being thrown in the path of danger, so this time I managed to ask myself the pertinent question a lot faster even if I was in a state of growing panic. It seemed I always asked myself *What would Tom Cruise do?* to reach the same conclusion: RUN. So, I did. If only I'd put even an infinitesimal amount of effort in my training of what Tom put in his, maybe I wouldn't be so slow.

I could hear the Prius getting closer and closer but didn't look behind me and kept running. I was heading for the trail again where the car would not be able to follow and run me over. I felt like Cary Grant in the most adrenaline-fueled scene of *North by Northwest*, only convinced that I wouldn't find a way to get my pursuer to crash against something and take himself out of my way like Grant does in the Hitchcock flick. And then I heard the loud clash, realized I was in one piece and not hurt at all, and I finally allowed myself to turn.

I recognized my sister's car right away. She has a pastel-blue custom-painted electric SUV. I can't stress enough how unmissable it is. It had bumped into Fred's Toyota on the passenger side. I started running to my sister to make sure she was okay when I heard police sirens in the not-so-far distance.

"Elena!" I heard yells coming from my sister's car. "Are you okay?"

"Of course I'm okay, are you okay?" I helped her open the door and get out of the car. She gave me a big hug and nodded. She was garbed in bright-pink Disney-princess pajamas and Koala-shaped slippers.

"How did you know?" I managed to say, still confused and enveloped in a sea of sweetness.

"David," my sister answered, and I think both of us were a bit shocked. But she was pointing to the passenger side of her car.

I didn't let go of my sister, grabbing her hand and running to the other side of her car. I've been told I was yelling David's name by then, but given my tendency to remain cool as a cucumber in all situations, I think that's highly improbable and a total fabrication.

David, thank goodness, was completely unscathed and was just now getting out of the car. He'd been trying to recover from an acute case of car sickness. Marta's aggressive driving can make even the most immune-to-car-sickness passengers feel queasy. And I could only imagine that must have been a bumpy ride.

"Are you both okay?" he asked me and my sister. His golden skin looked grayish, and he was unbalanced, keeping a hand on the car door. I tackled him in a hug and buried my face in his chest, inhaling his smell shamelessly.

"¿Habéis hecho las paces, entonces?" My sister wanted to know if we had reconciled, and that brought me back to reality. I was still holding one of her hands and pretty much the whole of David's body.

"Have we?" David asked me, tentatively.

"I cannot be mad right now, but we still need to have a long chat," I said, looking at him.

By then, the police had made it to the crash area and some uniformed officers approached us. I recognized Detectives Clooney and Moreno between the agents. They didn't care as much for us and went straight to the Toyota Prius.

"Shoot! What happened to Fred?" I asked.

"I'm sure he's okay," my sister said. "I didn't even hit him so hard!"

"But he didn't flee, right?" I asked. We'd been so distracted making sure we were unhurt, we hadn't paid any attention to Fred. I now realized the driver's door on his car was open. "Detective Clooney, that's the guy who killed Dashing Henry!" I yelled, pointing to Fred in sudden anguish. He was running toward the trail and making good progress.

"Rooney," both my sister and David whispered.

"Oh, I don't care!" And I really didn't.

Detective Moreno ran after Fred with a cadence and graceful style that made me realize she probably was more of a runner than I had ever suspected. A few of the uniformed officers followed her closely. Detective Clooney seemed to think about it and decided there were already too many people getting sweaty. He came toward us instead.

"You again, I see," he said, referring to me and David. "And this would be . . . ?" he addressed my sister.

"Marta Freire Valls," she said, and she sounded like a total boss. "I'll be representing Ms. Elena Freire Valls and Mr. David Ramos until their other attorney gets here. He's on his way." She was typing on her oversized phone and not missing anything.

"I see. You really like your lawyers in the family, huh?" Clooney asked.

"We do," I said, and I would have smiled but I was too worried about something else. "Fred is escaping!"

"Don't worry. Detective Moreno is into trail running and that sort of thing. No one outruns her," Clooney said, but I wasn't convinced. "We'll be able to wrap this up and arrest him shortly."

"You got my message, then," David told Clooney.

"We did. We'll still need to talk to you, but you're suddenly looking a bit less suspicious. Now, can you tell me what happened here?"

Marta signaled to David and me to shut up, and we acquiesced.

"A bit after 7 a.m., Mr. Ramos, while pursuing his professional investigation of Mr. Dashing Henry's murder, found a piece of evidence that linked Fred Appleton to the scene of Henry's death," Marta explained.

"What evidence?" Clooney asked. He was taking notes.

"You saw the sticker, right?" I intervened, asking David. That's how I'd figured out Fred's involvement.

"What sticker?" David's brows drew together.

"The Procedural Writers Association of America sticker that Fred has on his car. The first time I saw the Prius on CCTV, I thought the sticker was a red star over a green background, then I realized it's the ugly-ass logo of the association. It's not a star but a quill and inkwell," I explained.

"As usual, you lost me," David said. My sister and Clooney seemed to be following our conversation as if it was the most engrossing tennis match.

"This isn't even a pop culture reference. The only reason I know the fucking logo is because I'm a member of the Procedural Writers Association," I added.

"I know you're a member, but no. I hadn't realized about the sticker or logo or whatever," David said. He was starting to get his natural glow back but still looked a bit ashen.

"Then how did you figure it out?"

"With the CCTV from the parking area, but the one from the camera you noticed at the garage." David didn't mention that we were breaking into Henry's car when I saw that particular camera. "We hadn't fully watched all the footage the first time, but I did it this morning and recognized Fred Appleton at the parking area of the Eastern Columbia."

"You recognized him?" I asked, confused. He wouldn't be able to tell Ryan Gosling from Ryan Reynolds, or Chris Pine from any of the other Hollywood Chrises. Hell, David wouldn't even know how many Hollywood Chrises there were or that they were a thing. And he recognized a showrunner?

"He was your boss," he said. And that explained it. It also told me that even if I had been convinced he didn't pay any attention to anything Hollywood related, he did when it came to my career. Because he cared.

"What I don't understand," my sister started telling Detective Clooney while David and I were still having a moment, "is how my client was able to find a crucial piece of evidence for this investigation that puts Fred Appleton at the scene of the crime while you couldn't and actually, in fact, were about to arrest Mr. Ramos."

"We never saw that particular CCTV footage, the one where you see Fred Appleton. We'd seen the ugly-ass sticker and were wondering what it was. In fact, we'll need your client to surrender the CCTV with Appleton in it," Clooney said, defensive. "How the hell did you get it?" he asked David.

"From the security guys at my building," David explained. "They told me the police had also been there and they'd also requested the videos."

"We did," Clooney said. "We watched everything. There's no Fred Appleton anywhere."

"Even in the video from the camera pointing toward the elevator?" David asked.

"I don't think we got that video," Clooney admitted. "And we were told we'd been given *everything*."

"I think the guys told me they'd just installed that camera a few days ago. They must have forgotten about it," David said.

David had probably gone out of his way to be extra nice to the security team working at the Eastern Columbia. And the fact that I had seen that camera and he was able to ask specifically about it had gotten us more CCTV material than the cops.

"My client will share the extra CCTV material with you," my sister said.

"Will he now?" Clooney said. "Will he also share how one of my partner's informants brought us Henry's stolen Patek Philippe today?"

Both me and my sister looked at David with extra curiosity.

"I would advise my client not to make any statement about that particular subject until his whole legal team is able to confer with him," Marta finally said.

"I see." Clooney chuckled. "Have your client and the *whole* legal team drop by the station in an hour, will you? For now, care to finish telling me what happened here?" Clooney pointed to the car crash.

I cleared my throat. "I was summoned to a 7 a.m. walking meeting with Fred Appleton. He angered the hell out of me, and I had a sort of epiphany to start saying *no* and speaking my mind more often, not that's relevant to you or anything. I also deceived Fred into believing that I was close to uncovering Henry's killer. When we said goodbye, he tried running me over with his car. My sister appeared out of nowhere and stopped him," I summarized. "How did you find me?" I asked David and Marta.

"We read the messages you wrote to Marta and then stalked your location," David explained.

"Stalked my location?" I asked, confused.

"Remember how I set a system with the Find My thingy on iPhone for the whole family to see where the others were?" Marta said matter-of-factly.

"You mean all this time, Mamá has been able to follow my every move?" I asked in panic.

"Seriously, Elena. We save your life, and all you can think about is Mamá finding your whereabouts." Marta shook her head.

Clooney seemed to agree with my sister. He was chuckling when he decided it would be better if I joined David at the police station for further questioning.

...

After dealing with the car insurance and the tow truck that would take care of Marta's car and dropping by my parents' house for a quick pit stop so my sister could change out of her pajamas and into a three-piece pinstripe suit, we were all aboard my dad's vehicle en route to the police station.

David and I were in the rear seats while my dad and Marta were going over the legal strategy in the front of the car.

"There's something I still don't understand," I told David in an almost whisper as I hoped my family/legal team wouldn't hear us. "I met the Hot Neighbor."

David gave me a blank stare.

"Andrew," I explained.

"Who's Andrew?" David asked, still not seeming to understand.

"Our neighbor from 10D. Didn't you see him the night of the murder?"

David shrugged. "We never talked. No idea he was called Andrew."

"Then how come he said he'd met my boyfriend?" I prodded. I knew David wasn't responsible for Henry's death, but I needed to know what had happened there. Had he knowingly lied to the police in an attempt to have more of an alibi, or was he simply confused about his recollections?

"Technically," David said with a smoldering face, "I'm not your boyfriend. Victor is."

Oh my god. Of course! Andrew had met Victor. He'd come to my place the previous week to drop off some hideous clothes my mother wanted me to try on. I'd dismissed them only by looking at them but had kept them somewhere anyway. And Victor had probably met the Hot Neighbor on his way out. I had just assumed that, since David was the most agreeable and sociable person—always willing to meet new neighbors—and Victor was eternally buried in his cell phone, it was David who had chatted Andrew up, not the other way around. But David hadn't said a word to the Hot Neighbor when he saw him the night of the murder, and Andrew had probably already forgotten about him, while Victor seemed to have chatted the Hot Neighbor up and made an impression. Also, David was right. Technically, Victor had been my boyfriend. But by then I knew why I had decided to understand something else entirely.

"He's no longer my boyfriend," I said. "Technically or otherwise."

...

We were once again seated in the interrogation room in urgent need of a paint job and some redecorating. Only now it was four of us on one side of the table, as my sister was helping my dad in our representation, and only Clooney sat in front of us.

"Is Detective Moreno still chasing Fred?" I asked. After my former boss had tried running me over, I wanted him behind bars *pronto*.

"I heard an arrest is imminent. The sucker has managed to outrun us as apparently he knows the geography of Griffith Park pretty well," Clooney offered.

I decided that, for once, I should trust the professionals even if I still felt uneasy about the whole situation and Fred being at large.

"You'll be glad to know we found marks and scratches on Fred Appleton's car consistent with the hits on Dashing Henry's body," the cop started.

"So you're prepared to charge him with the murder of Henry and drop our clients from this investigation," Marta said. She was looking quite smart in black-rimmed glasses, and it appeared my dad would assist her and not the other way around.

"There's still the matter of the watch," Clooney said.

"What about it?" Marta asked.

"We'd like to know how it came into our possession. As I mentioned before, an informant delivered it to us this morning, but we believe the informant may also be one of Mr. Ramos's sources. We think it was him who gave it to the informant and would love to know how that happened."

"I think you better stop speculating and start investigating," Marta concluded.

"I see," Clooney said. "Both your clients should be more cooperative. We still have video evidence of them breaking into Henry's car."

"It is our understanding that the video shows two individuals garbed in white jumpsuits, wearing face masks and hoodies. How are you able to identify my clients?"

Clooney clasped his hands on the table. "The individuals in the video match their height and build."

"That hardly narrows it down," Marta said. "Both my clients are quite common in that regard."

Ouch! Even if being a common height and build was perfectly okay and convenient at the moment, I still almost got offended.

"Let me just tell your very *common* clients," Clooney said, and I didn't appreciate the tone, "that if they decide to share whatever they could have found inside Henry's car, *if* they were indeed the ones breaking into it, we wouldn't be pressing any charges. But they only have twenty-four hours to come to their senses about it."

36

David asked our lawyers to drop us at the *LA Gazette* newsroom, which was not far from the Downtown police station. I was going to say he should stop there to talk to his editor or finish his article or whatever he wanted to do, but I needed to get home. But he pleaded with me with his eyes, and I wasn't able to deny him even if—and I apologize if I'm getting tedious in my basicness—I hadn't showered in two days, I probably had slept a total of eight hours in as many days, and I was still craving a thorough fuck.

But ten minutes after leaving the LAPD police station and having been reassured for the umpteenth time that Fred Appleton would be in custody at any moment, I was by David's side at the newsroom of his former newspaper. John Diaz, his editor at the *Gazette*, was flanking him on the other side. We were all going through David's copy. I negotiated my way into an article bylined by both me and David after writing a few paragraphs. And John demonstrated an iron hand as an editor. He deleted, rearranged, and asked us the right questions. David had always talked about him in stellar terms, saying that good editors are difficult to come by because they needed to be selfless and make someone else's writing better. I understood what he meant then.

The trepidation was such that I told David it should be him, and not me, who hit the publish button when the article seemed ready. Or as ready as it would ever be. Then I realized John would do it.

In the end, I warmed up a bit to David's former boss and present editor, especially when I saw them working together and after John offered David his old job back as a freelance contributor at the *Gazette*. David politely thanked him and told him he'd think about it, but I intuited what the answer was going to be. The whole professional scene reminded me that my own career was on the line as I still owed my agent an answer of some sort before that evening. But I gathered, or more precisely I hoped, that the whole kerfuffle with Fred Appleton trying to kill me and still being on the run may buy me some sympathy—and time. After all, there could hardly be a *NYC Misconducts* show with the showrunner being accused of murder, no?

Ten minutes after David and I had left the newsroom of the *Gazette* and a couple of hours after getting there, our article was published on their website.

LA Misconducts Showrunner Fred Appleton Will Be Charged in the Death of Actor Dashing Henry

The LAPD is about to make an imminent arrest of the television writer and producer. Fred Appleton's Toyota Prius was revealed to be the car that killed Dashing Henry. Appleton tried running over screenwriter Elena Freire Valls early this morning.

By Elena Freire Valls and David Ramos

Don't believe everything you read in other, less reputable publications. None of the writers involved in the reporting of this story are responsible for the killing of Dashing Henry. And the *LA Misconducts* star, while dead, will remain an uncovered sexual predator who made unwanted advances toward several of his colleagues and subordinates.

On the evening of Wednesday, February 21, *LA Misconducts* showrunner and producer Fred Appleton followed actor Dashing Henry to the Eastern Columbia, the downtown building where the reporter David Ramos resides. Celebrity superfan Marky Fitzsimmons, also known by the moniker LA Troubelmakr, witnessed a car matching Appleton's silver Toyota Prius tailing Henry's car into the building's parking entrance.

Fitzsimmons had been engaged by Henry to follow Ramos and warn the actor about the journalist's whereabouts. Henry visited the Eastern Columbia with the intention of confronting Ramos regarding the articles the reporter had written about him that had unveiled him as a predator. The actor sued the journalist for libel and the trial was set to start next week but, according to legal experts, the trial would have in most probability been dismissed. Henry had been recently fired from *LA Misconducts* for his behavior. As a result of that firing, the show was canceled and Appleton was preparing a spin-off set in New York.

Dashing Henry's Involvement in the Weird Circumstances Around His Death

Henry had been resentful against Ramos reporting and had leaked a series of fake emails pretending the journalist summoned him at the Eastern Columbia the night of his death. Henry's intention was to get the journalist to look suspicious ahead of the trial. Proof about said emails being fake and written by Henry was found inside of the actor's car in a USB-C pen drive that has already been surrendered to the LAPD. Henry's car, a bronze-painted Mercedes-Benz AMG G63, was registered under Henry's assumed name and left at the parking garage of the Eastern Columbia for a few days before being searched by the police.

In the CCTV material obtained while reporting this article, Henry can be seen outside his car in the parking area of the Eastern Columbia. Appleton lambastes him from inside his silver Toyota Prius. Evidence indicates Appleton would run over Henry, kill him, grab his $80,000 Patek Philippe watch to make it look like a possible robbery, and flee the scene with his car. The motives behind Appleton's actions were not clear at the time of publication.

After reading several articles that implicated Ramos in the killing of Henry that had been published without reasonable proof, Appleton took advantage of the confusion and decided to further incriminate the journalist. On Friday, February 23rd, and while Ramos was at the Downtown LAPD police station making a statement, Appleton broke into his apartment at the Eastern Columbia and planted Henry's Patek Philippe.

Ramos was able to obtain CCTV material of the building from that Friday where Appleton can be seen taking the elevator and exiting the Eastern Columbia fifteen minutes later. Both the watch and the CCTV material have already been surrendered to the police with all other pertinent evidence.

Appleton's Attempt on One of His Former Employees

On the morning of Saturday, February 24th, Appleton demanded the presence of screenwriter Elena Freire Valls for a "walking meeting" in Griffith Park. Freire Valls had been a writer on two seasons of *LA Misconducts*. Appleton had offered her a writing position on the staff of his new spin-off TV show, *NYC Misconducts*.

When the walking meeting was over and after Freire Valls shared with Appleton that she'd been investigating the death of Henry, the showrunner tried running her over with the same Toyota Prius involved in Henry's death.

Appleton remains at large and was last seen running from the LAPD at Griffith Park shortly after making an attempt on Freire Valls's life.

After leaving the newspaper, we realized we had been running on fumes and empty stomachs, so we stopped by Cabra for sustenance in the form of Peruvian tapas.

"I can't believe you brought me to another rooftop restaurant in a swanky Downtown hotel," David said while we were seated at a tall round green-tiled table with views over Broadway street and its many Art Deco buildings.

"Oh, shush!" I dismissed him and I was immediately reminded why I loved the downtown area of Los Angeles so much. It was inconvenient, at times packed, chaotic, and sometimes even grimy, but no one could dispute its cinematic qualities.

"Try and enjoy the beauty," I ordered David.

"How do you even find out about these places?" he asked. "It's not like you can walk around and discover a bar on top of a building."

"I subscribe to at least three local publications, and they all have a great food section," I explained as we were served veggie empanadas, avocado dip, and a mango pineapple berry salad.

"Thanks for keeping my business afloat," he said as I doused a taro chip with avocado and devoured it while making a very audible sound. "Hungry?" David joked, and I was glad he didn't inquire whether any of those publications were the *Voice* or the *Gazette*. The truth was, I subscribed to both of them but had been actively avoiding any section where I could encounter his writing.

"More like famished," I said, my mouth still full of food. "This whole investigating stuff is too stressful. There's no time for anything! I don't know how you can do it."

"Well, it's not always this . . ." David said, and I knew he was looking for the right term to describe it.

"Fucking crazy?"

"I couldn't have put it better myself," he conceded. "Plus, I'm normally not a suspect and wanted by the police. That also helps keep things a bit more manageable."

"Don't forget the part about the man-child following you around and then chasing us down, please." I attacked the tomatoes from another dish that had just been served and avoided the chorizo in it.

"Technically, he wasn't chasing us around," David said with a smile. "He was just looking for answers about his beloved icon."

"He still scared me to death," I said. "But since we seem to be done with the frightening episodes. Do you want to talk?"

"Aren't we talking?" David asked, playfully.

"You know what I mean," I said, even if I knew he wouldn't take that for an answer.

"I don't actually," David said as I rolled my eyes. I knew him so fucking well.

"Us, Scribe. Let's talk about us."

"Are you still mad at me for not finding the time to tell you I had been offered a job I wasn't going to take?"

"I'm not mad," I admitted then ate a mouthful of berries —only realizing what he'd just said after and being forced to speak again with my mouth still full of food. If only my mother could see me, she'd be so disappointed in my lack of table manners. "What do you mean you weren't going to take the job?"

"I don't think that's relevant now. I heard Gloria Kingsley was offered the position," he said.

"Gloria Fucking Kingsley."

"Gloria Fucking Kingsley," he repeated. "But since I'm still pretty much crazy about you, I don't think I could have taken a job where one of the conditions was to stay away from you."

I dropped a forkful of some veggie or other headed for my mouth. The food landed on my jeans, the table, and the restaurant's floor. I grabbed a napkin and cleaned myself as well as I could. I suddenly had the urge to make myself a bit more presentable—and attractive, if possible. I took my hands to my eyebrows, combing them to make them look brushy. And I raked my fingers through my knotted, messy hair. Where was a mirror when one needed one?

"I'm happy to hear you're still crazy about me," I said, and I tried keeping my voice calm and sexy but I could hear my heart racing. "Because I too have a massive crush on you."

"Do you think we could give *us* a second chance given the reciprocating feelings?" You may be thinking: Nobody talks like this. Well, he does. And it's definitely part of the turn-on for me.

"And disregarding the long list of grievances and irreconcilable differences?"

"I didn't even know there was a long list," he said.

"I can fill you in, if you really want, but I think I liked your last proposal a lot. It could work for us."

"Remind me again?"

"No more fights but, especially and please, no more misunderstandings," I said. "We need better communication from now on. It shouldn't be so hard as we both specialize in communication, no?"

"No more secrets?" he asked.

"No more secrets," I said, and there was an understanding between the two of us.

"So absolutely no misunderstandings but fights are okay-ish?" he said, jokingly.

"Not ideal, but from time to time and if they aren't so massive that we can't ever recover from them. They can help keep things interesting, no?" Not for nothing, our last big fight—our breakup—seemed to be bringing us closer together now. And it had been just what our sex life needed.

And that's when we decided we wouldn't be having dessert after all. We finished the rest of the food in record time, asked for the check, and headed home.

We entered one of the elevators at the Eastern Columbia five minutes after leaving the restaurant. David pressed the button for the tenth floor but not the second.

"I should probably let you know that I haven't showered in . . . two, no, three days now," I told him as my newly nourished body seemed to have only one desire at present. And it wasn't getting that much-needed shower.

"You smell quite delicious to me," he said, while he got closer and started smelling my neck and collarbone. Then he licked me behind an earlobe, and I almost melted. "You taste quite delectable too."

The elevator thankfully made it to the tenth floor and the doors opened. By then, I was drenched in lust and not caring about anything else.

"Are you coming inside?" We stood in front of my front door, and I was somehow in early stages relationship mode. This communication thing was so rousing but so strange somehow.

"The police made a complete mess at my place when they were looking for me. So I'm not looking forward to going there. And there's not a chance I'm going to let you out of my sight right now." He leaned closer and kissed me. My back was against the wall, his body on mine. The feeling of being in the open, on the landing where a neighbor—probably George from 10B—could see us made the whole situation sexier.

I guess I should have realized then that something was amiss—since my front door was unlocked. But I was tired and had only one thing in mind: getting David undressed as soon as possible, and me with him. Also, I'd left the place in a rush that morning. I wouldn't put it past me to have left it unlocked. And perhaps I did.

We got inside the apartment in a long, extended kiss that looked almost like that sequence in *Notorious*, where the camera gets up close to Cary Grant's and Ingrid Bergman's faces and follows them while they're making out.

"Please stop with this premium-cable quality sex scene choreography," a voice said, and it sounded like someone I knew . . . but it couldn't be. "You know physical intimacy makes me cringe."

Fred Appleton stood in my living room, pointing a crooked smile toward David and me. No, there was no gun in sight. Yes, the fact that a semi-perfect non-stranger had sneaked inside my apartment was still terrifying. You may say I'm a selfish brat and shouldn't wish any harm on David. And I really don't. But I was so happy not to have come home alone for once.

"You couldn't just let it be, right?" Fred continued. "You couldn't just leave Dashing's death alone, take the great job that was being offered to you, and be grateful?"

"Fred, what the fuck are you doing at my place?" The shock must have gotten a hold of my system because I wouldn't shut up. "I don't remember inviting you. I don't have a habit of having guests over who've tried killing me. Also, for the record, it wasn't a great job. It was *a* job, I'll give you that, but I wouldn't have taken it even if it was set in Los Angeles, which it wasn't, so—"

"Elena," David, of course, tried navigating the situation in a more diplomatic way. "Perhaps don't antagonize the uninvited killer, who we know is dangerous. What do you want, Fred?"

"That was my fucking line!" I snapped at David. "Can you please stop always taking control of the situation?"

"Seriously?" David asked me, frowning. "Are we fighting *now*?"

"We wouldn't be fighting if you weren't so annoyingly diligent, organized, and rational," I said, and believe me, I know I sounded deranged. But I think by now it's been amply established: I don't react well in threatening or stressful settings.

David scoffed, confused by my attitude. "Being diligent, organized, and rational is a bad thing now?"

"Can you two stop bickering and pay attention!" Fred yelled. He was visibly exasperated, and I didn't blame him. David can have that effect on people.

"What do you want, Fred?" You have to admit, it was my rightful line to deliver. Also, I sounded bored, which made Fred twitch with annoyance. That alone made it the most worthwhile.

"I'm here to make a statement for that article the two of you have written," he said. I didn't see that one coming.

"A statement?" David double-checked and, I kid you not,

he started looking around for a notebook and pen. He could have found them expediently as I keep writing utensils scattered all over the house, but instead he took his cell phone and pointed it to Fred. "Care if I take notes?"

"Go ahead. I want to know what's all this BS you've written in your article where it says: 'The motives behind Appleton's actions were not clear at the time of publication.'"

"Apologies for that, we should have probably tried contacting you and asking for a comment," David said. "We just didn't think you would as you were being chased down by the police. Care to make a comment now? We can add it to the article."

"Oh my god! You're so annoying! Don't reason with the psycho!" I told David.

"Elena, don't antagonize the psycho," David said, patiently.

"I'm not a psycho!" Fred protested.

"I'm sorry for the inappropriate use of language," David said, and I rolled my eyes harder than I'd done in years. Probably in my entire life. And I'm an avid eye-roll practitioner. "You were saying you wanted to make a comment?"

I was going to protest again at David's incapability of leaving his work alone even in the most extreme of circumstances, but he grabbed my hand with his free one and squeezed it. I understood right away: *I'm just trying to make some time. Please stop antagonizing the psycho. I'm scared too, but we'll get through this. Together.*

I shut up even if I would have gladly continued telling Fred a thing or two he probably didn't want to hear.

"I'm a perfectly functioning individual and an extraordinarily talented writer," started Fred, and David squeezed my hand again because he intuited I was about to lose it.

During my tenure at *LA Misconducts*, I'd been quite open with David about what I thought of Fred's writing skills: They were nonexistent. The only thing the man was good for was taking credit from junior writers and copying the works of previous screenwriters. "Do you really want to know whose fault it is that I ran over Henry? Yours," Fred said, referring to me.

"I don't follow." And I really didn't.

"I was only in the damn building to tamper with your water heater," Fred explained.

"It was you!"

"I knew you'd say no to the job offer because you're a spoiled brat who doesn't like to work away from daddy and mommy. I needed you to feel slightly uncomfortable to realize life is hard and you can't always bank on your rich and influential parents for everything. You needed to grow up and get a real job. Nothing reminds us of that more than when everything we take for granted starts falling apart. I was going to meddle with your Wi-Fi next."

"What kind of depraved maniac does that?"

David softly squeezed my hand again. He really wanted me to shut up. But how could I?

"Excuse the language, again. So you happened to come to the building for *other* reasons and then realized Dashing Henry was also here?" David asked.

"He was on a path of destruction. I pleaded with him to make a bow and withdraw his accusation against you," Fred said, referring this time to David, and almost implying my journalist lover was to blame. "To stop meddling around, go quietly, and let me develop the new show. He didn't listen."

"So you ran him over?" I asked, still confused—and sore about my heater.

"I wasn't planning on it, but he came here looking for

trouble. He was drunk on Fernet and wanted to confront David. He was hoping David would try to get rid of him in a violent fashion, maybe even punch him. He wanted to sue him for assault."

"Assault?" asked David. "I haven't punched anyone in my life. Not sure I even know how to do it!"

"He was set on getting you hooked for something. That's why he drank all that awful stuff. At the latest, he wanted to get you for making him drink against his will."

"How do you know all this, Fred?" I asked.

"Because he told me all about it when I found him here and confronted him. I tried to dissuade him from exposing himself any further. He didn't listen, took the elevator, went to knock on David's door, didn't find him, and finally came back to the garage. I'd been waiting for him. Thinking."

"Why did you care what he did? You'd already fired him." Something wasn't adding up.

"He was going to ruin the legacy of *LA Misconducts*!" Fred made it sound as if that was enough cause for murder. "Our argument got very heated."

"So you ran him over before he could make a fool of himself?" David had an eyebrow raised, as confused as I was.

"I'll protect the show's legacy at all costs!"

"I didn't exactly ruin any legacies, so can you tell me why the hell you tried killing me this morning?" I asked.

"Isn't it obvious?" Fred said, and I guess my face told him what I thought of that. "When the police started investigating, I wasn't worried. They're a bunch of overworked incompetent idiots who eat donuts by the dozen. We've covered all of it on *LA Misconducts*. They're corrupt, they're dumb, they're lazy."

On the one hand, I wasn't sure he actually believed what he was saying. On the other hand, over my years in Los Angeles and working in Hollywood, I'd met so many self-centered people in the business who thought prime-time dramas were akin to documentaries, that Fred's words didn't surprise me that much.

"I wasn't worried about the press either. They're all a bunch of click-grabbing bozos. Newsrooms are notoriously understaffed. Journalists are hurried, underpaid, and exhausted. Who was going to have the time, or energy, to dig into this other than superficially?" I must have been stressed and exhausted because he was starting to sound reasonable and actually make sense. "But then there was the rumor you also had started investigating with that ex of yours," Fred said in disgust, while David kept holding my hand. He was still taking notes on his cell phone frantically. Seriously? Did he really want to get all that crap? "And I knew I'd be doomed. If there was someone who could pull this off, it would be an *LA Misconducts* alumna. Your time as a writer on the show has provided you with all the necessary insight and know-how to follow the leads and unmask me."

Okay, maybe Fred wasn't sounding so reasonable, or *sane*, after all. David remained buried in his cell phone, but when he realized I was no longer talking—I guess my brain was trying to find out what to say or how to react—he took charge.

"And you planted the watch in my apartment to further incriminate me?" he said.

"Of course." Fred looked immensely proud of himself. "The press had decided you were the killer. You were my easy way out of this, my path to my future in New York."

"You realize that, just because they have actual winters

there, New York is not like a different country without an extradition treaty, right?" I asked Fred. "The police would have eventually figured it out and arrested you. Especially once you decided I also had to go."

"Pity they still haven't done it," Fred said. "Because you still have to go."

38

F red looked at me and David with a deranged stare, even more so than before. Cold sweat traveled down my spine. Fred took his hand to the pocket of the hideous parka he was wearing, and I realized there seemed to be something big and heavy there. Could I've been wrong when I'd assumed he was unarmed? Also, why had I assumed such nonsense?

I panicked, holding David's hand tighter. Without even the hint of a warning, David yanked at that hand and made me move to the side and away from the front door, pushing me to lie on the floor and landing on top of me.

Detective Laura Moreno barged into the apartment then. She wore a bulletproof vest and was followed by at least ten uniformed police officers. All of them pointed guns at Fred Appleton.

It all got blurry. Fred started yelling, but he wasn't the only one throwing loud remarks. David buried my body under his and dragged us slowly behind the couch. Someone knocked Fred out. The police finally handcuffed him and read him his rights. He kept protesting, even battered and in handcuffs. They took him out of the apartment and most of the agents left with him. Detective Moreno came to me and David then.

"You two okay?" she said, while we made our way up to sit on the couch. I felt exhausted.

"Considering I never liked him as a boss and he's tried killing me *twice* in a day," I said. "Absolutely. Never been better."

"The sucker has been ahead of us all day." Detective Moreno seemed to share my dislike for Fred, and that made me like her for the first time. "Glad he finally decided to stop."

"By showing up here?" She had to be fucking kidding me. Perhaps I didn't like her after all.

"By being stupid enough to show up here and let your *periodista* use his cell phone," Detective Moreno explained, pointing to David. I liked that she referred to David as "my *periodista*." It had a nice ring to it.

"You weren't taking notes?" I asked David, realizing what he'd been doing all along.

"What? Of course I wasn't taking notes! I was texting Detective Moreno, who thankfully wasn't too far from here. She gave us her card the first time we went to the police station, remember?"

"And you memorized her number in your burner phone?" I was still confused.

"You never know when it may come handy." For once, I was so happy he was the most methodically annoying and organized person I'd ever met.

"Need you two to come to the station again and go over what happened," Detective Moreno said.

"Nuh-uh," I said, shaking my head.

"Nope," David agreed. "You have it all there in writing,

on the several detailed texts I sent you. I don't think I can put it better than that. Believe me, I'm the most eloquent in writing. And if you *really* need us to tell you what happened, we can drop by the station on Monday morning. But we're done for the day."

"I really need a shower." I decided not to tell her what else I needed, but the unmade bed in my apartment was staring at me with lascivious eyes and calling the word *siesta* at me.

"Okay, I'm gonna let you off the hook this time," Detective Moreno conceded, checking her cell phone and presumably going over David's communications. "Try to get some rest. You two look at least five years older than the first time we met."

Ouch! Seriously, ouch!

She made us promise we'd be at the LAPD Downtown station at 9 a.m. sharp on Monday. It had taken us a couple of minutes to convince her she really didn't want me there at 7:30 on Monday because I would be completely useless so early in the morning, and extremely pissy.

"Good luck with your love life, by the way," David told her while she was leaving. "I hope it stops being a complete mess soon. Life tends to have a way of taking us by surprise. I say that from experience."

"I doubt it. I'm going to be undercover in a few weeks, and that's hardly the time or place to meet anyone," she said.

David shrugged. "You never know."

When we finally finished saying goodbye to Detective Laura Moreno and closed my apartment's door—and bolted it—David turned to me.

"Such a skilled detective," he commented.

"Oh my god!" I said. "Have you ever met *anyone* you

didn't like? She just said we've aged five years in two days! Why are you so nice?"

"Is that a problem? One of our many irreconcilable differences?" he asked with a smile.

"Not really, I guess," I said, and I realized I meant it. For the first time in months—no, years—I didn't mind him being the nicest, preppiest person I knew. "It's just, she's been eyeing us, more particularly you, as the culprits for this Dashing Henry debacle for days. And you still manage not to hold a grudge against her and think she's good at her job! She only deduced Fred was the killer once he tried killing me the first time, remember?"

"You do realize she just saved our asses, right?" David sounded quite reasonable.

"She was just doing her job, which, if the LAPD had done better, wouldn't have permitted Fred to try and kill me *twice*."

"Do you think that's what he was going to do?" David said, with a chill.

"Can we not talk about this now?" I really needed to watch some videos of cute kitties, get a deep tissue massage, and do some breathing exercises or some other extremely soothing activity.

We were still standing by the front door. David got closer, his eyes soft and fixed on mine.

"Do you want to pretend the last hour didn't happen?" Perhaps he also needed to take a yoga class or do some journaling or whatever he did to unwind. "We were just inside the elevator. You haven't showered in two days."

"Three days," I corrected.

"Who's counting?"

"I am," I said. "But please continue."

"I was thorough enough to check not only that you smell

great," he said, his breath warm on my neck, "but you also taste great. I'll have to sample you again though." He kissed my clavicle and then bit my earlobe.

"And we've just made it home," I said, joining in the fantasy.

"We have," he smiled, still working on my neck. "And not only are we on speaking terms for the first time in two years, we've also not had sex in a room where you could actually see anything in as many years. So I'm particularly into the idea of getting myself reacquainted with your body."

Even in my constant state of horniness, I would have always said that I am not one to have sex—or even feel mildly lusty—in any circumstance where stress plays such a big factor. As it turns out, I was wrong and didn't know myself well enough.

Also, David had a point. After months where the two of us hadn't been uttering anything more than guttural monosyllables during our encounters together, it was nice to have a conversation while feeling sexy and getting to undress one another.

He also was right about the bit of fucking in plain daylight. It's nice to not only be able to see your partner's face for a chance, but his entire body.

It looked like the shower and sleep would have to wait—for now. But I was ready to embrace all of David's thoroughness.

39

There are more important things in life than your next byline, especially if you ask your lover to start writing a script together.

"Forget about the Pulitzer, Scribe. We're gonna get an Emmy!" I told David after I woke up from the most pleasant and restorative of siestas. I may have been almost killed twice that Saturday, but it was not going to be the day I also became a writer deserted by her agent.

"Huh?" he asked, confused and still battling sleep. "Can we still get a Pulitzer as well?"

I suspect he was still too sleepy to have heard my mention of the Emmy that Fred Appleton's story was going to get us, because who cared about the Pulitzer. But that tale really had everything: a deranged villain, a victim no one was going to mourn, a true crime angle, a Hollywood backdrop, and a couple of sexy writers pining for each other and managing to solve the case.

I checked the time and realized it was almost 3 p.m. I texted Beatrice right away.

The woman was ruthless and replied immediately.

"Feel like writing something else with me?" I asked David. He was still lying in bed. I was sitting up. He turned to me, propped his face over his flexed arm, and gave me the most sultry of smiles.

"Are we going to almost get killed again?"

"No, but we're going to write precisely about that," I said. "There's a prestige TV movie in this mess we've found ourselves in these last few days, and I think we're the perfect people to write about it."

"Sounds good." I have to reiterate here that his smile could be described as smoldering. "But can I think about it?"

"Of course you can. But I really can't. And I'm gonna need a dress!" There was no way I was going to drop by an awards red carpet wearing ratty jeans and a stained top.

So I left David naked in bed, put some clothes on—probably the aforementioned ratty jeans and stained top—took the elevator down, and went straight to the Acne Studios store that resides at street level on the Eastern Columbia.

To the untrained pedestrian walking by, it could look as if the Downtown location of the Swedish-based minimalist brand was closed. I knew better.

Among the industrial-looking metallic hangers and the fluffy black ottomans, I rummaged through the selection of designer clothes with an edge. Fortunately, I was quick at finding the perfect garment for what I was going for: put together but not too fancy, glammed up with an attitude. For a moment there, I had a bit of trepidation. Could I possibly pull this somewhat daring dress off? Of course I could. I was so glad that I-don't-give-a-shit-and-I'm-dumbly-sure-about-everything Elena was back.

Ten minutes after that, I'd bought a figure-hugging black satin dress with thin straps and an adjustable tie-up detail at the waist. It would go great with my battered classic Dr. Martens boots and the vintage Chanel mini flap handbag my mother had so generously gotten for me months before. I still hadn't been social—and grown-up—enough to take it out of the closet.

I was running the pitch for Beatrice in my head and feeling energized and creative in a way I hadn't experienced in months. I was so absorbed, I even took the stairs. By the time I made it to the landing of the tenth floor of the Eastern Columbia, I'd come up with the perfect elevator pitch for Beatrice. I know, it was paradoxical considering I hadn't taken the actual elevator.

"You haven't heard, have you?" said a recognizable bass voice. My next-door neighbor was standing by my front door with an expression that said: *Ready for chatting up.*

"Probably not," I admitted.

"They figured out what happened with the fire alarm the other day," George said in a hushed tone.

"Didn't someone trigger it by mistake?" I dismissed him, not even trying to conceal my boredom.

"It wasn't by mistake but clumsiness," said my gossipy neighbor. "It was Andrew."

"What Andrew? Hot Neighbor Andrew?"

"Yep. On Thursday morning, he came home much later than usual after his shift at the hospital ran long. He was so numb after working nights for the whole month that he didn't see there was a corpse in the garage. Not only that, he triggered the alarm thinking it was the button to call the elevator. He was wearing noise-canceling headphones and didn't even hear the sound. He went home and slept through the whole thing while we were out there freezing." George chuckled in disbelief, but the thing was, I could see myself doing the same. Only in my case, I wouldn't have triggered the alarm thinking it was the elevator because I'd been working for hours in a hospital but because I was too drunk. So I decided not to judge Andrew. He was only human after all.

As I looked at George, something occurred to me. "Do you have an agent?"

"What do you mean, do I have an agent? Of course I do! I'm a *working* actor!"

"Pity, I was going to introduce you to mine. I think you'd like each other. You both always seem to know everything."

"I pay attention," George dismissed me. "Information is power."

"Yes, so says my agent."

"You went shopping?" George changed topics. He didn't miss a beat and was eyeing my shopping bag.

"I'm in desperate need of a makeover." For some reason, I wasn't feeling quite as vindictive with him. But I was fully aware I'd been way too social and congenial with him.

"I can see that," he said, and I suddenly remembered why I'd never liked him. "Are you guys also humping like rabbits during the day now? Let's just hope that means less of a racket late at night and after midnight. You were quite loud before."

"You can hope whatever you want, George," I said. "But I may set my alarm to hump at 3 a.m. if only to get back at you for talking to the fucking press."

"Aren't you actually humping a reporter?" George asked, but I could see he was disturbed by the idea of being woken up in the middle of the night.

"Which is precisely why I'm on a revenge path, George." I opened the door to my apartment. "You talked to a competing outlet," I added, then closed the door dramatically in his face.

"You're back?" David said from bed. He was still naked, propped up on pillows while reading the latest steamy rom-com novel I'd been devouring the night before when I couldn't sleep. And he was wearing my glasses. Needless to say, he looked irresistibly pretty. All my wild fantasies about a sexy naked librarian materialized in front of my eyes. "Come back to bed. We haven't reconciled adequately enough." He patted the mattress.

I took my glasses off his face—I'm sure they weren't even the right prescription for him—and that only made it a little bit easier. It was arduous telling him why I couldn't join him in bed and why he needed to get out of it and get changed into whatever presentable clothes he had. *Pronto.*

"I'll pick you up at your place in ten minutes," I told him.

He somehow found his favorite UCLA T-shirt while looking for the clothes he'd come in. He took it and showed it to me with a face I understood right away: *May I take this one?*

Leave it here, my eyes told him. *We can share it.*

"If you want me to be your pretty plus one for a fancy

party, I'm going to need at least half an hour to get ready," he said.

"Seriously?" I couldn't believe his vanity. "You have fifteen minutes. Be ready."

Before leaving my apartment, he tugged me close and kissed me—slowly and methodically.

"You've got only fourteen minutes now," I said, still in a daze. He left with a grin.

40

Have you ever showered—okay, I guess *cleaned* is the more appropriate verb here. Have you ever cleaned yourself with a make-up remover wipe? Don't judge me if I tell you that's exactly what I did that afternoon before getting into the dress I just bought. I then had a video phone consultation with my sister who helped me rein in my hair into what she called a *chignon* that was held together with lots of hair pins and even more hair wax. I was feeling so fancy, I even put some foundation and mascara on.

"You clean up well," David said when he opened the door to his apartment a few minutes later. He gave me a stare that it was impossible for me to misinterpret: *You look HOT.*

"I'm not technically *clean*, and we should definitely do this more often," I said, appreciating him unabashedly. He wore a slim-fit two-piece black suit over a white shirt open at the collar. He looked like a rebellious dandy.

"Drive or walk?" he asked at the landing as he was locking his front door. "Parking is going to be a nightmare."

"Scribe, even if none of us are wearing heels, the Shrine Auditorium is almost an hour walk from here." I checked my cell phone. "The Uber should be here in a minute, and we'll barely make it there as is."

"Fine, but you owe me a walk around the city." He was definitely the most avid pedestrian born in LA I'd ever met.

...

"All glitzy feel-good stories should always include a bit where the protagonists get all glammed up to go to a silly party," I told David as we were being dropped off in front of the 1920's auditorium with a Moorish Revival style where the SAG Awards were about to start.

"Make sure to add this part to the script then," David said, smiling. He held my hand while we walked toward the red carpet area.

"Wait, is that Pedro Pascal?" I stopped in the middle of the street, pulling my hand out of his to put it on his chest. Let me clarify—David's chest, not Pedro's. "What is he wearing?"

"I literally don't know what or who you're talking about," David said. "You do realize there's a security checkpoint to access the red carpet, right?" He brought me back to earth and forced me to stop ogling in Pedro's direction.

"No te preocupes," I told David. "We'll be fine."

We approached the check-in point and I did what I hadn't done ever before: embraced my family connections.

"Elena Freire Valls," I told the security people. "Plus guest. Should be on the list. I'm the mayor's daughter."

Two of the security people looked at each other in resignation, as if saying, *Here we go again.* I guess they were going to ask me for proof of identity, but it wasn't necessary.

Aurora Valls herself descended that instant on the Shrine Auditorium followed by an entourage of personal assistants and bodyguards, and by a swarm of cameras and journalists. I know she's my mother, and you may think I'm not the most objective person when it comes to her, but the whole thing was like your typical deus ex machina plot device. Plus, she did look goddesslike.

"I thought you'd said you didn't want to come," my mom told me as a way of greeting. I realized it would appear that two people had invited me to that particular party, but I'd been too absent-minded to remember.

"Oh, I'm not coming," I replied. "But I need you to get me through security. I'm meeting my agent at the red carpet."

"That's highly atypical and bizarre." On principle, she was against all things that couldn't be labeled *normal*.

"I'm atypical and bizarre." Let me tell you, this self-assured feeling was the best high I've felt in a long time.

"I guess you are, bitxo," she said. She hadn't used the Catalan pet name with me in a long time.

"Don't have time to go over a therapy session with you right now and ask about the use of that particular word at this particular time. I see Beatrice, and we need to talk about work," I told my mother, and I knew if there was someone who appreciated hard work, it was her.

So she got me through security with expediency, asked for a kiss on the cheek, and let me go.

"Aurora," David greeted the mayor while I dragged him behind me.

"David," my mother replied with a nod.

But we didn't have time for the two of them to dislike one another overtly in public, as I was walking in Beatrice's direction with David in tow. I was going over the pitch in my mind but once in front of Beatrice, I somehow ended up saying something absolutely different and not rehearsed at all.

"Before we go over the pitch or you hijack the conversation, let me tell you, I hate air kisses and hugging people who aren't my family or close friends. Also, I don't appreciate being threatened," I told Beatrice. "And don't call me *honey*."

"Honey," Beatrice started, flapping her hands, clearly flustered. "I mean, Elena, I'm sorry if I ever made you feel uncomfortable—"

"We don't have time for this right now. We're not staying," I told her. "I'm writing a movie about Dashing Henry's death. It'll have murder, an investigation, chases, one or two deceptions, and quite the amount of suspense and sex. It's *LA Misconducts* meets true crime, with a dash of *Spotlight*. Can you sell it?"

"Oh my god! I'd love to play Elena's role in the movie," a familiar voice said behind me. When I turned, I saw Amelia decked in the most exquisite gown and having obviously pulled all the stops required for the perfect red-carpet manifestation. Everything had been curated and produced from the hair, to the nails, to the make-up and the accessories. She looked flawless. I was so used to seeing her fresh-faced and in jeans that I almost didn't recognize her.

"Is that a verbal commitment for a possible attachment?" Beatrice asked Amelia behind me.

"If you can sell it," Amelia said.

"You're asking me if I can sell a script of the story that's kept LA obsessed for the last three days? With Amelia Sanchez, Elena's real life friend, playing Elena. And let's not forget to mention Elena is the mayor's daughter." I could see the dollar signs in Beatrice's eyes.

"Yes, please. Let's not forget to mention it or to focus on that while designing the promo campaign for this," I said, but I knew, even if I didn't want it, there was no way my family wouldn't be alluded to.

Beatrice looked at me, still clearly uncomfortable. She wasn't used to my snark being expressed out loud.

"Of course I can sell it," she said, and she looked like she was already mentally cashing her commission.

"I may be interested in buying it," said a nasal voice behind me. When I turned around, I saw a tuxedo-clad man of about fifty, perfectly groomed and about my height. Archie Eisenberg.

"The question is, how soon can you have it?" Archie continued. He seemed to echo Beatrice's sentiment.

"Am I to assume that you're going to continue working as a producer even without Fred Appleton as a partner?" Beatrice asked Archie, and I was reminded why I had stuck with her as an agent for so long even if she got on my nerves half the time. She knew how to ask the uncomfortable but necessary questions.

"Of course!" Archie said, and he sounded almost offended. "I've always been more of a classic producer than he was. I hustle to find the money, get the right team, make sure everything gets shot without delays, ask for the cuts and trims that need to be made, and even carefully oversee the press side of things."

"To that last part I can attest," David joined in the conversation. "You oversee the press even to the detriment of freedom of speech."

Ouch. It looked like Archie Eisenberg was indeed the one who tried stopping David from publishing his exposé about Dashing Henry, and it also looked like David did hold on to at least *some* negativity. He hadn't exactly forgotten or forgiven Archie.

"You two know each other?" Amelia asked David and Archie, not missing a beat.

"Briefly," said Archie, with a polite smile.

"Not really," added David with an expression so unreadable, I tried to interrogate the clenching of his jaw for some hints. "But I know he is not a fan of my reporting."

Beatrice laughed nervously.

"And you two," she said, pointing to me and David, "are writing this movie together, right?"

I was about to reply for David with something non-committal since I'd promised him he'd be able to think about it. Plus, I wasn't sure he'd want to join in at all now that it seemed Archie Eisenberg could be our potential boss. But David was faster than me. And I was quite taken by the answer.

41

An hour after the red-carpet affair, I was dropped by an Uber a few blocks from home. I thought the walk would clear my mind and would be the perfect occasion to make a couple of necessary calls. But I didn't anticipate how dark—and cold—it was going to be even after a gloriously sunny and warm afternoon.

Brenda picked up at the second tone, and we exchanged the customary greetings. Fortunately, I had seen her and Amelia the previous weekend and I didn't have to bother with many civilities. So I cut to the chase.

"Remember how over Christmas I babysat those furry monsters who are your children, and you said you owed me one?" I asked my former colleague at *LA Misconducts*. I loved spending time with Brenda and Amelia's dogs, but they were the most spoiled and demonic canines I've ever met.

"Of course. It was a glorious week in Bali," Brenda said. "Troglodita, sit. Sit. Sit. SIT! Bimbo, no! Leave it!" she yelled, not at me but at little demon number one, the red merle Australian Shepherd aptly called Troglodita; and little demon number two, a feisty, overweight Corgi named

Bimbo. Bimbo was unafraid of showing teeth whenever she didn't feel happy, which was often.

"I'm ready to collect," I told Brenda, and I was so happy Troglodita and Bimbo were being their usual worst selves because Brenda had to be very aware that those ten days I spent with her two furries weren't easy. "What are you wearing?"

"The navy silk pajamas Amelia gave me for my last birthday," Brenda said.

"Great, you don't even have to change. You can dress that up. Just put some heels on and a little bit of rouge, will you?"

"Where am I going exactly?" Brenda asked.

"I need you to be your wife's plus one at the SAG after-party because I really need a bath right now. Tell her I sent you."

"You're shaming me into being a dutiful wife?"

"Of course not! I'm going to tell you that I've been not giving a shit what everyone thinks about me for the last few months, and now I've even learned how to tell everyone what I think about them. It's pretty awesome," I told Brenda, as I kept walking alongside Broadway Street. "So get out of the house and don't even think about the press taking pictures of you or comparing you to Amelia's previous partners. You get to spend your life with her. You are amazing and always look amazing."

"Even in my pajamas."

"Even in your *fancy* pajamas. Oh, and you can take the dogs to the party with you! Just tell them they're your emotional support animals, and if anyone tells you they can't be there, call my mom or Victor. They'll sort it out. They just passed some municipal ordinance that's going to be a nightmare for anyone with a dog-hair allergy, but it gives animals and dog owners a lot more rights."

"I always liked you, but I think I like this newer version of Elena more," Brenda said.

I preened. "There's something else: Thank you."

"For entrusting my overindulged fur babies with you?"

"That as well, I suppose. But I meant for talking to David so many months ago and being brave enough to expose Dashing Henry," I said. "Your testimony meant he was able to publish the article."

"Henry needed to be exposed," said Brenda. "David simply gave me the perfect vehicle to exorcise some of my demons by talking about what Henry did. And we exposed him."

"That article brought David and me back together." The thing that changed inside me that day six months before when I went to David's studio for the first time in the middle of the night was that he'd just published the article that exposed Henry and would keep him at bay for other people like me.

"I didn't know you two were back together." Brenda sounded surprised.

"We weren't," I said.

"But you are now?"

"It's a long story, and I promise to tell you and Amelia all about it. But now, chop, chop. You need to get ready. Big hugs to you and the demons."

I continued strolling and called my sister next.

"You're calling me to let me know you're not coming to tomorrow's brunch at the Four Seasons, and you want me to tell Papá," Marta said the moment she answered. "He'll be disappointed."

"What makes you think that?"

"I figured after almost being killed twice in a day, you'd

like some peace and calm instead of Mamá telling you you need a haircut and a photofacial."

"Don't forget about the closet overhaul," I told my sister with a chuckle. "Wait, how do you know about the second time Fred tried killing me?"

"I'm reading the *Voice*'s latest article written by Gloria Fucking Kingsley. Apparently, you and David have been strutting your stuff all over town," Marta said. "Oh and congrats on the new project."

"What new project?"

"The movie you're writing," Marta said. "It's going to be so meta. I want to see it already, and Amelia playing you is the best."

"Don't you think she's a bit tall, statuesque, and high-cheeked to be me?" I asked, suddenly insecure about the comparisons.

"There's nothing wrong with the placement of the cheeks on your face," my sister protested. I was so glad she was back at being my most ferocious cheerleader and then realized she'd never quit being it.

"What time is that thing tomorrow?" I asked.

"1 p.m. *sharp*."

"And you're going to be there?"

"Unlimited matcha margaritas." I loved that we could be so different yet so similar for certain important things.

We hung up after exchanging a fair amount of hugs, kisses, and all manner of affectionate reassurances as I arrived at the Eastern Columbia and sighed in relief. I was finally home and about to accomplish a much-needed feat.

42

Are you still there? Because I'm still inside the bathtub. Do you need a recap? I started this tale coming home tired and smelly. My water heater wasn't working, but I managed to heat some water myself and fill the bathtub. I was taking a bath while narrating this story. What comes next is what happened after telling you how I found myself in such a peculiar situation.

The whole bathroom smelled like pineapple and plumeria as I'd found one of those bath bombs you buy at Lush, thinking of giving it to your mom for her birthday with a nice selection of Eve Babitz books. But then you decide to keep everything to yourself. I was about to fall asleep, still craving some comforting greasy food, when I heard the front door open.

"The place was packed!" David said from the living room. "I had to fight with half of the vegan population of Los Angeles—which is probably *half the population of LA*—but I got us dinner."

"Can we have it here?" I yelled from the tub.

"Sure, where's here? I don't see you anywhere." His voice was getting closer.

"I'm in the tub!"

"So we're eating and bathing at the same time?" He came into view, smiling. He handed me the much-craved lentil burger with extra avocado. He left the side of sweet potato fries on the tub's ledge.

I devoured everything while watching David undress.

"Aren't you hungry?" I asked him.

"Starving," he said. "But I figured the right way of doing things was getting undressed first and eating once inside the tub."

"There's no protocol, really." I popped a fry in my mouth. "But you'll have to be careful with the soap. It leaves a bitter aftertaste."

"You know that even if you blink, I'll still be here when you open your eyes, right?"

"Sorry. Seeing you has just not been an option these last few months. And I missed your body," I said. My mouth may have been full, but no one was telling me not to eat and talk at the same time.

"It's not like you've been deprived," he said, hamburger in hand while submerging in the tub in front of me.

"I have been, actually. I was deprived from looking at you too unrestrainedly."

"I didn't buy your feigned indifference for one second," he said, smiling.

"What indifference, Scribe?" I splashed him playfully, and he held his burger out of the way. "I was visiting your place even more frequently than you were coming here. For someone who wasn't supposed to be into you, I sure was interested."

"You were only showing interest at night, then not talking to me and keeping a boyfriend on the side," he said.

"Fake boyfriend."

"Seriously?"

"Why are you so feisty? It's almost as if you want to pick a fight," I told him.

"You're doing it again," he said.

"What am I doing again?" I had no clue what he was talking about or why he was being so difficult.

"Avoiding the conversation we should be having. You asked me to write a script with you. I told you I needed to think about it, and now you're pretending like you never asked."

"Scribe, I was giving you time. You told me you needed to think about it, and I'm letting you do that." I polished off the sweet potato fries.

"It's been *hours* since you asked me." He bit into his burger.

"Precisely," I told him, mouth full again. "It's *only* been a few hours. I was still going to wait for a couple of days for your answer."

"Days!"

We looked at each other from across the tub, letting our legs find themselves and fit together under the water.

Is this one of those cases in which things are done differently in your line of writing and in my line of writing? my eyes asked his.

I think so, his told me.

"So screenwriting deadlines are clearly a lot looser and longer than journalistic ones," David said. "And Beatrice said this had to be quick. I don't even want to imagine."

"Don't be sassy." I was about to splash his face with my foot, but he caught my ankle and leaned closer. "So, are you writing this with me? You told Archie and Beatrice we'd only do this if we had total creative freedom and could pick a director. So I somehow assumed you'd be in . . ."

"Do you want me to write this with you?"

"What do you think?"

"It's one thing to want me in your bed," he said.

"And my bathtub," I added.

"And your bathtub," he conceded. "It's another to want to write something together."

"We've already done it once."

"This would be a longer process," he said.

"Are you admitting that writing a script takes longer?" I asked.

"We've just established that."

"You can still try to get as many Pulitzers as you want on the side. You know you can keep working as a journalist, right? I know you want to take John's offer at the *Gazette*."

"That's not an offer, that's an open door to keep writing for them here and there. Nothing that'll keep me completely occupied."

"So you can work with me as well?" I teased.

"You know we're going to fight because we're working together," he said, and I knew then *that* had been the one thing really bothering him.

"Then we'll have to reconcile. I like reconciling with you," I told him. "Is this why you didn't say yes before?"

"Maybe," he said and looked at me with eyes that said, *Yes*.

I ran my foot along his under the water. "You know the rules: no more misunderstandings, but we can spar from time to time."

"And you really think this isn't a terrible idea?"

"What could be worse than three days of unshowered anxiety and surviving a deranged showrunner?"

"Writing about it *together*."

"Nuh-uh," I told him. "For one, the only danger we'll be running into is the overuse of adjectives. Plus, all I've been desperately needing these past three days was to bathe, sleep, and have you make me scream. I'm sure we'll be able to keep accomplishing such three simple goals."

They sound reasonable enough, his eyes told me.

He sealed his agreement with a kiss.

Thank you for reading *Love, Lines, and Alibis*. For a bonus Elena/David chapter visit this link: https://BookHip.com/GHRZLFM

And please leave a review of the book on Amazon, Goodreads, TikTok or your favorite platform. ¡Gracias!

ACKNOWLEDGMENTS

I had every intention of starting this by thanking Pacific Gas & Electric for the two days in the winter of 2023 when our power was out—and with it, the ability to take a hot shower. I also wanted to tell you about the day in the summer of 2014 when I almost had to interview Clive Owen unshowered. Those moments gave me the first glimpses of what Elena's story could be.

But as I was editing this book, a series of fires were devastating Los Angeles—a city I simply love, where I've always felt happiness, and where dreams always seem possible. So instead, I'm going to start by thanking Los Angeles for being the most inspiring place, even for those of us who no longer live there.

Xavi, thank you for keeping my sanity in check, giving me valuable notes, helping me every step of the way, and, most importantly, believing in me. I couldn't do this without you.

To the Martas in my life—thank you for always being there. One day, you all have to meet each other. Marta Franco, I'm perfectly aware that romance is not your preferred genre, yet you read my early drafts and keep encouraging me as a writer. Marta Gené Camps, I still think you should charge me every time you read one of my manuscripts and tell me everything I can improve. And Marta Puentes, thanks for having perfected the art of being the best younger sister.

Mary Weilage, thank you for helping me when I first took the plunge and started writing in English. I wouldn't be here without your help, generosity, and friendship.

Darinka Gadikota-Klumpers, I don't think you realize how much your words have encouraged me to keep doing what I do these past few months. Thank you for being there!

Ale Ramos, for being the most reliable WhatsApp correspondent and for keeping me young(ish).

Emma Colt, meeting a fellow romance writer from Barcelona has been one of the many rewarding highlights of this journey. Thanks for the chats and for sharing your experiences.

Joan Griffin, thanks again for being such a generous author and person. Every time we talk, I learn something new.

To Brenna Bailey-Davies at Bookmarten Editorial—for always pointing out where my protagonists could improve before readers get a chance to meet them, and for being the best editor.

Ashley Santoro, thank you for the amazing cover and for always knowing exactly what I want, even when I can't quite explain it.

And finally, to every reader who has given this indie author a chance—thank you.

ABOUT THE AUTHOR

Patricia Puentes is a Barcelona native, expat, and recovering entertainment journalist who has been calling California home for almost 20 years. She can tell many funny (or just plain surreal) stories about the frequent times she has interviewed celebrities, but she mostly gets wowed by writers—and doggies.

She writes open-door romance mysteries with a Hollywood setting and where the leads have non-stop banter. You can check her previous rom-com mystery, *Cluelessly Unscripted*.

She lives in Oakland, California, with her romantic partner and their rambunctious Border Collie, Boira (aka Peluchín diabólico).

Find her online at www.patriciapuentes.com/lovelines. To subscribe to Patricia's newsletter, visit this link: www.patriciapuentes.com/newsletter.

TikTok: @patriciapuentesbooks

Instagram: @patriciapuentesbooks

Goodreads: www.goodreads.com/patriciapuentes

www.ingramcontent.com/pod-product-compliance
Lightning Source LLC
Chambersburg PA
CBHW071406300726

48976CB00006B/2004